Considering how Paris had to put up with Harley, she figured she deserved every bit of cash he gave her and then some. She ran fingers through her freshly touched-up tresses and smiled to herself. It was a good thing she didn't have to foot her own bill at the salon. She'd be out of over four hundred bucks a month. She didn't always rely on the same person, but she never considered taking her own checkbook out for daily expenses. Besides, it was all a part of the package Harley and all her other "sponsors" enjoyed. Paris remembered the turning point in her adolescence when she'd began concentrating on her looks. It had taken a while, but slowly she'd begun to see potential when she looked in the mirror.

# *UNDER THE CHERRY MOON*

*CHRISTAL JORDAN-MIMS*

Genesis Press, Inc.

**Indigo Vibe**

An imprint of Genesis Press, Inc.
Publishing Company

Genesis Press, Inc.
P.O. Box 101
Columbus, MS 39703



ISBN: 1-58571-169-1
Manufactured in the United States of America

First Edition

Visit us at www.genesis-press.com
or call at 1-888-Indigo-1

# *DEDICATION*

*To my mother, Jacqueline.*
*I'm everything I am, because you loved me.*
*To my AJ.*
*From the beginning to the end, my best friend.*
*And to DR who passed away without realizing how much he would be missed.*

# *ACKNOWLEDGMENTS*

I thank my Lord, Jesus Christ who is forever faithful.

I thank my husband, Sean, for being the definition of the word partner. You've taught me so much about unconditional love. You believe in me even when I don't believe in myself. Because of you, I believe in fairytales. I have my own chocolate Prince Charming. You will always have my heart. Chanelle Edryce and Stone Erickson, you are the light of Mommy's life.

Big thanks to my Granny who taught me God helps those who help themselves. Special thanks to all friends old and new who encouraged me to chase my dreams. Hey Stacy! Sheila J. we're headed to Chicago one way or another. My play sister Jayme Broome, I love you and am so proud of you and my goddaughter Jayvin. Solid Foundations Preparatory Academy is about to blow up! Keep doing your thing. What's up Ebony T., girl finally. I'm looking out for you. Alice B. I'm forever indebted to you for your encouragement and perspective. Delores, Amaya, Karen, Cindy and Monica R. CSC will always have a place in my heart. Also many many thanks to my agent Sha-Shana Critchon (Critchon & Associates).

To the Essence Reading Group and everyone else back in Tulsa, OK, it's been awhile, but I miss you all. To all my baby girls from Women of Tomorrow, respect is just a minimum, never settle for less. Keep reaching for the stars; you'll catch them. That includes, you James Dawson, Jr.

Last, but not least, I want to thank Niani Colom and Genesis Press for allowing me to tell Paris' story and my editor, the brutally honest (smile) Deatri King-Bey for helping me tell it effectively.

*To everyone out there following their dreams...the most beautiful rainbows are birthed from the darkest storms.*

Be blessed,
Christal

**Curves**

*I've been searching for love in all my curves;*
*Hypnotizing and oh so tantalizing, they cause men's necks to curve,*
*when they see the curve*
*of my mouth; setting up the curve*
*of my neck; which leads to the curve*
*of my breasts sitting proudly on my chest; enhancing the curve*
*of my onion; leading eyes around to the curve*
*of my hips; drawing eyes downward to the curve*
*atop of my calves as it extends proudly from the curve*
*of my ankle;*

*Caught up in all my tempting curves,*
*you could miss the subtle curve*
*outlining somber eyes; surrounded by the curve*
*of eyelashes damp, with the curve*
*of tears making their way down the curve*
*of my forlorn cheek.*

*They witnessed the curve*
*of my mother's back as she struggled to nurture the curve*
*in her stomach; which she knew would have to embrace the curves*
*of life without you.*
*I wonder if the curves*
*of my body, the shrine to my femininity are invaluable;*
*because previously I hoped they would curve*
*attention around themselves, and into the curve*
*of my soul.*

*But when they see my many curves*
*they reside for brief, while before curving*
*onto the next, in a long list of curves*
*looking to put the same curve*
*on rejection as myself.*

*Because just when I think the curve*
*of my outstretched arms, leading to the curve*
*of my fingers prepared to grasp and curve*
*around love, drawing it into the curve*
*of my bosom, it curves*
*away leaving me with nothing but empty*
*curves.*

by Christal Jordan-Mims

For Paris and the many Daddy's girls growing up without a Daddy.

# *PROLOGUE*

Paris rushed out of the indigo-colored building. Eyes quickly adjusting to the dark of night, she checked her peripheral vision to ensure no one followed. Steps away from the deserted parking lot, she paused to squint up at the scripted sign. It blazed "Under the Cherry Moon" in red neon lights. She'd spent the last three years of her life here, but tonight had been her last shift. She fingered the cold metal in her soft leather purse then pushed teased hair out of her face. Tonight she would get answers to the haunting questions that plagued her all of her life.

Black t-strap heels three inches high made click-clack noises on the hard pavement as she made her way to her black Porsche Boxster with the vanity plate *CARAMEL*. She'd gotten the plate after her boss had taken one look at her and exclaimed, "Add butterscotch to chocolate and you get caramel." Paris smirked at the memory of his unexpected and unnecessary comment, then focused on more imminent matters.

Pressing the black button on her key ring, her Porsche bleeped, the headlights flashing in response. Paris input the personal code then paused as the door unlocked itself. She had a long drive ahead of her, so she hastily secured her safety belt and spared a quick glance to check the location of her mirrors. She'd stopped at the gas station earlier where she'd filled the tank, gotten a routine oil change, had the engine flushed and had her tires rotated. Pleased her car had received a clean bill of health; Paris knew there wouldn't be any interruptions in her journey. Paris slid the key in the ignition and smiled as the powerful engine trembled underneath her fingertips, resting on the steering wheel.

Every time Paris sat behind the wheel of this car, she appreciated it all over again. The power was intoxicating as it flowed from the engine. She felt empowered; driving at top speed always provided an immediate heady rush. Backing out of the parking lot, she checked her make-up in the rearview mirror, eased the car into the street then gunned the engine, taking off for the nearest exit. Paris was off to see her father.

# *CHAPTER ONE*
# *KEEPING IT REAL*

The phone rang loudly, interrupting Paris from her sleep. Irritated, she reached over and knocked the phone off the hook. It was two-thirty in the afternoon, and she was in the middle of enjoying a good sleep.

"Hello?" a female voice called out from the misplaced receiver.

Paris groaned as she extended a slender brown arm from her plush comforter to search for the phone.

"Hello?"

"Hi, Momma," Paris grumbled.

"How are you, baby? You must be sleeping. I can hear it in your voice."

Her mother's warm voice pulled Paris out of her sleep and provided the initiative to sit up in bed. Amidst the darkness, she rubbed her eyes and tried to focus on the surroundings of her bedroom. Her chocolate shades, pulled severely in attempt to block any cunning rays of sunlight. Outfits from last night's performance were strung over the back of her Queen Anne lounger in the far corner of her room. The closet was ajar, revealing a mirage of Size 6 lingerie, costumes, and casual clothes. La Perla Size 4 silk panties and 34C-sized brassieres decorated her wooden dresser and armoire. *I really need to clean this place up,* she reluctantly admitted to herself.

"Yeah, Momma, I got in really late last night." She stifled a yawn.

"Baby, I wish you would reconsider that late night job. A young lady doesn't need to be coming in that late at night. I worry about somebody following you home or something."

Even though she experienced a brief stab of guilt due to her mother's incessant worrying, Paris smiled. She shuddered to think what her mother would do if she knew what she was actually doing at her midnight job. She led Deanne, her mother, to believe that she worked the graveyard shift at a twenty-four hour customer-service call center. Though she hated lying to her mother, she knew it would kill Deanne to know her true profession. There was little chance that Deanne would discover Paris's secret because her mother lived in a tiny backward county in Mississippi and wouldn't dare travel all the way to racy, upbeat New Orleans.

The imaginary job wasn't the first misconception Paris planted in her mother's head, but merely the biggest in a rich history that spanned as far back as Paris could remember.

Deanne Jackson had been a single mother with an iron fist, narrow mind and a propensity to hide behind her stern Baptist teachings. Paris and her brothers learned early on to rely on their imagination when dealing with their mother's intolerant rules. Now, Paris constantly reminded herself that as a twenty-six year old woman, she should be able to look her mother in the eyes and tell her she was a grown woman whose choices were hers and hers alone, regardless if Deanne approved or not. Unfortunately, one disapproving look from Deanne could still make Paris feel like an eight-year-old with an unfinished homework assignment and no pre-packaged alibi.

Her twin brothers Ivan and Sharp lived in Atlanta. Georgia was far enough from Deanne to keep her from being confronted by their less than conservative lives, but close enough for them to make it home for major holidays. The boys were three years younger than Paris. She had always been fiercely protective of her brothers and had travailed over the decision to enlighten them on her career choice, especially Ivan. Although Ivan was only a minute-and-a-half younger than Sharp, it seemed like years. Growing up, she and Sharp had recognized Ivan's naïveté and had tried to shield him from kids that would take advantage of him.

She had told Sharp of her true profession, assuming that he would do her dirty work and relay the bad news to Ivan. His accusatory response had temporarily bruised her ego, but it was what she should have expected from Sharp.

"You know that's fucked up, but hey you're grown. I hope you realize that won't last for long though, and then what are you going to do?" Sharp had asked.

It was almost a year ago since she'd told Sharp her secret, and Paris hadn't paid his question much thought at the time. She also hadn't told him how much she made in a week, that being one of the biggest factors that convinced her to slowly disrobe in front of a room full of obnoxious men.

Paris considered her relationship with her brothers as close, but even in that, she kept them at arm's length emotionally. Sharp was very much the same way, and the two of them shielded Ivan's emotions. When she was around her family, Paris kept quiet most of the time to keep from slipping up and revealing too much about her lifestyle. She never allowed herself to think about how her brothers would feel if they saw her perform. It was much easier for her to keep those parts of her life separate physically and emotionally.

Not wanting to deal with the hassle of being distant this year, Paris wormed her way out of Easter and had a plan for getting out of Thanksgiving in a few months, but there was no way Deanne would let her off the hook for Christmas. She was going to have to drive her old Camry, which would mean leaving her beloved Porsche in the covered parking at her building,

Paris smiled to herself, imagining her brother's jaws dropping if they could see her convertible limited edition Porsche. Sharp would be extremely impressed, as he was much more materialistic than Ivan. She almost laughed aloud at the thought of Sharp's milk chocolate features turning green with envy. Fortunately, for him, she would never be able to drive her car anywhere near her family. There was no way she could justify having such an expensive car on her salary to her mother, and even if she could hide the fact from Deanne, the car would cause tongues to wag in Cleveland, Mississippi. So, although Sharp knew she was a dancer, she wouldn't be able to share her prized possession with him either. Paris and Sharp were kindred spirits, and she knew he'd never admit how much it bothered him that she was stripping for a living. If anyone understood doing everything in one's power to avoid ending up powerless and without, it was Sharp.

"Baby, are you there?" Deanne's question snapped Paris out of her daydreaming.

"Yeah, Momma. I guess I'm really tired."

"Alright, baby. I'd better let you get back to sleep. Call me later in the week all right?"

Paris returned her mother's goodbye, replaced the phone and pulled her down comforter over her eyes. She hoped sleep would not evade her as it usually did once her groove had been interrupted. It was Friday, and that meant she'd have to endure hell at the club tonight. The weekend would produce hordes of men who were ready and willing to spend their hard-earned cash on any and everything but their wives and children.

Paris still found it hard to believe that her customers spent so much money at the club. Many dancers told stories of exotic trips and grossly expensive jewelry lavished upon them by besotted customers. The majority of these men were married, and it was obvious by their constant offers that their wives were totally in the dark.

Last year a silver-tongued Italian executive from New York whisked Chocolate away on an all-expense paid tryst to Belize. Chocolate told Paris the man called his wife three times every day and even answered a cell phone call from his daughter while they were engaged in what Chocolate described as physical recreation.

The lies never stopped with these men, from secret credit cards, covertly written-off expenses, surreptitious phone numbers to elaborate love nests and exorbitant cash advances. Their intricately spun web of lies magically avoided intersecting, leaving their wives and families none the wiser.

A very-married customer who owned an exotic car dealership talked Paris into test-driving a brand spanking new Porsche Boxster. He generously offered to help with the down payment on the car, then informed Paris that she would be the culmination of every man's secret fantasy driving the phallic-symbol of a car. After posing in several pictures for his dealership surrounded by various new Porsche models, Paris decided she liked the way she looked and felt sitting behind the wheel of the car. She fell completely in love with a sleek black convertible, and so the next week her auto dealer friend helped her put a hefty down payment on a '99 Porsche Boxster.

Paris bought her Porsche a month after the Mardi Gras celebration. The infamous New Orleans holiday was easily her favorite time of year, as she made the bulk of her yearly salary that week. The hedonistic French Quarter were bombarded with freaks and perverts, who, surprisingly enough, had tough competition outdoing the average Joes ready to shed coordinating suit coats and slacks for a week of unadulterated fun. Since much of the celebration included strip bars and private parties, Paris, along with her co-workers cleaned up righteously. This year she'd worked twelve private parties, and that was working the Sunday before Mardi Gras through the Wednesday after. She cleared over twelve thousand dollars, and got another twenty-five hundred at the club that weekend. With that money, and help from a couple of friends who enjoyed her company, she managed to pay her penthouse off completely.

While Chocolate reminisced about how nice it must be to have someone love you enough to want to give you their last name, Paris reminded her it was much better to be on this side of the bank account. There was no way she wanted to end up being played out like the wives of her clients.

# *CHAPTER TWO*
## *www.underthecherrymoon.com*

"Don't forget, I need you in early today. We got that photo shoot right before your set," Kenton, Paris's boss, reminded her over the phone. The sound of Kenton's authoritative tone reminded Paris of how much of a prick he was. Kenton had the reputation of having the best strip club in the South, which was no small feat, considering Atlanta and Miami were infamous for their gentlemen's clubs. While Kenton was a glorified pimp for most of the girls on his roster, he and Paris had a much different relationship. She knew he respected her ability to separate business from pleasure, even if he wasn't exactly sure what in her past made her such a hard ass. She also knew he was aware that the respect was mutual. For all his arrogance, Paris respected Kenton as a shrewd businessman. He only valued that which produced results, and results meant everyone got paid and paid well.

Paris groaned but assured him she'd be there two hours early. She couldn't forget about the impending photo shoot if she'd wanted. The tracks she'd added to her thick waist length hair yesterday were expensive reminders. Kenton believed in going all out to stimulate his customers' fantasies. He had scheduled a celebrity photographer to take pictures of his top four performers. This particular set was for the club's website, which was currently under construction, awaiting the newest and sexiest pictures Kenton could put on a public website without surpassing the pornographic boundaries. The quintessential businessman, Kenton didn't want to exclude anyone from being allowed access to the club's website. There was, however, a more in-depth pornographic internet tour one could get for the annual price of $49.99 that would allow access to more revealing pictures of some of the dancers.

Looking for the outfits Kenton requested she wear for the pictures, Paris rummaged through her closet. The theme for the website was

"*Indulge yourself on cherries and cream at Under the Cherry Moon.*" The girls wore various pieces of red and cream La Perla lingerie. Paris and Chocolate were paired up as usual, with Sundae and Jezebel completing the foursome. The red g-string with matching string bikini top was not Paris's favorite, but there was no choice. She dropped the set in her silk garment bag and added a lacy red teddy. After finally locating both of her scarlet four-inch pumps, she relished the opportunity to relax alone before heading in for what promised to be an extremely trying night at the club.

After taking a relaxing bath and treating herself to a facial, Paris decided to do her own make-up instead of relying on the make-up artist Kenton hired. She knew he had them working on the other girls, but he trusted her ability to do her face for photos. She knew she needed help with her hair, as Kenton was anal and insisted on absolute perfection. No matter her thoughts about her duties tonight, she couldn't begrudge Kenton's business sense. His shrewd insight helped secure her and Chocolate a lot of money outside of the club from private appearances and shows.

The money was good, but sometimes Paris thought the price was a bit too high. She swallowed the feelings that often arose in the pit of her stomach each time she let Kenton talk her into doing something a bit more risqué for profit. Since working at Under the Cherry Moon, he'd cajoled her into crossing more than a few boundaries she thought she'd never cross. The biggest example was his request that she and Chocolate do what was for all practical purposes a lesbian act. Kenton managed to put her in the same predicament he'd rescued her from years ago, still Paris allowed herself to be convinced for the sake and security of her paycheck.

She took a deep breath to steady her nerves. There was no doubt she'd be asked to do some suggestive posing with Chocolate and the other girls during the shoot today. Staring at her reflection in her vanity, she willed the fear and shame from her eyes. As long as she made choices that benefited Paris Renee Jackson, she had nothing to be ashamed about. Fear meant that she wasn't in control, and she couldn't have that. Once she was certain her eyes reflected their usual steely determination, she resumed getting ready for an evening at the club.

As usual, Paris and Kenton ended up in a heated argument once she'd finished her individual pictures. She'd insisted he was trying to make them too pornographic. They'd bumped heads over pornographic pictures before, and every time, Paris stuck to her resolve of not taking her clothes off in front of a photographer.

"You take your fucking top off every night. What's the damn difference? Everybody in here sees what your titties look like, up close and in person. You think these niggas in here don't remember what you look like when they leave?" Kenton asked, mocking her. "I see what's up."

"Maybe they do, maybe they don't. I don't give a fuck. All I know is, I'm not taking any pictures that could end up anywhere on the freaking planet. I don't want to live the rest of my life like that," Paris shot back angrily.

"Oh so you thinking about pulling an Analise on me and getting hitched up with some sucker too, huh? The pictures may ruin that white picket dream you got, huh?" Kenton challenged.

"Don't play me like that, Kenton. You know that's not me," she retorted irately, storming out of Kenton's office.

"Paris, hold up." Kenton stepped out from behind his desk.

She threw her extensions over her shoulder and pushed past Kenton toward the dressing room. She rolled her eyes as Kenton rushed behind her. He put a hand on her shoulder to attempt to turn her to face him, but she threw his hand off.

"So what is it? Hell, it pays. It pays damn good. That's usually all it takes to get your ass to do something."

Paris abruptly swung around to face him and slowly extended her middle finger.

Kenton laughed. "Classic, Paris. Why you always got to be so damn difficult?"

"Because I said I don't want to do it, that's why. I don't do shit that I don't want to do." She crossed her arms over her chest

Paris mentally prepared a comeback for Kenton's usual statistical spill referencing what sales of a pornographic mini-magazine could do for Under the Cherry Moon. He took a deep breath, but hesitated as the two of them locked eyes. She broke the gaze and unlocked the door to the dressing room, letting it close in his face. She heard him open the door and follow her over to her vanity, but she ignored him. The stares of the other dancers made the room thick with tension, but Paris was determined not to give in. She congratulated herself on gaining a bit more control of the situation when instead of responding, Kenton shook his head and left the dressing room without lapsing into his usual rant.

An hour later, Paris and Chocolate were positioned provocatively across each other on a white bearskin rug.

"Now bring Sundae in. I want her right behind Paris," the photographer instructed.

His male assistant motioned for the other dancer to kneel behind Paris and place one hand precariously close to her breast.

"I'm sorry, Paris," Sundae whispered as her hand brushed Paris's left breast.

Paris just pursed her heavily glossed lips. These photo sessions really worked her nerves. *There is no way Kenton or any other man would submit to this type of humiliation for an hour and a half,* she fumed internally. It chapped her to no end that Kenton stood to make much more money off this shoot than she or any of her colleagues did. Still, she reminded herself, the money would be good, and it wasn't like these pictures were being seen by anyone except a bunch of pathetic horny men. Why was she stressing over something that had already been seen by clients of the club, and was putting money in her account. Kenton, the photographer and the other men on set were just waiting for one of the girls to lose it, especially her. There was no way she was giving them the satisfaction of seeing her break.

The photographer proceeded to place Jezebel between Chocolate's legs with her head resting atop Chocolate's stomach.

"Are we about ready now?" Paris asked sarcastically.

"Please tell your dancer I cannot have this type of energy coming from her right now." His emphasis on the word dancer let Paris know he thought all the ladies posing for him were a joke. "All that ghetto girl attitude is coming straight through my lens, taking over my beautiful pictures. I can assure you, your customers don't want that. Men don't come to this club for attitude."

Paris rolled her eyes at the photographer's dramatic response. Clad in pink silk pants, his petite legs flitted back and forth around the small set.

He was a flaming homosexual, and Paris found his imitation female falsetto extremely annoying. The only reason Kenton booked him was because he was the best, constantly in demand for fashion magazines and commercial advertising.

"I know his precious little ass didn't just call me ghetto," Paris snarled.

"Can you please just chill, Paris, so we can get through?" Kenton asked through gritted teeth.

Paris narrowed her eyes and shot an evil glance his way. *It's damn easy for his ass to say chill, he's not sitting with two other dudes hands all over his body*, she thought angrily. The hot lights, coupled with the thick extensions added to her hair, had Paris drenched in sweat midway through the shoot. She sucked her teeth, but resigned herself to cooperating for the sake of getting out of there as soon as possible.

"We're almost through, girl. I feel you though," Sundae agreed.

"Now give me the eyes," the photographer instructed. "I need all four sets right here. I want your eyes to follow any viewer that pops onto this site."

Obediently, Paris and the other dancers focused on the camera and tried their best to seduce their internet audience. The camera whirred and clicked for five minutes straight as no one on the set moved a muscle.

"Beautiful, absolutely beautiful," the photographer purred.

His assistants agreed, uttering oohs and ahs between his words.

"That's money in the bank," Kenton added from the back of the room.

"You're going to have every heterosexual man with a PC down here spending his hard earned money," one of the assistants said slyly.

"You're always welcomed to join us," Sundae offered, making eyes at the light-skinned assistant with a long curly ponytail.

"Not my type of party, girlfriend, but thanks for the invite. You all are simply fabulous!" he exclaimed, slapping the other assistant a high five.

"Ain't that some disappointing shit?" Chocolate whispered to Paris and Sundae. Paris laughed, in spite of her pre-disposed bad mood.

As soon as the girls heard the camera shut off, they began the task of untangling stiff limbs, heavily laden with body pancake make-up from around each other. While the other dancers huddled around the laptop, getting a first peek at the new proofs, Paris pushed through the studio doors and made her way to the dressing room. All the way in the back of the club, the dressing room would probably be empty. She needed to get her mind right for her sets tonight. Scolding herself for letting the photo session rattle her, she fought to convince herself that she hadn't done anything she was overly uncomfortable with. *In reality, they just created some tricky illusions.* She smirked to herself as the photographers rhetoric played over in her mind.

"We're just creating illusions for the men whose ultimate fantasy is to be the only man in a roomful of accommodating lesbians," he explained to the girls as if they were completely devoid of a brain.

At the time, his words hadn't done much to calm Paris down, especially considering the condescending delivery, but now she acknowledged he was right. Even though she and Chocolate did things on stage she didn't enjoy, she knew she wasn't bi-sexual. If the performance gave the illusion that she was, then so be it. Their double performances always brought in double the money she usually made. What did it matter if she didn't enjoy it in the least? Most of the time she didn't feel sexual at all, especially after performing.

"Shake it off, girl," Jezebel cut into Paris's musing. "You know them pictures is just a thang."

The unexpected comment took Paris off guard. She turned and glared at Jezebel as the rest of the dancers made their way into the empty dressing room.

"Paris, your pictures were the bomb for real," Chocolate congratulated as she put an arm on Paris's shoulder and shook her slightly. "What's up?"

Paris brushed the hand off her shoulder and glared at Chocolate. "Nothing's up. I just wasn't feeling that shit that's all," Paris offered smartly.

"It's not like we were naked or anything," Chocolate consoled.

"Who cares if we were naked? We're naked in here all the damn time." Jezebel shrugged as Chocolate's eyes pleaded with her to stop needling Paris.

"Chill, Jez, not everybody wants to be featured in *Black Tail.*"

"Whatever, *Black Tail* pays my bills," Jezebel retorted sassily.

"Different strokes for different folks," Chocolate relented.

Paris remained quiet throughout the conversation, moodily removing some of the tawny colored pancake she'd applied for the photo session. Jezebel's barely five-foot voluptuous frame was oozing from a brilliantly white garter set which set her bronzed skin off to perfection, while her face was hidden obscurely behind blond curls. Jezebel was a dark-haired Latina, but it was hard to know exactly what she was with the blonde hair and heavy make-up. Looking at the smug expression on her face, Paris thought she was a joke.

"Are you ready, Sundae?" Jezebel asked.

Sundae ran a reassuring hand over her pasties, smiling at herself in the mirror. Not bothering to change out of the scarlet boy-cut panties and demi-bra she'd worn for the pictures,the two of them whispered to each other, giggled, then headed out to do their set.

"Don't worry about them. Jezebel don't bring in near as much money as either of us, so she has to do stuff on the side. I ain't mad at her though. She does have mouths to feed at home. I mean, everybody has to do what they think they have to do to survive, ya know?" Chocolate put a reassuring hand on her shoulder.

Paris shrugged it off, again. "Damn, I thought you would have had enough touching for one day."

"Forget you then. I was just trying to make your evil ass feel better."

Eyes closed, Paris attempted to calm the anger boiling in the pit of her stomach. Drawing in a deep breath, she re-adjusted her focus on the task of dancing for the next four hours, then opened her eyes. "I know you're trying to make me feel better. I was just trippin'. I'm cool now."

Paris stood and surveyed herself in the wall-length mirror. Getting home to take the extensions out of her hair couldn't come fast enough. Excessively long and thick, she worried that because the weave was sewn so tight, it might somehow damage her natural hair. Peering over at Chocolate to see if she'd accepted her effort at an apology, Chocolate's eyes met hers in the mirror. Instead of speaking, Chocolate just shook her head.

# *CHAPTER THREE*
# *SHE'S GOT EVIL EYES*

"I want you to work with her for the first couple of weekends, then we'll see how she does on her own," Kenton instructed, watching Paris expertly apply lip liner in the wall-length mirror.

"Is she green?" Paris asked, pivoting to face him.

"Her interview was pretty tight, but it's an entirely different game once you get out there," Kenton commented.

Paris glanced over at the young girl dressed in cut-off denim shorts and a revealing midriff sweater. Part of Paris and Chocolate's responsibility as head dancers was to choreograph new routines, then coach the new girls until they could choreograph their own shows. Some girls were naturals, but others completely freaked out as soon as the stage lit up and the house lights went down.

Paris walked over to the girl and introduced herself. The girl's nervous response told Paris she was intimidated by her aggressive approach. This kid looked freshly sixteen, and stood a statuesque 5'9" without the high heels. Guessing the girl was probably a wanna-be model taking the strip club detour, she must've been unaware that an almost non-existent percentage of girls made the complicated transition from stripping to modeling.

It was no secret that some of the dancers had mentalities like Jezebel and considered modeling in *Black Tail* and *Players* as breaking into the illustrious modeling business. The ambition was usually there, alongside youth. But, as age caught up with numerous failed attempts, the girls' motivation fizzled out, and they became content dancing in a high-class gentlemen's club. After experiencing the high of having temporary control over customers, most girls became consumed with their own sexuality and could easily be convinced to pose nude, which was a hop, skip and short jump from turning the occasional trick. The girls also became addicted to the quick cash that was received nightly, as opposed to waiting for the 1st and 15th of the month.

While Paris hadn't totally rejected the idea of one day posing nude, there was absolutely no chance she would turn tricks. Just about all of the dancers she'd ever worked with either had been or soon would be persuaded. The money was simply too hard to turn down. Paris had no qualms with taking men's money in the club, but sleeping with clients would put her in an emotionally vulnerable position that she didn't want to be in. As a rule, Paris avoided vulnerability like the plague, and so she only slept with a few choice male friends who understood her need for privacy.

She wouldn't consider sleeping with any man who was a regular at the club. Although often propositioned with big bucks while doing private dances, she knew if she gave in, the customer would be in control. Control was the one thing Paris valued more than money. As a young girl watching her mother cry over her father, Paris vowed never to let a man have control over any aspect of her life.

"I'm Keisha," the café-au-lait girl said, extending a slender hand with three-inch manicured nails.

Taking in the girl's passive non-verbal signals, Paris shook her hand firmly. "Call me Caramel when we're in the club," Paris informed her.

"You're in good hands." Kenton smiled and smacked the girl on her rear. "I'll see you when you get back."

Keisha giggled playfully as her innocent eyes stared longingly after Kenton's retreating presence. Paris rolled her eyes and continued applying her lip liner, leaving Keisha standing in the middle of the dressing room.

After the aroma of Kenton's cologne had wafted from the room, Keisha awkwardly walked over to Paris's dressing area. "I think I may be a little scared or nervous at first, at least until I do it a few times, but I know I'll be really good. I mean once I get used to it," Keisha rambled nervously. "How do you deal with the vibes from the men when you're up there? I mean, they can be really loud sometimes, not to mention really rude," she asked, attempting to make eye contact with Paris through the wall length mirror.

*Great, this one doesn't have half a brain*, Paris thought dryly. Keisha stared expectantly at her, resembling a baby bird seeking morsels from its mother's beak.

"Every man out there is pathetic. You give a pathetic man a little ego massage and a smile, and his dumb ass is at your disposal," Paris explained flippantly.

"Excuse me?"

"If you just concentrate on how pathetic somebody has to be for them to be in here giving you all their hard-earned money, you'll do fine." The girl's eyes widened. Paris continued, "Would you give a man who had absolutely no interest in you all your hard-earned money?"

Keisha swallowed slowly then shook her head. "No, I guess I wouldn't." She paused. "I mean, if we were involved, maybe."

Her voice was full of uncertainty, and Paris immediately took that to mean Keisha was an easy target. Her questionable self-esteem and naïveté immediately categorized her a fish, and the men who frequented Under the Cherry Moon sought out and quickly took advantage of fish. In Paris's experience, even the most colorful fish didn't do well in these shark-infested waters; only the sharks survived. The money, power and influence their customers possessed outside the walls of the club gave them a tremendous edge over any dancer. You had to be one of the smartest sharks to maintain your sanity, and one of the biggest sharks to keep from being mauled and labeled a victim.

"Remember, it's all mental," Paris instructed. "Watch and learn," she threw over her shoulder, adjusting her pink pasties as she headed out to center stage.

Paris was objective as she watched Keisha performing behind a small window in the sound booth.

"What do you think?" Kenton asked.

"You can tell she's been a dancer and taken lessons for awhile. She needs to loosen up, though. She's a little stiff. She probably needs to rehearse a routine to start with and get used to doing the same movements until it comes naturally." Paris studied the young girl as she moved from patron to patron. "And tell her to stop looking each trick in the eyes."

"Give her a break. She's just nineteen," Kenton said. Paris glanced over at him and rolled her eyes.

"Are you sure she's nineteen?" Paris noticed an innocence in the girl's eyes while they were talking that made her trust her previous suspicions that Keisha was closer to sixteen than nineteen. Whatever her age truly was, it didn't matter much now. As long as the girl didn't give Kenton any tangible reason to doubt her age, there was no way he would push for the truth.

Judging by the way Kenton was salivating over Keisha, Paris was sure the girl would end up being his flavor of the month in no time flat. Kenton, after all, was the biggest shark in the water.

"You think you can work with her?" Kenton asked, flashing a devilish smile.

"We'll see. I'm not a magician you know."

"You just do your part. I'll work the magic," Kenton countered, ogling the girl's behind as she sashayed off the stage.

"You are so damn trifling," Paris spat, disgusted with Kenton's lack of control. Kenton flashed his tongue suggestively at her.

"Been there, done that. Don't want to go back." She flipped her hair over her shoulder, dismissing Kenton's insinuations.

# CHAPTER FOUR
# AN UNWANTED KNIGHT IN SHINING ARMOR

Paris read the addressee labels while skimming through the mail on her coffee table, methodically separating bills from catalogs and magazines. Her work week was Wednesday through Saturday, and Mondays were reserved strictly for downtime. She usually stayed in the bed until noon and rarely ventured out of the house for anything other than to retrieve her mail and newspaper.

Kenton interrupted her solitude this morning, calling with an offer that pushed her out of the bed and made her restless. There was going to be an oil and gas company convention in town, and one of the attendees had visited the club on a prior business trip. He'd been so enchanted with Paris, he'd asked Kenton to book her for a private performance for himself and five of his clients. Paris had done this type of party before, but no matter how many times she did them, she was uncomfortable until the festivities were over. Always striving for control, she had made a strict rule of never doing any of these jobs by herself, so Kenton had told the men they would need to book two dancers and the bouncer if they wanted to seal a deal. The man was more than willing to agree to those terms as long as Caramel was one of the dancers. Kenton informed her that he had taken the liberty of approaching Chocolate with the deal, and she was willing to do it. He threw in a guilt trip about Chocolate needing the extra money to buy something for one of her kids. Kenton wasn't aware of it, but Paris had little sympathy for Chocolate's or anyone else's situation. The way she saw it, everyone had choices, and in the real world, choices came complete with consequences.

The chime of the doorbell shocked Paris out of her disturbing recollections of perverted men pawing all over her during private parties. She pulled her silk robe tighter around her body and smoothed it out to its full length at mid-thigh.

"Grey," she sighed, visibly disappointed at his unwelcome reflection staring at her through the peephole. Grey Lucette would be considered heaven sent by any other woman. Standing 6 feet even with a butterscotch complexion and grayish blue eyes, he was the definitive pretty boy. Unfortunately for Grey, Paris was the one woman who remained undaunted by his looks or his impressive bottomless wallet that reflected his job as senior partner at one of New Orleans's most prestigious law firms. She cracked the door partially open.

"Pretty in Paris," Grey said, smiling down at her.

"What's up?" Paris asked, fully opening the door so Grey could follow her into her luxury condo.

"I know Monday is your off-day, so I thought I'd stop by and bring you lunch."

Knowing Grey always offered his motives upfront to deter her mood swings, she smirked.

He sat on her cream sofa and produced a brown paper bag from behind his back. "I got your favorite, orange chicken and fried rice."

He withdrew two cartons and chopsticks from the bag and pushed her boxed dinner across the table at her. Paris smiled briefly at Grey, then plopped on the love seat facing him. He'd succeeded in slipping past her usual annoyance at his invasion of her serenity-promised Mondays.

"You didn't have to do this," she said sweetly.

Grey constantly attempted to win her over. Usually, his presence bored her, but today his intrusion was a welcome distraction, especially since he came bearing her favorite Chinese dish.

"What have you been up to?" she asked, taking a bite of her chicken. Eyes closed, she savored the sweet taste. Opening her eyes, she found Grey staring intently at her.

"What?" she asked coyly.

"You're really enjoying that chicken."

She smiled at him then took a prim sip of her diet cola. "It was really thoughtful of you to come all the way out here on your lunch hour and bring me something. I needed the distraction."

"Oh, I've got good timing now, huh? So tell me, what has you needing some distraction? Usually you'd have laid some lame excuse on me to leave by now." His voice was good-natured, but his eyes belied his disappointment in their relationship.

Paris debated if she should share her dilemma about doing the private party. She felt like Kenton was taking advantage of her, and while she wanted Grey's opinion, she knew this could quickly turn into something he could use to try to persuade her to stop dancing.

"Kenton wants me to do a private show with Chocolate for a corporate group in two weeks. I'm just not sure if I feel up to doing another one of those right now," she said, avoiding Grey's intense gaze.

He put down his chopsticks and leaned his elbows on beige slack-covered knees. "Paris, I don't know why you won't listen to me. I've told you repeatedly, you don't have to live like this. You don't have to dance at that ridiculous club another night. Let me take care of you."

Paris stood up and stalked angrily on bare feet over to the window. "I'm not getting into this with you again," she said in a clipped voice.

It was just like Grey's dumb ass to go and ruin the mood. She'd been tolerant with him, and he just had to go and spark her fire, bringing them back to this explosive discussion. She chastised herself for not following her first mind by keeping her situation to herself. Now, she regretted even allowing him in the house. On several occasions, she'd made it crystal clear that in no way, form or fashion was she interested in signing up to play the monogamous game with him.

She'd stopped sleeping with him six months ago because he was becoming harder and harder to shake after the fireworks were over. She'd only slept with him four times, but it felt like a mistake that she'd be indebted to for the rest of her life.

"I don't understand you. It's obvious you don't want to live the rest of your life like this. If you did, you wouldn't be so worried about doing another private party. You don't have much time left in this business. Pretty soon there'll be another younger Caramel dancing at that club, and then what are you going to do?"

"That's none of your concern is it, Grey? And furthermore, that club is where I met you, so it can't be that ridiculous if your snooty ass was up in there." Paris narrowed her eyes at him angrily.

As usual, he was persistent and completely unfazed by the insults she hurled his way. "I just wish you would seriously think about your future. You're better than that, Paris. You're different from all those other girls in that club. Anyone can tell you that. You don't belong there."

Paris sucked her teeth irritably. Grey was always complaining about the rest of the "hood rats" that worked at the club with her. He absolutely hated Chocolate. He was constantly climbing atop his personal soapbox proclaiming Chocolate to be the typical ghetto single mother who didn't take care of her children. His ultra-conservative argument claimed she was setting a terrible example for them and ultimately the rest of society.

"Grey, no one tells me how to live my life. I have my reasons for dancing. If you feel so strongly about this, maybe the two of us need to go our separate ways." She folded her arms across her chest. Grey was tap dancing on her last nerve. His plan for her life consisted of her accepting him as her savior. He wanted to be the knight in shining armor that rescued the wayward little girl, dressed her in white, put her in a storybook house and have her pregnant before the honeymoon was over. This would, of course, make her indebted to him for the rest of her life. There was no way she would go for that. Paris had managed to be her own knight in shining armor, and she intended to give herself a life of luxury and security.

She sucked her teeth again. *Grey has to be mentally disturbed.* There was no way she was buying into his delusional dreams of her becoming Mrs. Grey Lucette. He was silent after she voiced an undeniable truth she whipped out whenever she'd had enough of his self-righteous talk. The bottom line was, even though he found strippers disgusting and claimed men didn't respect them, a stripper had his nose wide open. Paris never let him forget that, ultimately giving her the upper hand in their relationship. For all Grey's complaints, he wasn't going anywhere until she'd had enough of his platinum credit card and was ready for him to go.

"I'm sorry," he conceded. "I shouldn't keep pressuring you. I just want you to know if you ever reconsider..." he trailed off.

"Don't hold your breath. When we met I was dancing, and when you're gone, I'll still be dancing," she said smartly.

He lowered his head and closed his eyes. The defeat she read in his posture brought a smug smile of satisfaction to her face.

# CHAPTER FIVE
# THE BENEFITS OF FRIENDSHIP

Paris met Grey when the partners at his law firm decided that renting out the club during lunch hours qualified as a business lunch. Furthermore, they reasoned, the corporate credit card would be able to withstand the exorbitant amount Kenton charged them for interrupting his daily lunch crowd money. The meeting was a two-fold celebration, as the firm had just won a huge settlement for a local client and had brought on two new partners. Grey Lucette was introduced as a phenomenal new talent, and the bosses were treating him and their other prized protégé like royalty.

"Now you ladies be good to these two gentlemen. They are the biggest assets we've acquired in a long time. I want you all to give these fellas as many lap dances as they can stand without ruining their slacks or falling in love," the older man had joked.

Paris was immediately aware of Grey because unlike most of the corporate men who visited the club, he was quiet and non-aggressive. He didn't lose himself in the party as most of his co-workers had. Paris was familiar with the company, and most of the men were standoffish around her. She didn't encourage patrons to touch her unless their money was within her reach. She absolutely never gave bargains, deals or specials, as most dancers would. It made sense to most girls to give their loyal customers a break or even a freebie every now and then, if they knew they were coming back to spend more money. Even Kenton agreed with the practice, assuring the girls he was overcharging patrons enough with drinks and cigars to ensure the club wasn't taking anywhere near a loss. Kenton referred to it as keeping everything on the up and up. On occasion, he hinted to Paris that perhaps she should give a client a break on a table dance or a lap dance, and she laughed in his face.

"Please. I don't get a break on my car note, my touch-ups at the beauty salon or my electric bill for that matter. My clients respect me for not compromising," she countered, blowing his reasoning off.

Paris's standards were understood throughout the club, and she was rarely asked to "hook a brotha up".

"You gotta come correct if you trying to get at Caramel," was a popular saying around the club.

Paris continued to watch Grey and his interaction with his new co-workers. The firm consisted mostly of Caucasian men of upper-middle class and age. Most of them wouldn't dare approach a black woman on the street, so they frequented Under the Cherry Moon to live out their exotically urban fantasies. Because they weren't used to talking to black women on a romantic level, white men tended to be a little nervous and uncomfortable until they'd had a few drinks and a little encouragement. Some of the dancers would coddle the men to loosen them up and make them feel more at ease, but that wasn't her style. If you were paying, she was dancing. Paris didn't have time to hold some old white man's hand and convince him she was down with a little jungle fever. The way she saw it, that was a lot of extra work for very little extra pay. When catered to, most men ended up trying to get over or became convinced they could entice the stereotypical poor little black girl with their superiorly Caucasian expensive gifts and cars. They knew their platinum blonde trophy wives would be mortified if they discovered their husband's were dipping their stick in chocolate syrup, so the thrill was the best money could buy, in more ways than one.

In the midst of his over-anxious colleagues, Grey appeared unusually calm and observant. His chameleon grayish-blue eyes studied Caramel curiously. While she found his eyes disturbingly unique, she felt comfortable under his scrutiny. She was used to men leering at her, and it usually was followed up with some serious cash. She just wondered if he would cough up any dollars as a result of his observation. She had completed two sets before he approached her and asked how much a private dance would be. Paris informed him that his company worked out a deal with Kenton to where their lap dances were free. Unfortunately, she and Chocolate were unavailable unless he was willing to fork out his own money. She insisted there were several dancers that would be more than happy to accommodate him.

"I want you," he replied simply.

"I'm sorry, but my services weren't included in the deal," she countered.

"What if I want to buy a dance from you? Only you? How much will that be?" he asked, enunciating each word slowly.

Paris gave him her rates while staring him squarely in the eyes. He pulled a crisp fifty-dollar bill out of his wallet, unfolded it and primly handed it to her. As soon as the money exchanged hands, Paris's demeanor changed. Her suspiciously calculating eyes transformed into smiling, flirty ones.

"I'll be right back," she cooed, winking at him.

She quickly deposited the money then returned to find Grey at an isolated table. Paris smiled into Grey's, eyes but her brain followed the words to Toni Braxton's hit "You're Making Me High." She noticed that his eyes stayed focused on her face, even when her hands moved suggestively to her breasts and thighs.

"Are you allowed to talk, while you're doing this?" Grey inquired.

Paris chuckled lightly at his naïveté.

"Of course, I can talk. What do you want to talk about, baby?" She rolled her hips over his crotch, methodically imitating a sexual grind while licking her lips.

"I mean can you sit down and talk?" he asked anxiously. She could tell that her sexually explicit movements had unsettled him and his cool exterior was slowly beginning to melt.

*Finally,* Paris congratulated herself. It had taken her longer than usual to get a rise out of him. He seemed anxious to talk, which wasn't unusual, except most patrons waited until after the lap dance was over to strike up conversation.

"Do you want me to sit down and talk now?" She stopped moving, as that was the apparent cause of his distraction.

"Yes, I'd like that better I think," he agreed quickly. "It's not that I don't like your dancing. It's very nice, but I would prefer to talk to you right now."

Paris thanked her lucky star for the break and quickly removed her legs from either side of Grey. It wasn't often she got an easy one like this, and she would enjoy it for as long as he shelled out the dough.

"Do you like doing this?" Grey asked as he leaned across the table to study her.

She had to admit, he did have the most beautiful eyes she'd ever seen. They resembled cool liquid pools, very still and calm. It would've been relatively easy for a woman to get lost in their beautifully unique color. *This one is a real catch.* She took the time to scan his hands for a ring or an inconsistency in the color of the skin on his ring finger that would indicate he owned a wedding ring. Wedding rings were notorious for relocating during club hours to a coat pocket or glove compartment. Her check came up empty-handed. His hands were smooth, with skin the color of pale honey. *He really is a good-looking man,* Paris repeated to herself. She noticed that he'd taken out four more fifty-dollar bills, straightened them out neatly, and carefully laid them out, then folded his hands neatly on the table. She smiled coyly, thinking there must have been a sky full of stars feeling her tonight. Not only was this one nice-looking with a body to match, but he wasn't skimping on the cash.

"Do I like this?" she repeated the question to give herself more time to come up with the answer she thought he wanted to hear.

If she were able to be honest, she could've explained how repulsed she felt by the men's touches. She could've told him that many nights she left the club feeling sick to her stomach after having money shoved in her panties and bra for five hours. She also would've been able to share with him how on some nights, she felt so much anger she honestly believed she could kill every warm-blooded man in the club for spending money to objectify women who could care less about them and neglecting their families at home. She would've told him that every once in a blue moon when a patron was being especially generous, she wondered if her father had frequented clubs like this, giving his money to strippers while her mother struggled to raise her and her brothers. On those nights, she got a high from taking the money of strangers who assigned more value to a shot at her tits and ass than her father had placed on to her heart.

"I enjoy my work," she answered simply.

Disbelief flickered in Grey's eyes, but was quickly replaced by the cool calmness they'd displayed before. The millisecond it took for Grey to conceal his emotions would have been lost on anyone besides Paris. She made it her job to thoroughly read her clients verbal and nonverbal behavior, unbeknownst to them. *Okay, so this one is not the average dumb-ass. I'll have to go the extra mile with him.* She filed the information in her mental rolodex for future dealings with Grey.

"You are a very beautiful woman," he stated slowly.

"Thank you," she returned sweetly. "You're very handsome. I'll bet you have lots of beautiful women dying to be with you. Obviously you're successful. Good-looking, successful, and I'm also sure, very nice. What more could a woman want?"

Grey smiled, and subtle laugh lines appeared in the crinkles of his eyes.

*So he does have a lighter side.*

"Do you really think so?" he asked.

"Definitely."

Out of habit, she leaned toward him to give him a better view of her cleavage spilling out of a black bikini top.

"What is a woman like you looking for?" Grey asked pointedly.

Paris closed her eyes and pretended to ponder the question. She knew this was another instance she couldn't afford to be honest. The truth was, Paris wasn't looking for a man at all. She had no intentions of ever giving her heart to a man and experiencing the disappointment that came along with heartbreak.

"Umm, definitely someone like you." She smiled sweetly at him.

Grey didn't return her smile as she'd predicted. Instead, he pushed his chair back and zeroed in on her eyes. "I think I'll take another dance now."

Paris stood up and paused to catch the rhythm of the song. Britney Spears was singing, "I'm a Slave for You." *You got that right girlfriend,* Paris agreed, before lowering herself onto Grey's lap once more.

Paris wasn't sure when Grey had made the transition from client to friend, because as a rule of thumb she never allowed that to happen. It was the equivalent of mixing gasoline and fire. She had seen more than one dancer find herself in a precarious position after they let a client get a little too close. The male ego was notably ultra fragile, and they couldn't stand to see another customer getting attention from a girl they assumed was reserved specifically for them.

After consistently frequenting the club for two months, Grey continued to appear physically uncomfortable in the environment. Most nights Grey would pay up-front for a minimum of two hours, and they'd spent the time talking and getting to know each other. He seldom requested a dance and never gave any of the other girls the time of day. Whenever he came in the club and she was servicing another client, he would disappear until she was finished.

Grey was from a historically affluent Creole family, with a blue-blood family tree spanning back four generations. Aside from his obvious distaste for everyone else in the club, Paris surprisingly didn't find him too pretentious most of the time. He was actually proving to be someone she enjoyed talking to, but didn't take seriously. It was obvious from hints he threw out during conversation that he was looking to turn their relationship into a long-term arrangement. Paris had had men attempt this in the past, and it was only a matter of time before they saw it was useless to try to change her mind. Eventually, they all accepted the parameters Paris placed on their relationships.

Six weeks into their meetings, Grey began hinting that he was willing to help her out financially if it would save her some stress at the club.

"You shouldn't have to work so hard," he'd say before presenting her with an envelope with neatly folded hundred dollar bills. Sometimes he substituted the bills for a check, but the sum was always to Paris's liking.

Grey's complimentary envelopes became a regular source of income. One night he laid things on the line and admitted to her that he felt uncomfortable coming to the club.

"This isn't my scene. You know I just come to see you. Isn't there a way I can see you outside of this place? I don't have to come to your house. I'd just like to meet you somewhere. Take you someplace," he offered gallantly.

Paris was hesitant at first.

"I have to go to a gala next week on behalf of my firm. I'd like you to be my escort, if you wouldn't feel too uncomfortable."

Still debating on letting Grey become more than a patron of Under the Cherry Moon, Paris smiled.

"Of course I would pay for anything you needed." He produced a platinum credit card from his wallet and pushed it across the table to rest in front of her. "I'm sure you'd like to buy a new dress, shoes, bag, jewelry...anything you need to feel more beautiful, just charge it," he said matter-of-factly.

Paris picked the card up and examined it. "Are you sure about this?"

She raised a questioning eyebrow at him, replacing the card face up on the table.

"If you'll accompany me to the gala, then by all means I'm sure."

Paris picked the card up again and slipped it into her bustier, convinced she had just embarked on a beautiful, mutually rewarding friendship.

Grey ended up allowing Paris to keep the platinum credit card for her personal use. He never mentioned the bill to her and told her it wasn't necessary to report to him every time she decided to use it. He encouraged her splurging on luxurious items for herself and only required she spend a little time with him in return. Though she hated to admit it, the time with him was a pleasant relief after a long day of being pawed, grabbed and disrespected at the club. Sometimes, the pampering and expensive trinkets she received allowed her the mental luxury of feeling cherished. It was how she envisioned it must've felt to be a Daddy's girl.

There were only two other men she allowed to escort her places outside of the club. One of those suitors was Harley Cox, a professional football player. The other was a hip-hop rapper that went by the pseudonym Dey.

Dey qualified as the lowest maintenance by far. He spent the majority of his time on the road touring. When he came into town, he was considerate enough to give her a decent notice. While he was on the road, he regularly sent gifts via Federal Express and UPS. He never pressured her about a relationship, and when he was around, he treated her like a high-priced mistress he enjoyed dressing up and spending money on. She assumed it fit right in with his "baller" status and was happy to oblige him. Every so often, he would ask her to fly somewhere to be at an appearance. On these occasions, there was always a first-class ticket awaiting her arrival at the airport. Once, she'd agreed to be an extra in a rap video with him. While the scene didn't appeal to her, she was agreeable to humor him every once in awhile if the price was right.

She did tell him she wasn't doing another rap video, because the experience had been far from enjoyable. It began with her sitting in a lobby crowded with at least five hundred beautiful girls. Paris's frayed nerves sent her right over to the video producer to ask for Dey. After one of the casting directors rescued her, per Dey's request, she was lead to a tiny overheated room with fifty other barely-clothed, catty women. Unlike the dancers at the club, the dancers had all been vying for key spots in the production. Dey had listed Paris as one of the main girls on set, but she entertained herself by watching the other girls size each other up. After the spots were assigned, Paris assumed the competition would be over, but she was mistaken. The chosen girls began fiercely competing for the attention of the rappers in order to secure stand-in spot parts in their upcoming videos. It had taken over five hours just to shoot the first scene the "video girls" were in. Paris ended up sitting poolside, while a thugged-out rapper she didn't know, lip-synced dangerously close to her ear, making several gestures to her breasts. Dey had mysteriously been incognito the entire time, and she really wasn't feeling the other rappers.

As a personal rule, Paris didn't get involved with men in the music industry because she wasn't into doing the groupie thing. There just wasn't enough hours in her day to spend catering to an extremely inflated ego and pretending to be awed by the "street" front most of them were desperate to sell their public. She associated rap with the clubs she danced in, so she wasn't a huge fan of the music or the artists in that genre. Most of them encouraged "hooking up their homies," and if you were a stripper, they looked at you like you were strange if you weren't more than happy to sleep with their entire entourage.

Dey never asked her to do anything she didn't want to do, and most of the time he was too high to function sexually. She knew that for him, the most attractive thing about the relationship was the fact that he got props from his colleagues for having someone like "Caramel" on his harem. He'd first approached her when his producer hired several dancers from Under the Cherry Moon to dance onstage in cages at an album release party. That was two years ago, and they saw each other about four times a year.

There was definitely no reason for Dey and Grey's time to overlap, and so she didn't worry about that arrangement interfering with her newfound sponsor. Harley was a very different story. He was not as high maintenance as Grey, but he did have the tendency to want to control her. Paris knew that Harley's motives were selfish when it came to him wanting to be her only lover. If there was anyone who should've been down with her no-strings attached rule, it should've been Harley. For all his ridiculous attempts to trick her into believing he was only interested in her, Paris knew there was no way he would ever be faithful to any woman. Harley was just a dog with a capital D. After seeing as many men cheat with dancers as she had, Paris seriously doubted any man could be faithful, but if there were such a creature, it surely wasn't a professional athlete, and certainly not an athlete as fine and charming as Harley Cox.

Whenever Harley started talking that nonsense, Paris rolled her eyes and laughed. Harley would present her with a pricey gift, then pout if she didn't appear overly grateful. He was addicted to the challenge she presented, then became irate and moody when he couldn't gain control of the relationship. Paris had little patience for his temper tantrums and mood swings. The upside to Harley was that he was finer than Zeus himself. His rock hard, chocolate ripped body was every woman's dream, and the advertising was honest, as he was incredible in bed. Harley's bad boy ways definitely brought out the song in Paris's body; even the ice queen herself needed a satisfying physical release every now and then. Because of his schedule, Harley was out of pocket much of the year, and that suited Paris just fine. She didn't have to worry about him until football season was over, and by mid-summer, he was inaccessible again preparing for the upcoming season.

Initially Paris thought the juggling of three men might be getting in over her head, but had quickly pushed the thought aside. The bottom line was, she hadn't promised either of them anything, and did not intend to do so—ever. There was no way they would convince her to change her rules about men; she'd drain their banking accounts bone dry first.

Carefully hanging her new clothes in her closet, she took out the plastic bag with the evening gown she'd purchased to wear to the gala with Grey. The beaded gold gown had cost over four thousand dollars, and that wasn't including the matching purse and shoes. Grey acted insulted when she'd repeated the offer to show him receipts, so she'd tossed them and treated herself to a fur vest she'd been eyeing since last season. The dress was the most beautiful thing she'd ever seen.

Earlier that day, she'd gone to the spa and treated herself to an aloe vera body wrap along with manicure, pedicure and facial, compliments of a cash advance from Harley. After showering, she took her hair down, applied her make-up, then gingerly took the dress out of the plastic bag. Sliding into the gown, she realized it was heavier on her body than she remembered. She'd have to remind herself to check her posture because the dress had to weigh at least fifteen pounds.

Grey arrived promptly and immediately began complimenting her on her appearance.

"You are absolutely breathtaking," he said.

Paris would definitely have described him as gleeful as he placed the sheer gold shawl carefully around her shoulders. His overt enthusiasm turned her stomach, but she kept the pasted smile on her face, let him put his arm around her shoulders and lead her to the limo waiting outside her home. Ecstatic that she was on his arm, Grey blushed when offering her champagne in the limo and bumbled over himself in conversation. In the club, he was more laid back and reserved. Paris realized he was like all the other men who came in the club, and got an ego boost from having a trophy on their arm in public.

"I'm just so pleased you decided to come."

Paris was starting to get a cramp in her cheeks from smiling sweetly across at him, so she welcomed the opportunity to talk.

"Did you really think I would cancel on you?" she asked coyly, sipping her champagne slowly.

He nodded ruefully. Paris launched into a pre-rehearsed conversation with him that she'd worked on a couple of nights before. She could sense there was a need to tread lightly with Grey. His pockets were obviously deep, but she didn't want him to get the wrong impression about their future. He was just a little too pleased with himself that they were attending a public function together. She planned to show him that their relationship was most beneficial to them both if they kept it right where it was. She nodded mechanically and leaned in closer to him as she realized he was confiding in her about one of his clients. His expression told her he was flattered she seemed so interested in what he was saying. Paris smiled sweetly, knowing he'd read the smile wrong and think she was happy to be there with him. He probably thought he was slowly melting her resolve by exposing her to the finer things in life. If only he knew the truth, she thought to herself, watching him drink in her smile. There'd been many Greys before, all vying for the same prize, her heart. Paris took a sip of her champagne and looked away. She knew she had him completely under her spell this evening. Just like her work in the club, she was feeding him an illusion. She could do this in her sleep. She was in control and everything was fine.

# CHAPTER SIX
# A RECIPE FOR CARAMEL

Paris couldn't remember the last time she'd spent time thinking about her future and refused to delve deeper into the painful memories of her past. Her first day of kindergarten, she'd taken one look at the other children's brand new clothes, Disney themed backpacks and lunch pails and made an important mental contrast to her own faded second-hand store threads and makeshift school supplies. She went home to Sharp and Ivan, and proclaimed, "We don't have nuthin'."

A severely broken heart had transformed their pretty mother, Deanne, into a bitter, narrow-minded Christian by the time the Paris and her brothers were in school. Deanne took the rejection from Richard, their father, hard, but did the best she could for her babies. She took the children to church regularly and tried to feed them deferred hope that included a stepfather and a nicer place to live one day. Instead of finding her prince after her breakup with Richard, Deanne ran into several toads and experienced several extreme disappointments before finally giving up on having a man in her life.

Unfortunately, Deanne conceded after her daughter had ingested her mother's pain and disappointment at the hand of the opposite sex. The worst of these experiments occurred when Paris was seven. She had snuck out of bed late one night and seen her mother being drug by her hair at the hand of her last prospective stepfather. Deanne caught a glimpse of Paris standing in the doorway of her bedroom and had tearfully begged Paris to go back to her room. That morning, Paris walked into the kitchen and watched her mother flipping pancakes for her and her brothers with two black eyes and a defeated look in her eyes. After that, Deanne had sworn off men, oblivious that her daughter had also.

Looking back, Paris now realized that Deanne's failures at love went against everything she learned at church on Sunday, so finally she gave up and surrendered to a strict Christian lifestyle, banishing all possibilities of a "happily ever after" for her family.

Deanne was determined to keep her children from adopting what she referred to as the "attitude of poverty". She stressed to her daughter the importance of not giving in to one's circumstances. Just because they were poor, that didn't mean they had to look or act like it. Although their clothes were old and usually purchased from second hand stores, Deanne made sure her children were always clean and neat. She did everything in her power to be the best mother she could, but Paris knew her mother was lonely. Many nights, Paris went to sleep listening to her mother's soft sobs from underneath a closed bedroom door.

Paris learned from observing the families of friends at school and church that there was a component missing from her family. After school, she and her four friends would wait for the school buses to come and take them to their apartments, and everyday Paris, Shelly, Opal and Janay would wait together for their prospective rides. Shelly was considered the luckiest girl in the entire school because she had the prettiest mom, the neatest clothes, was picked up in the shiniest car and always had extra lunch money.

As the girls stood in a huddle waiting to be picked up, Shelly reminded them she had something to show them. She reached into her blouse, pulled a delicate gold necklace from around her neck, and held it out in her tiny palm. Three pairs of eight-year-old eyes took in the beautiful necklace with visible envy.

"Ooh, that is sooo pretty," Janay cooed.

As Paris reached out to touch the charm at the end of the necklace, Shelly moved it out of Paris's reach.

"I just want to read what it says," Paris countered defensively.

Shelly smiled coyly, shrugging a fat shiny curl over her shoulder. "Here," she said, leaning forward. "Just don't touch it."

"Daddy's little girl," Paris slowly read the inscription. She looked bewildered at Shelly and the other two girls playing with them.

"My daddy bought it for me," Shelly stated proudly. "He gave me this so everyone would know I'm a Daddy's girl."

"What does that mean?" Paris inquired.

"It means my daddy will buy me whatever I want 'cause he loves me'."

Paris took a step back from Shelly and lowered her head. It was obvious just by looking at Shelly's pressed and curled hair, new clothes and snobbish attitude that she got whatever she wanted. The other two girls joined Paris in pretending not to be impressed with the gold necklace.

"So what?" Janay challenged. Her bottom lip trembled as she dared Shelly to take her on in a physical challenge.

Shelly shook her head, ensuring her curls flounced around her face. "So that means I get whatever I want," she responded smartly.

"My daddy buys us stuff, too. He comes sometimes on the weekend and brings me and my brother toys," Janay said, smiling in her own defense.

To Paris's eight-year-old mind, Daddy seemed to be a synonym for Santa Claus.

"For Thanksgiving my daddy is taking us on a family cruise," Shelly boasted. "He said my mommy and me can go to the store and pick out new clothes for the cruise. I'm going to get a brand new pink swimming suit."

"What's a cruise?" Paris asked.

Shelly laughed and took another opportunity to toss her curls in the girls' faces.

"It's when you get on a really big boat that has hotel rooms in it, and the boat stops at really pretty places," Shelly explained.

"If you go swimming, your hair is going to get all messed up, then you'll look ugly even if you do have on a new bathing suit," Opal said, bursting Shelly's spoiled bubble.

"No it won't, silly. Mommy's taking me to the beauty shop. I'm getting braids put in my hair for the trip, so I'll look pretty the whole time." Shelly laughed snobbishly.

Opal made a face at Shelly then retreated from the conversation. A shiny blue car trimmed in silver pulled up at the curb, and Shelly's hazel eyes brightened.

"There's my daddy. I'll see you guys tomorrow."

Paris, Opal and Janay watched in silence as Shelly ran toward the luxury car, her curls bouncing and designer knee-high boots kicking behind her.

"She thinks she's better than everybody, but she's not," Janay announced to her friends. Opal shrugged her shoulders. Paris was star-struck as she watched Shelly waving from the passenger seat in the most beautiful car she'd ever seen. Shelly's beautiful father waved, then smiled a comment over at his equally beautiful daughter before pulling away from the schoolyard curb.

"Shelly's dad seems really nice," Paris said as she got a glimpse of Shelly's father.

A neatly trimmed mustache enhanced his smooth café au lait skin tone. Paris thought his charcoal gray sweater was much more exquisite than anything she'd seen her mother wear.

"Who are you talking about?" Janay asked.

"Shelly's dad. He's probably the best daddy in the whole world," Paris said more to herself, than her playmates.

Opal turned cold eyes on her.

"How do you know? He's probably just like everybody else's dad. He just has more money. He'll probably divorce her mom soon anyway. Then she'll be just like us." Paris and Janay looked blankly at Opal. Paris didn't understand what had triggered so much fire in Opal's eyes.

"I gotta go, my sisters are here." Opal grabbed a tattered Barbie backpack off the ground and scurried after two older girls in short skirts and too tight T-shirts.

"Her sisters are so pretty," Janay sighed.

She watched in amazement as Opal's sisters walked alongside two slender young men who appeared to be carrying their books.

"I can't wait until I'm a teenager like them. I'm gonna have the cutest boyfriend in the whole school. I guess you could have the second cutest boy," Janay said, smiling.

Paris chewed on her bottom lip, processing the whole incident with Shelly and Opal's angry outburst.

"Don't let her make you mad. My brother told me Opal's parents are getting divorced because her dad was cheating on her mom. That's why she's sad. I wasn't supposed to tell anybody, so promise you won't tell."

Paris shook her head. "I won't."

"Pinky promise?" Janay asked, extending her pinky finger.

Paris stuck out her pinky finger and crossed it with Janay's. "Pinky promise."

"Come on, here's our bus." Janay nudged Paris toward the big yellow school bus that was pulling up.

When they boarded the bus, Janay immediately took a seat with an older girl who occasionally rewarded her young fans with stories about boys in junior high school. Paris took the first seat behind the bus driver so she could sit by herself and mull over her own thoughts.

Days later, Paris still couldn't get the image of Shelly and her father out of her mind. She closed her eyes and saw them laughing together, their identical hazel eyes crinkled with laughter. She could remember seeing Shelly's family once before at a parent-teacher meeting. While the other moms seemed tired and hurried, Shelly's mom stood out like a beautiful gem. Her hair was always perfect, and her clothes were beautiful. She smiled and shook every one of Shelly's friend's hands, while Shelly's father carried her baby brother on his shoulders.

Paris thought they looked like the doll family that came with the dollhouse she'd wanted for Christmas last year. She hadn't gotten the dollhouse or any of the people. In fact, there hadn't been much of anything under the Christmas tree except socks and underwear. For a minute, she wished she was Shelly's sister and could go home with the beautiful family, but one look at Deanne and Paris regretted her thought. Her mother worked hard, and Paris loved her with all her heart.

"We can go now, Mommy," she whispered to her mother.

Deanne looked thankfully over at her while hastily wiping Ivan's face, then his twin brother's with a damp washcloth. Paris knew after taking the bus home with the three of them that Deanne would have to bathe the boys, then prepare them for bed. She felt selfish for even asking Deanne to come to parents' night, but her teacher had insisted. Paris pressed her face against the windowpane on the bus, closed her eyes and wished the city bus would take her anywhere but back to the apartment complex where she and her family lived.

Although she realized her family was poor, Paris didn't understand exactly what made them poor until she got to junior high school. Besides Shelly at school, most of the kids in her neighborhood were in the same economic situation as her family, so there wasn't anything to compare to until she reached the sixth grade.

Her mother had enrolled her in a newly formed middle school with a mission of merging impoverished children with their economically superior peers. Paris compared her family to the families of her new friends and finally came up with the one component her family lacked: a father. It wasn't that all her new friends lived with both their mom and dad, but just about all of them had a father somewhere. Deanne had never told Paris much about her father other than, "He ain't about shit," prior to her being born-again, and after that it became a sympathetic, "Unfortunately, we don't get to pick our fathers."

During her sixth grade year, Paris's curiosity about her absent father bubbled up inside of her until she could no longer take it. She finally walked into the living room one evening after her brothers were asleep and stood behind the sofa her mother was sitting on.

"Why don't me, Ivan and Sharp have a daddy?" she asked in a small voice.

Deanne stopped watching St. Elsewhere, something she never did unless there was a dire emergency, and looked over at her twelve-year-old daughter.

"What made you ask that?" Deanne asked, peeking at Denzel Washington's young face on their 13" black-and-white television.

"Everybody at my new school has a daddy. Some kids' daddies even come and pick them up on weekends and take them to fun places and stuff," Paris said, her big brown eyes shining with amazement. "Why doesn't our daddy do that?"

Deanne tilted her head to one side, looking like Paris had just asked her to explain the mystery of the birds and the bees. She was quiet for so long, Paris thought she had decided not to answer her.

"Well, baby, not everybody's daddy wants to do stuff like that with them," Deanne said slowly.

Her eyes made contact with Paris's, then broke away just as quickly. Paris didn't understand why her mother was having such a hard time answering her questions. After all, it was *her* problem, not her mother's, wasn't it? Her mother had a father. Paris remembered hearing her talk about him.

"Why doesn't our daddy like us?" she asked, her bottom lip trembling.

Deanne shook her head, pursing her lips like she used to when she was trying not to curse.

"He's a sorry something, Paris. That's all I can say about it. Maybe one day you can ask him yourself. Don't worry about him though. You all are fine without him," Deanne said, returning her attention to Denzel and St. Elsewhere.

Paris knew that was her mother's way of telling her that the discussion was over. She walked down the dingy hallway to the room she shared with her brothers and cried until her head hurt almost as much as her heart.

A week later, Deanne sat Paris down and told her everything she wanted to know about her father. Deanne met him through a mutual friend two years before she got pregnant with Paris. She thought he was nice enough, and after he pursued her for over a month, she gave in and started dating him. According to Deanne, Richard Dennison was a light-brown athletic guy with dimples to die for. What he didn't have in traditional good looks, he made up for in persistence and an engaging personality. Deanne thought the two of them were destined to get married and live happily ever after, as most eighteen year olds do when they fall in love for the first time, especially when they are in love with an older, more stable man. Deanne considered herself lucky to have snagged the much older Richard, who was twenty-six at the time, and had what was considered a "good job" working in a glass factory.

Unfortunately, the stereotypes dooming young love are too often correct. When Deanne told Richard she was pregnant, his engaging personality turned cold and non-responsive. He told her he didn't believe the baby was his and began flaunting other women in her face.

The day after Paris was born, he and one of his best friends visited Deanne in the hospital room. Richard's quiet mood expressed his disappointment that the baby was a girl all too well. While Richard had been less than eager to have a baby, he never considered the possibility that he would have anything other than a boy. According to Deanne, she and Richard hooked up after that just enough for her to get pregnant once more and for him to take that opportunity to act an even bigger fool.

Paris couldn't understand why Deanne ever took Richard back. If one of the boys in her class treated her like that, she'd never speak to him again. Deanne told her she didn't know the answer to that question, but she agreed that she should have left Richard alone long before she did.

Deanne explained that a few months after Ivan and Sharp were born, she decided she was finished with Richard for good. She went to the local child support agency to inquire about getting child support for her three children. Richard was furious with her, especially since he never got around to being involved with any of the children. Depending on his mood, he would boast to his friends about his twin boys. He didn't do anything for Sharp or Ivan, but Deanne told Paris that Richard thought it made him look like the man to have twin boys who looked so much like him. It certainly made it impossible for him to deny them the way he did Paris. Deanne said Richard hired a lawyer that drew up papers saying that if Richard paid Deanne $1,000, she could never approach him about the paternity of Paris again. Knowing her electric bill and rent were past due, Deanne felt she had no choice but to take the money and tackle the issue of Sharp and Ivan later.

Deanne tried to explain the humiliation she felt that prevented her from approaching Richard later about child support for Ivan and Sharp. Deanne gazed into Paris's eyes, her own filled with compassion, but the last thing Paris heard was that her father had gotten rid of her for a measly $1,000 dollars.

Paris had been overjoyed when her grandmother informed her she would be spending her thirteenth summer in Jackson, Mississippi. Deanne had fallen sick and had no choice but to take the children back to Jackson to stay with their grandmother, Louise. Feeling obligated to do the right thing, Louise called Richard and told him the children were coming. Louise later admitted to Deanne that she thought Richard would change his mind about being involved in the children's lives, or at least feel a bit of guilt if he had to look into their faces and see how much his absence hurt them.

Louise sat the children down the night they arrived and let them know that she'd contacted their father, and he'd agreed to come to see them. Paris could barely get to sleep the night before. She tossed and turned fitfully the entire night. She was too excited over the prospect of seeing her Dad for the first time since she was a baby. Studying her thirteen-year-old reflection in the bathroom mirror, she frowned. Recently introduced to puberty, she had just gone through a nasty bout with acne, and her face was spotted with scars and small bumps. Trying to separate her features from the acne, she stepped farther away from the mirror.

"I'd probably be really pretty if not for this acne," she reasoned aloud to her reflection.

She swiped a heavily medicated pad over her face and scowled at its sting. If only she could wish this acne away, once and for all. She desperately wanted her father to think she was pretty. Maybe then he wouldn't be so disappointed in the fact that she was a girl. She knew that he would probably love Sharp and Ivan. Men in the community housing addition where they lived were always slapping high-fives with the two of them. Paris often watched with envy as they called out with either "What's up, little man?" or, "Hey, little partner" to Sharp and Ivan as they walked home from school or to the corner store. They never even glanced her way. In fact, Paris had observed, the only time men paid women or girls any attention was if they thought they were pretty.

"That girl is gonna be bad when she gets older. If only she were a few years older man. She's gonna be fine," she'd heard an older man saying that about one of the older girls in her junior high class.

Paris just knew if she were pretty enough, her father would be proud to have her for a daughter. She stuck out her tongue at her reflection. There wasn't much hope of that happening with her face. She looked at her pubescent shape. She wasn't even starting to get hips or anything yet. The only thing there was a little leftover baby fat from elementary school. An unexpected tear made its way down her chubby cheek. She swiped it away, angrily. She wouldn't cry. There had to be a way to get her father to notice her, and there had to be something about her that was better than Sharp and Ivan. She just needed to find out what it was.

Six hours later, the three of them lined up at Louise's window, waiting to be reintroduced to their father. Two hours past the designated visiting time, a brown Cadillac pulled up with a stocky bright-skinned man and a young white woman.

"There's your father," Louise said. "I can't believe his trifling ass, gonna be six hours late and then bring some honky with him," Louise muttered under her breath.

"Hi. I'm Lisa," the slender brunette girl said, extending her hand to Paris.

Paris's spirits perked up as she looked the woman up and down. To be her father's girlfriend, this girl didn't look like much at all. Paris summoned a mental picture of her mother. Deanne was much prettier than this pale, mousy-haired girl was. Maybe her father wasn't into pretty girls after all.

Just as Paris suspected, Richard took a liking to Sharp and Ivan. His eyes shone with pride as Sharp told him about Pee Wee football and Ivan talked about little league and soccer practice. Paris thought if she heard another "That's my boy!" she would throw up. Richard and Lisa took them to an amusement park and bought them ice cream cones. While she didn't get the attention she was after from Richard, Lisa made several attempts at conversation. Paris was shocked to learn that the woman her father had brought with him was only six years older than she was.

"What grade are you in?" she asked.

"I'll be in seventh grade in the fall," Paris replied.

She decided to go ahead and be nice to the girl. It was obvious her father cared about her a great deal, so it would probably be wise to be nice to her, at least until she was able to talk to her father.

"I didn't finish high school," Lisa said, staring at her butter pecan ice cream cone before taking a nibble. Paris rolled her eyes skyward. Not only had her father snagged a young white girl, but on top of all that, she was a dumbass, too.

"Why?" Paris asked, feigning curiosity.

Lisa shrugged, flipping mousy brown hair over her shoulder. "I thought about going back to school. Do you think I should?"

Paris looked incredulously at her then shrugged. "I don't know. If you want to."

She couldn't believe her father's white nineteen-year-old girlfriend was actually asking her if she should go back to high school. This was a bit too much for her thirteen-year-old brain to process.

Taking notice of her father's unwavering interest in her brothers, she managed to fake interest in the rest of Lisa's pathetically mundane conversation. Finally, the rendezvous was over, and they headed back to Louise's. The car ride back was filled with male laughter. Paris noticed, with some joy, that Lisa seemed just as out of place as she did. Richard made a point of letting the kids know that he was up on all the latest music and videos. He even joked about how beautiful some of the girls were in one of the latest rap videos to Sharp and Ivan's delight. Paris couldn't understand why her forty-year-old father was listening to the same music as they were. Deanne surely didn't. Deanne wouldn't even let them play most of their music when she was in the house. Richard seemed to be trying to impress her brothers, while she'd been worried about impressing him.

"Are we going to see you again, Daddy?" Paris asked, unbuckling her seat belt.

"Yeah sure," Richard said.

He gave them all hugs, ruffling Sharp and Ivan's hair, then shuffled his stocky 5'8" frame back into his Cadillac and backed out. Paris stood on her grandmother's porch, watching as the headlights made a path down the residential street.

Three weeks later the kids were back with Deanne. Sharp and Ivan hadn't talked much about the trip or their father. Paris overheard Sharp telling Ivan that Richard didn't want to be bothered with them.

"At least he likes you all. He had so much fun with you," Paris said, sulking.

"He must not have liked any of us that much, cause he didn't come back to see us," Ivan reasoned out loud.

Paris looked over at Ivan and smiled. He was so adorable with his big brown puppy dog eyes. He was a bit young for ten years old, and Paris was very protective of him. Cynical by nature, Sharp had always known how to take care of himself.

"Ivan's right," Sharp said. "He don't care nothing about us. He just came over there and took us out because Grandma Louise made him. I heard her tell Uncle Byron that she called him and told him he better come see us."

Ivan's eyes got big, then he looked away, concentrating on the baseball mitt Deanne had bought him for his birthday two weeks ago. Paris collapsed down on the bed next to Ivan and playfully shoved him. It hurt her to think that Ivan and Sharp were hurting over their father just like she was. It was one thing to hurt her, but as the oldest, she didn't like seeing her baby brothers hurt.

"Fuck him," she said solemnly. Both boys looked at her as if they'd just seen a ghost. Paris knew they were wondering how she could say such a bad word in Deanne's home. Once Sharp was backhanded for slipping and saying "damn" in front of her. At this point, Paris didn't care if Deanne had heard her. Whatever Deanne would do paled in comparison to what her father had just done to her. Her biggest fear had materialized during their visit. Her father had rejected her again, and there was no way he would get the chance to do it again.

Paris narrowed her eyes, bit her lip and vowed never to speak to her father again. If he died and the next time she saw him was in a casket, it would be too soon for her. She wished they'd never gone to see their grandmother. Before, she'd been hopeful about a reunion with their father. She had always talked to her brothers about the possibility that their father would change his mind and decide he wanted to be in their life. Now they all knew there was no more room for hope. Richard Dennison wanted no part of being their father.

"Yeah," Sharp echoed, "fuck him."

# *CHAPTER SEVEN*
# *DEALING WITH TEMPORARY SETBACKS*

Paris and the twins slowly began to move past their hurt over Richard's apparent lack of interest in them. Their healing process would come to a screeching halt, due to a letter that arrived four months after their visit to Mississippi. Paris's heart began hammering against her chest when she discovered the informal white envelope with her father's name in the addressee corner. Her first thought was to open the letter and devour the contents all by herself, but when she put her finger to the envelope to tear it open, she clammed up. Stiff with a heavy sense of foreboding, she held it away from her body and marched into Deanne's bedroom.

"What's this?" Deanne asked, motioning toward the white envelope Paris held awkwardly out to her. Unable to speak, Paris stared wide-eyed at her mother and then again at the envelope. Deanne slowly took the envelope. "I guess we better see what this is about," Deanne said slowly. Paris could hear the sadness in her mother's voice, although she knew Deanne was trying to shield it from her.

Deanne called the boys into her room, then sat her children down to read a letter from their father which had arrived in the mail. Paris's eyes brightened with dim hope. Maybe Richard had come to his senses and was writing because he wanted to begin a relationship with them. It certainly would make sense for him to come to that conclusion after spending time with them. Even if he wasn't impressed with her, maybe he had taken somewhat of an interest in her brothers. It was fine with Paris if he returned to them because of Ivan and Sharp. Eventually, she would find a way to win his heart herself, she reasoned. Paris had concocted an entire storyline, when the sound of her mother clearing her throat reminded her there was no reason to rejoice just yet.

Hesitantly, she leaned in closer to listen with her fingers crossed behind her back. Deanne began reading, and three expectant brown faces fell simultaneously. Richard was letting them know that Lisa was pregnant with his child. Not only was he rejecting them, but he was providing them with a mental picture of their replacement. Now, Paris was confused at his reasoning for writing the letter after all. He didn't say anything about seeing them ever again or about them being involved with the new baby's life. Deanne folded the thin white piece of paper then reluctantly looked into her children's eyes.

"I know this hurts, but no matter what Richard does, he is your father, and I feel you all deserve to know the truth. Many times in life, the truth hurts. Does anyone have anything to say?" she ventured slowly.

Sharp angrily shook his head no, and Ivan imitated him.

"Can we go outside now?" Sharp asked, avoiding his mother's probing eyes. His handsome features were set as calm as stone, but Paris was perceptive enough to witness the trembling in his bottom lip. That meant he was struggling to hold back his emotions. Within minutes, she knew all signs of vulnerability would be gone and Sharp would have internally filed this new disappointment away with the rest.

"Yes, baby, just don't stay out too late. I'll have dinner ready in a few minutes," Deanne said sadly.

Paris sat still as her brothers grabbed their jackets and basketball and went outside to play. She felt Deanne's eyes on her, but wouldn't meet her eyes.

"Are you all right?" Deanne asked.

Paris didn't respond. She didn't know what to say. She was slowly becoming used to the idea that she would never have a father, but somewhere deep down it had felt better knowing he didn't have any other kids he was being a father to. Now, she knew he would have another child that he was taking care of, giving all their love to.

"I guess he just doesn't love us. He must not have liked us very much when he met us again this summer," Paris said, biting her bottom lip.

Deanne shook her head then sighed loudly.

"It's nothing you all did. Your father doesn't know how to love anyone but himself. Maybe he'll learn with this new baby. Maybe he'll try to be a father this time. Lord knows he didn't do right by you all."

She laid a sympathetic hand on Paris's shoulder then got up to prepare dinner. Paris watched her walk to the kitchen. She disagreed with her mother. She didn't want him to be a father to this baby. She knew she was being selfish, but if he couldn't be her father, she didn't want him to be a father to anyone else. Paris angrily rebuked herself for hoping against everything that her father was changing his mind about them. She couldn't ignore the pain that seared through her heart after this fresh rejection. If only she'd left the wound intact and not gotten her hopes up, the pain wouldn't be fresh all over again.

After registering in her head that a reunion with their father was not going to happen, Paris adopted a new wish. Whenever she spotted a single man, she would instantly size him up, wondering if he would make a good partner for her mother. Paris thought her mother was the strongest, most beautiful woman in the world, but even Deanne couldn't hide the fact that being a single mom could be lonesome Paris would silently watch as men ogled her mother, only to have Deanne shoot them down as soon as they made a move. Deanne's warnings to young Paris concerning men were backed up by the fact that she never made the mistake of getting herself involved again.

Sharp and Ivan weren't bothered by the fact that their mother never became involved again, but Paris was. As the oldest and only girl, she had a different perspective on the future of their family. Paris knew one day they would all be grown and living their own lives. At a young age, she worried that there wouldn't be anyone there to take care of their mother. When she was younger, Paris remembered her mother being hopeful on the possibility of one day getting married, but as time went on and the children grew older, their family dynamic seemed cemented and unlikely to change. Deanne resigned herself to being single for the rest of her life, and told her teenaged daughter she was single by choice.

Little by little, Paris began to adopt her mother's philosophy that men were a lot more hassle than necessary, and avoiding heartbreak completely was far better than taking chances on love.

After the news from their father, Paris's family struggled more and more with finances. Ends had always been tight, but Paris had never felt the brunt of their poverty until she started high school. Deanne seemed overwhelmed by the task of raising a teenage girl and two preteen boys. When the kids were younger, Deanne worked overtime trying to keep them on the right track, but after Paris became a teenager, she noticed Deanne's reins loosening. Where before Deanne was undaunted when it came to checking up on the kids and their grades, the older they got, the more she took their word without questioning. Paris knew raising her children alone and living paycheck to paycheck for years was starting to take its toll on Deanne. It saddened her, but she was also relieved, because this newfound freedom gave her the opportunity to spread her wings a bit.

Deanne tried to instill Christian and moral values in the children, setting them apart from the neighborhood children, but Paris felt she didn't fit in on an entirely different level. Trying to fit in with her friends at school became harder and harder the older she got. Not wanting to draw attention to herself or her situation, she was quiet and reserved. Besides not having the latest pair of designer jeans, she also struggled with acne. She was an honor roll student, but not as a result from her studying—she was naturally smart.

"Why don't you give anybody your phone number?" A classmate confronted her loudly in front of a large group of other girls one day. Paris blushed underneath her caramel complexion, but didn't answer. Deanne had trouble keeping up with their bills and the phone was usually the first to go.

"My mom won't let me give the number out," Paris answered.

Hoping the girl wouldn't continue with her investigation, she held her fingers crossed behind her back. She did, and Paris ended up blackballed from her group of friends after discovering that she was "poor". She caught the bus home that day, looking out of the small rectangular window, wondering why she wasn't more upset than she was. She had begun spending lunch hour in the library to avoid the speculation of others catching on to the fact that she didn't have lunch money.

Though she wanted to be liked by her classmates, girls had never been her friends of choice. She found boys much more intriguing to observe than girls her age. She had several male friends at school that stuck by her side through all the teasing and didn't care about her poverty. She wasn't interested in boys romantically, but she did like listening to them talk about the other girls they were involved with. Paris felt privileged to listen in on conversations between her male friends when they aired all the girls' dirty laundry. There were plenty of scandalous details of who had which girl sprung, or what this girl let them do when they'd walked her home. Silently, she would listen and then later at home she would replay their conversations in her head. She vowed to herself never to be stupid like the girls in her class. Why couldn't they see that the boys were just out to use them then talk about them behind their back?

# CHAPTER EIGHT
# THE ART OF DANCE, BIRTHS A BUTTERFLY

During her junior year in high school, Paris discovered that she could dance her butt off. Her first two years of high school, she would watch the older girls on her high school's dance team shaking and rolling their hips while the band played during football games. The girls wore black leotards with tiny royal blue skirts and ballet shoes. During the summer months, they wore revealing cropped tops and short shorts. Paris would watch in amazement as men who came to watch the football game would spend most of the time gawking at the dance team. She would sit near groups of men, listening to their rude comments about the girls' newly budding breasts, promising hips and the onions in training.

Paris considered most of the comments crude, but something about the way the men looked at pretty girls that intrigued her. Paris thought the moment a man looked at a beautiful woman he was under her power. Most of the girls didn't realize they had this power, but Paris watched in amazement as men would trip and fall over themselves to accommodate girls they were attracted to. Although Paris wasn't interested in entertaining conversation with men, she was intrigued at the possibility of having that power and control.

Making the school's dance team became Paris's number one goal during her junior year. She would go home, put on the hottest R&B records and practice making up routines. She had to do this while Deanne was at work, because there was no way Deanne would allow her to do the type of dancing she was practicing under her roof. Despite the danger looming ahead if her mother caught her, dancing felt natural and became a much-needed release of pent-up emotion for her. Paris would close her eyes and let the body interpret the beats, rhythms and melodies transmitted through the tiny speakers in her bedroom. Making routines became a challenging hobby she enjoyed, and one that allowed her mind to escape the constant struggles that Deanne was becoming unable to hide from her oldest child. Making the team would serve a dual purpose in her life; it would make her privy to attention from men, and had become a much-needed form of release. Most importantly, Paris felt dancing came natural to her. She knew she was good at something for the first time in her life.

Everyday after school from 3–7:30, while Deanne was at work, Paris practiced dancing. Her favorites were Guy, Janet Jackson and En Vogue. Sharp and Ivan often teased, saying she looked like a fake Paula Abdul or Pebbles. Instead of irritating her, she used their barbs as motivation. If she could impress her brothers, then she could definitely impress the judges at school.

That summer, Paris noticed changes in her body. After bathing, she would apply her lotion, then look in the mirror and take inventory. Sure enough, her breasts resembled juicy little peaches with pert black cherry tips, and her hips were rounding out. The best news of all was that her skin had done a 100% turnaround. Her caramel complexion glowed from her nightly facials. The reactions from boys around her neighborhood confirmed that others took note of her transformation also.

Dating didn't interest Paris, but her new figure boosted her confidence enough to actually tryout for the dance team. Deanne reluctantly gave her consent for Paris to join the team if she made it, but their agreement was that Paris would have to fund her dance and her own clothes for the school year. Money was still extremely tight, and Deanne had her hands full trying to deal with Sharp and Ivan, who were eating and growing at warp speed. Paris spent the summer practicing and babysitting in order to buy school clothes and pay dance team fees.

A week before school started, she got up the courage to dance in front of an audience. She rounded up her brothers and made them watch as she danced to Janet Jackson's "Miss You Much". The boys sat side-by-side on her bed, watching with straight faces until the song was over. After she finished, she turned off her small boom box and collapsed on the floor.

"So, what do you guys think?" she asked, trying to catch her breath. The twins were entering freshmen and had seen the dance squad perform a few times.

"You look like one of those video girls," Ivan said, smiling.

"You really are good," Sharp said simply.

"You think I can make the dance team?" she asked.

"Yeah you're better than most of those girls," Sharp admitted.

"Paris is going to be on Video Soul!" Ivan said happily.

Paris smiled at him. Ivan had always thought the world of his big sister. She knew regardless of her performance, he would be complimentary. Sharp's approval, however, gave her the push she needed.

Once school started, along with the appreciative glances from the boys, came jealous smirks from her female classmates. The unexpected attention took her off guard. Boys offered to take her to lunch or walk her home from the bus. Some even asked her if she would like a ride home. The newfound popularity didn't sit well with Paris, for the guys who once considered her "one of the guys" now saw her as the new topic for locker room discussions.

Auditions were the second Friday of the school year. Nervous, Paris skipped lunch, opting to hang out in the girls' locker room and perfect the routine she'd created for tryouts. She had decided to dance to "Miss You Much". Her hard-earned babysitting dollars were well spent on a pair of shiny black biker shorts and a matching black sports bra that would act as her top. Her calve muscles popped in the stylish blue and black Air Max tennis shoes she purchased at Foot Locker.

In the field house afterschool, she signed her name on the clipboard marked "Dance Team Contestants", then hid out in the bleachers while the judges took their seats. It seemed as if the entire school had turned out to watch the tryouts. The dance team was just about the most prestigious auxiliary a girl could join. The football and basketball teams took their places on the floor-side bleachers. While most of the girls were nervous due to the boys being there, Paris knew the boys were her biggest fans.

"Number twenty-one, Paris Jackson," Mrs. Moore called out over the loudspeaker.

Paris heard several girls in her class snicker at her name.

"I can't believe she has the nerve to tryout," a voice whispered smugly.

Paris confidently walked over to cue the football coach who was handling the music. She looked at the judges in front of her, calculating which would be the hardest sell. There were three women and two men, but three of the football coaches were sitting with them. She was certain the football coaches had some pull on which girls were selected, because they were the main ones ogling them once they were on the team. Paris felt totally relaxed as she pulled her over-sized T-shirt over her head, revealing her shiny ensemble. She heard sighs of approval from several football players.

"Damn, I want to go to Paris for real baby," one of them remarked.

"Damn she fine," another moaned loudly.

Paris smiled coyly, reached back and pulled her dark-brown hair free of its ponytail holder. She ran her fingers through it lightly then took a deep breath and cued the coach to start her music.

Paris danced naked in her bathroom mirror. She'd done a bang-up job at trouts and blown all the judges away. The evidence was in the raised eyebrows, and furtive glances exchanged between the five of them. By the end of her performance, she had every male coach's mouth hanging wide open. Paris felt the shift in power and congratulated herself. While before she'd been intrigued, in that moment she was hooked. She felt empowered and indestructible. She had the power.

Mrs. Moore wouldn't announce the new members of the team until Monday after school, but Paris already knew the results. She'd remembered all the tips she'd picked up from the videos: toss your hair, make eye contact, lick your lips and do it all very, very sexy. She'd heard *oooh, aahs* and *damns* from the mouths of the football and basketball players, and she reveled in the jealous looks on the other contestants' faces as she'd exited the gym immediately after her routine.

She held her hair off her face and narrowed her eyes in the mirror. She'd learned a valuable lesson that day. Although she'd been good, there were plenty of girls were just as good but received little or no feedback from the audience. Paris knew the response she received was due to her looks and her willingness to flirt with the audience. She determined that as long as a woman was attractive and knew how to charm men, she could have whatever she wanted. She could be in control.

That night Paris began her nightly facial ritual of astringent and blemish cream. It wouldn't do to have her acne spring back up, because she just knew this face and body were going to make her a star.

Fully into her senior year, Paris was totally pleased with her transformation. Being appointed captain of the dance team hadn't come as a surprise to her, and she was determined to have the tightest squad in the city. She had been so busy reinventing herself, she hadn't thought about dating or having a steady boyfriend, like most of her friends were. Of course after making the squad, she'd slowly begun to notice boys trying to get her attention. Because she didn't return their advances, many of them began adopting drastic measures to win her attention. Opal told her that some of the popular guys even had a running bet on who would "get" her first. Paris told Opal they were pathetic. She wasn't thinking about boys, she was focused on changing her life, and the dance squad had helped her to do just that.

She shifted her science and math books to her left arm, turned off the light in the activity room where her squad practiced, checked the door to make sure it locked then headed toward the main campus. She had exactly twenty minutes to make it down the hill to the school's entrance where she would catch the school bus home.

"Hey, Paris, wait up." Paris turned to see JaJuan Harris headed her way.

JaJuan was the captain of the basketball team and a star football player. Basketball practice had just ended, and he was still dressed in his practice shorts and matching muscle shirt. Paris held her hand up to her forehead to shield her eyes from the setting sun.

"What's up?" he asked after he'd finally caught up to her.

Paris squinted up at him but didn't respond. JaJuan had to be by far the best-looking guy at her school. With a blemish free milk-chocolate complexion, curly hair and a body that defied his eighteen years, he had the entire female population swooning.

"I'm on my way home." She turned to head toward the activities bus.

"What? You gotta ride the bus?" he questioned unbelievably.

Paris rolled her eyes skyward. "That's what it looks like."

JaJuan dribbled alongside her, his muscular thighs flexing as he walked. "Let me take you home. I know where you live."

"And why would you want to do that?" Paris questioned, not missing a stride on her path to the bus.

"I just do. Come on. Fine as you are, you shouldn't be riding that bus," he flirted. Again, Paris rolled her eyes, but she let him lead her to his jeep.

"Is this yours?" She settled into the worn passenger seat.

"Yup, I got it a couple of weeks ago."

She watched as he carefully checked his mirrors then pulled out of the school parking lot. It would make her life a lot easier if she had a car. She couldn't afford to miss one practice now that she was captain of the dance squad. She looked at the worn interior in JaJuan's 1980 jeep. It wasn't a bad car, but if she had to find someone to get her back and forth to practice and school, she would much rather ride in style. JaJuan's car was far from riding in style, even though he was one of the only guys with their own car at school. Still, he was a cutie-pie and she wasn't feeling riding the school bus. She knew there was no way she could afford to buy herself a car, so she decided there was nothing wrong with relying on the courtesy of strangers. After all, she knew the only reason JaJuan offered was that he wanted something from her.

"So," JaJuan started but didn't finish.

"So?" Paris repeated, looking blankly at him.

He flashed a perfect smile at her. "Who are you going to prom with?"

In spite of herself, she laughed aloud. "Prom's in the spring. It's only September."

"I know what month it is, and I know when prom is. I also know who I want to want to go to prom with," he said proudly.

"And who is that?" she asked, nodding slowly.

"It's the same person I want to be my lady." He let his hand brush against hers on the gearshift. Paris was amused at his attempt to win the bet, so she decided to play along for a while. Until she found another driver, JaJaun's services would come in handy.

"Your lady, huh?" Paris repeated.

"Why you trying to play me?" JaJuan asked, glancing over at her. "You know what I'm talking about. Why you tryin' to play me?"

"I'm not playing you. I'm just trying to see exactly what you're saying." She gave him an encouraging smile.

"I want you to be my lady. That's what I'm saying."

Paris laughed softly. "Why me?"

"Why not you? You're fine. You smart and you can dance your ass off. I think we make a good couple, don't you?"

"Because you're fine, too?" she questioned.

"You know what I mean, damn, Paris. What, you don't like me or something?" His confident smile let her know he didn't consider his question an option.

"I didn't say that," Paris responded smugly.

"So?"

Paris giggled at his persistence. It was obvious by the way he nervously toyed with the gearshift that he was less sure of himself than when their conversation started.

"So we'll see," she concluded. "This is me right here."

Paris gestured for him to make a right into her apartment complex. Two years ago, the rundown appearance of her home would've embarrassed her, but her newfound confidence made her oblivious.

"We'll see. What kind of answer is that?"

"We'll talk about it," she promised.

"Can I at least get your number then? So we can talk."

"You give me yours," Paris said, providing him with a piece of paper from her purse.

JaJuan scribbled his number on the paper, then pressed it in the palm of her hand. "You're gonna call me right?" he asked, confidence removed from his voice.

"I'll call." She reached into the back seat and grabbed her backpack.

"You need me to get that? I can walk you to your door."

"I'm alright."

Paris thanked him, then exited the jeep and walked toward her apartment.

He rolled the passenger side window down and honked at her. "When are you gonna call me?"

Paris laughed then coyly, waved goodbye then disappeared in the house.

"How are you going to play the finest guy at school?" Opal demanded. "Every other girl in a hundred mile radius would kill for him. You must need your eyes checked."

Paris focused on curling a strand of hair around her one-inch curling wand. "I'm just not feeling him, that's all."

"How can you not feel JaJuan Harris? You got problems for real. Let him ask me anywhere, I'd feel him all night long."

Paris shot a sidelong glance at Opal, but remained silent. "Let's just say, I'm holding out for the big payoff," she said. She released the curl and it bounced twice before settling around her shoulders.

"Humph, JaJuan is the big payoff," Opal muttered.

"You don't look at the big picture. I'm trying to make my life easier. JaJuan can't do that."

Opal shook her head in amazement. Paris chuckled at her friend's naïveté and picked up another strand of hair. Just because Opal and a bunch of other girls were head-over-heels for JaJuan didn't mean she felt the same. For her, JaJuan was a convenient way to get home after school, nothing more, nothing less.

During her past friendships with boys, Paris had learned that they were expert manipulators. They manipulated girls to buy them things, go out with them and eventually, give them sex. She knew JaJuan's interest in her had little to do with her personality and everything to do with the fact that she was captain of the dance squad and that every other guy at school wanted to go out with her. There was no way Paris was going to be manipulated by any dumb teenaged boy.

She'd seen enough girls give up their virginity, only to end up heartbroken after the guy dumped her. Their tears reminded her of the tears she watched her mother cry over her father some nights when Deanne didn't realize Paris was listening by her closed bedroom door. Paris knew that she wasn't crying any tears over any boy. If anything, she was going to be the one to get the best of them.

"You said you were going to curl my hair, too," Opal reminded her friend.

"When I'm finished. I've got to look perfect tonight," Paris said, concentrating on releasing the curl so it would automatically spiral.

A few games back, Paris spotted a group of older men that frequented their high school games on a regular basis. After listening in on a few conversations, she learned that three of the four young men had brothers that attended King with her. She'd watched the men for the past three games, and last week she'd made some serious eye contact with the one she thought most promising.

His name was Tariq Molden, and he was twenty-three years old. Everyone knew the Molden family owned two dry cleaners in town, and their father gave Tariq one in order to keep him from going off to school. She'd also learned that he managed the shop and attended college up at Jackson State University. Tariq drove a navy blue convertible Mustang and was one of the most eligible bachelors in town. During half time, she'd ventured to the concession stand where he was getting soda and a hot dog. She'd said hello and made blatant eye contact with him, smiling slowly as she watched him checking her body out in the skimpy dance uniform.

He shook his head at her flirting and nudged one of his partners. "Ay yo, these shorties are dangerous. Mess around and get a nigga locked up looking like that." His friend laughed.

Paris swung her hair behind her and pivoted to allow them better view of her pert backside in the high cut leotard and knee boots. She glanced back at Tariq and giggled. Making eye contact had been the first step in her plan; next, she'd seal the deal with conversation.

"Hurry up, Paris. You're not going to have time to do my hair," Opal whined.

Snapped out of her thoughts, Paris glared at her friend. She motioned for Opal to set down on her bed and began combing through Opal's light brown hair.

"You need a touch-up," Paris complained. "Your curls won't last."

"Just do what you can."

Paris shrugged, then parted Opal's hair into ½ inch sections.

"So what are you going to do about JaJuan?"

Distracted by Opal's nosiness, she bopped her on the head with the rattail comb. "I'm going to burn you if you're not still. Damn, Opal. Nothing. I'm not doing anything about JaJuan."

"So what's the big deal about tonight then?"

"Tonight is the big payoff," Paris said mischievously.

"You trippin' as usual," Opal muttered.

Paris didn't retaliate because she was busy planning her attack on unsuspecting Tariq. She'd found a more suitable ride to take her back and forth to dance practice.

Four months later, Deanne cornered her daughter after Paris dropped Ivan off in Tariq's navy 5.0 Mustang. Because the Molden's were a well-known family, Deanne knew whom the car belonged to and wanted answers as to why Paris had the keys in her hand. Paris assured her mother that she and Tariq were just friends, and he was the older brother of the guy she was interested in at school.

"He's like my big brother, Momma," Paris lied while smiling innocently at her mother.

"Paris, I've been meaning to talk to you about this. Some of the ladies at church are saying I need to rein you in a bit. People are saying your relationship with Tariq is much more than just friends. Now I know you aren't doing anything wrong, but the Bible teaches us to avoid the very appearance of evil, and it just doesn't look right for you to be running around with this boy all the time," Deanne admonished.

Paris ducked her head at her mother's intrusive gaze. "I keep telling you it's not like that, Momma. I bet I know who told you that. It's probably the mother of one of the girls who likes Tariq. You know he is really popular, and some of the other girls at school are mad because we're friends. Some of them just don't like me because I made captain this year," Paris explained.

Deanne narrowed her eyes at her daughter. "Paris if you are interested in this boy, you need to just tell me. You are at the age that—"

Paris cut her mother off. "Momma I'm telling the truth, I'm not interested in Tariq or any other boy for that matter. Have you ever known me to do anything like this before?" Paris challenged. "Are you going to believe those old nosy women at church over your own daughter?"

Deanne's eyes saddened at Paris's allegation.

"No, baby, that's not it. No mother likes to hear people saying things about their child. I believe you, but I also want you to know that if you do meet a boy that you are interested in, you can talk to me about it. I don't want you to feel you have to hide things from me, okay?" Deanne asked, raising an eyebrow at her daughter.

"I know that, but I don't think you'll have to worry about me wanting to go out with a boy anytime soon," Paris answered, trying to sound as truthful as possible.

"Momma, are you gonna help me finish this?" Ivan whined from the kitchen table.

"I'm coming Ivan. Sharp, you get back over here and let me check your homework before you turn that television on," Deanne ordered wearily.

Paris silently thanked her brothers for distracting Deanne. She wasn't convinced Deanne was totally off her trail, so she dropped Ivan's backpack, then sprinted off for dance practice. Once in Tariq's car, she pulled her shades down over her eyes and checked her reflection in the rearview mirror. The designer shades had been a gift from Tariq after he'd returned from school last Friday; today they shielded her from the guilt evident in her brown eyes. She hated lying to her mother, but didn't see any other way. Deep down she knew she was wrong in the way she was dealing with Tariq, but she felt justified in her actions. If she had to explain things to Deanne, she knew the guilt would take over and she'd be forced to admit that she was in the wrong.

Paris had been seeing Tariq for three months, and she was the envy of every girl in her town. The girls on her squad were so jealous, some of them stopped talking to her, except during practice and performances. Waiting for the big payoff had been the wisest decision she'd made since trying out for the dance team. After she'd convinced Tariq to take the risk of seeing her regardless of the fact that she was still in high school, things had taken off for her.

He'd been a bit standoffish at first, insisting that he was too old for her, and he didn't feel right talking to a girl his little brother and friends were vying for. Paris adamantly assured him she wasn't interested in his brother Tyrell or his best friend JaJuan Harris.

Unlike JaJuan and some of the other guys vying for her attention, Tariq wasn't trying to pressure Paris into being his girlfriend, which she had no intentions of becoming. Paris had become an expert at using what she had to get what she wanted out of boys. Although he was a bit older, Tariq was no exception. He enjoyed her company and bought little things to impress her. She enjoyed driving his car and the extra change he gave her whenever she needed something. She had avoided having sex with him thus far, not because she didn't want to, but because it was fun seeing how long he would go without pushing her. Paris knew Tariq was hanging around hoping that she'd let him be her first. It became a game to her to push him all the way, then chicken out at the last minute. The tortured expression on Tariq's face threatened to make her double over laughing, but she managed to keep a straight face.

"As sexy as you are, I can't believe you are a virgin," Tariq muttered the last time she turned him down. Tariq had gone to great lengths to make sure that everyone was out of his parent's house, and he and Paris had the place to themselves. Paris was surprised to see rose petals strewn from the front door leading to his bedroom upstairs. It was evident from the rose petals to the candlelight bouncing off the walls to the champagne chilling in a bucket on the kitchen table that Tariq was determined to take her virginity that night.

"Why would you say something like that?" Paris asked, feigning hurt.

"The way you be shakin' that ass on the field, I thought you were an old pro." His eyes followed his hands as they rubbed her thighs, which were exposed in a pair of shorts.

Paris slapped his hand playfully. "How do you know I'm not a pro?" she challenged.

Tariq smirked. "A virgin damn sure ain't no pro. I better watch out before I end up turning your little ass out," he said cockily. Realizing tonight wasn't the night for his conquest, Tariq blew out the candles on the coffee table in front of them and turned on the lamp next to them on the sofa.

Paris squinted at the sudden burst of light in the previously dimly lit room, and she twisted her face thoughtfully. She interpreted his statement as a challenge, and there was nothing she enjoyed more than a challenge. "We'll see who turns who out," she said pulling him back onto her and slowly flicking her tongue around her pouty lips sensually.

"Stop playing, girl," Tariq moaned then captured her mouth.

Paris let her fingers caress him lightly while he kissed her. She heard another moan escape him when her fingers sought out then caressed his sex. This was going to be fun, she thought. She had planned her first time down to each calculated kiss and caress, and there was no doubt in her mind who would be turned out when she was done. Unlike her friends, Paris was not looking forward to the physical aspects of sex for herself. She rolled her eyes as Janay and Opal talked about feeling good when a boy touched them or kissed them. Paris couldn't feel anything except a sense of accomplishment when she got something from the guy that she wanted. She would not allow herself to entertain enjoying anything about Tariq. Her plan was to make sure he enjoyed it because then he would be even more willing to give her things she wanted.

Paris's first time turned out to be as uneventful for herself as she'd predicted. When Opal and Janay pressed her for details about sex with the older and more experienced Tariq, Paris described it as "a means to an end." As much as she'd enjoyed toying with Tariq, she knew it was only a matter of time before he tired of waiting and moved on. While she'd managed to get quite a bit out of him without having sex, she knew giving him her virginity would clear her tab and she could start all over again.

After they had sex, Tariq's demeanor toward her changed, and he was confiding more about himself and his friends. He never approached the subject of them dating exclusively, but he would often ask her if she was his girl. Paris would smile sweetly at him and nod, giving him enough to keep him satisfied, but not enough to tie her down. Satisfied that she'd accomplished her goal of getting Tariq hooked, she decided it was time to move on.

Since they'd had sex, Tariq was becoming a little too familiar. He wanted her around all the time, and he wanted to have sex with her at every available opportunity. He was constantly giving her money and little gifts here and there, but Paris's eyes had begun to get bigger.

Besides things for herself, she would often buy things for Ivan and Sharp. They'd been so happy when she bought them a Chicago Bulls jersey to share. She made the boys swear they wouldn't let Deanne catch them wearing it. They were supposed to say it came from a friend at school if she somehow found it.

Paris hated the fact that she couldn't do more for her brothers. She needed someone that could give her larger amounts instead of nickel and diming her all the time. The twins were growing, and so were their feet. Keeping them in shoes became a full-time job. She began looking for a bigger fish to fry.

Tariq was a senior at Jackson State and was a member of Kappa Alpha Psi fraternity. On weekends, he started taking Paris with him to functions at school, while she was supposed to be babysitting to pay for dance uniforms. She made him promise he would take care of her fees if she agreed to hang out with him. Unbeknownst to Tariq, his attempts to show off his girl from back home slowly started to backfire as his frat brothers and friends began taking notice of Paris. Where most girls would ignore inappropriate looks from friends or frat brothers, Paris would meet them with a bold stare, challenging them to step to her. In her mind, she wasn't tied down to Tariq, and there was no commitment between the two of them. She didn't owe anyone anything besides herself. Her rationale was to keep her options open to move on to bigger and better things whenever the opportunity presented itself.

Nathaniel Johnson was the son of a heart surgeon and one of Tariq's frat brothers. Paris noticed that every time Nathaniel's girl Meri-Lyn came around, she was showing off something "her baby" had given her. Paris looked with envy at a charm bracelet Meri-Lyn delicately lifted out of a robin's egg blue Tiffany's box, the last time they double-dated.

Nathaniel was all-right looking, but his gold Lexus truck and expensive clothes are what caught Paris's eye. She knew that he had more money than Tariq and had no qualms lavishing expensive gifts on his girl. There was no reason Meri-Lyn should have more than she did. Besides, Meri-Lyn probably came from a wealthy family as well. She probably wasn't trying to buy tennis shoes for twin brothers.

Paris began looking for ways to get closer to him. The opportunity came quicker than she'd planned as Nathaniel ended up staying with Tariq over their spring break. Tariq got her a part-time job at his cleaners on the weekends, and he would stop by to talk with her whenever he got the chance. He brought Nathaniel with him one Saturday, and Paris slipped Nathaniel her number while Tariq went to check stock in the back. Nathaniel gave her a strange look at first, but then smiled devilishly and tucked the number in his back pocket. When the two turned to leave, Nathaniel glanced back at her.

Paris placed a finger to her lips and mouthed "Shhhh."

Again, Paris's pre-meditated plans worked smooth as butter, and she soon had both Nathaniel and Tariq calling her on a regular basis. Nathaniel gave her a pager because he said he wanted to be able to get a hold of her whenever he wanted. Paris congratulated herself on winning over such a huge prospect, as Nathaniel proved to be just as generous as she'd thought he would be. He showered her with jewelry and clothes, taking the gifts up a notch from Tariq. Besides the gifts, Nathaniel took her places his family frequented.

Disaster struck when he took her to see a performance of Dream Girls at a Civic center in Jackson. Unbeknownst to the two of them, the Molden's had a family member performing with the production. Paris was nestled in Nathaniel's arms leaving the theatre when Tariq and Tyrell approached them out of nowhere.

"What the fuck?" Tariq asked loudly.

Paris's eyes widened at the sight of him, but then she summoned her cool back.

"Hey, man, it's not what it looks like," Nathaniel attempted to assure his frat brother.

Tyrell's eyes shot daggers through Paris, but she refused to acknowledge her fear or guilt. She knew Tyrell hated her because of the way he thought she'd played JaJuan.

"What's up, Paris? You all up on my frat now?" Tariq asked her.

Paris narrowed her eyes angrily at Tariq. "Chill Tariq, don't cause a scene. It's not even that big a deal," Paris replied evenly.

Tariq balled his fists up at his sides.

"Come on now, man, it's nothing. Let's just talk about this somewhere else. I know you're family's in there. You're little brother's right here," Nathaniel reasoned.

"Fuck that. You been all up in my face and fucking my girlfriend all this time?" Tariq yelled.

"I'm not your girlfriend," Paris stated simply. "You know we're not even like that."

"You're right. You're not my girlfriend. You're nothing but a gold-digging bitch," Tariq spat. "Up here wearing the necklace I bought you for Valentine's Day out with my fucking frat brother."

Paris shrugged her shoulders. It was too bad that Tariq had to find out this way, but she knew he would eventually find out. Paris was actually amused at Tariq's anger. He was embarrassing himself in front of a bunch of strangers, not to mention his family.

"Tell that bitch to give me my fucking necklace back!" Tariq demanded.

Paris backed away from him but didn't make a move to take the necklace off.

"Man, come on now, this isn't the place. Let's just go back to my truck and talk about this," Nathaniel said.

"Man, fuck you nigga. Don't say shit to me," Tariq threatened.

"Go on. Give him the necklace back, baby girl. I'll buy you another one just like it or even better. It's not even worth getting into this all out in public like this."

Paris shook her head no. "He gave it to me. It was a gift, and now it belongs to me. Why would I give him something that belongs to me?"

Nathaniel huffed irritably. "Damn, shit," he said under his breath.

Tariq made a move toward Paris's neck.

Nathaniel stepped in to block him. "Come on, man. This shit ain't worth it."

"That bitch ain't worth this man," Tyrell yelled, trying to pull his brother away from a physical confrontation with the much bigger Nathaniel.

Tariq looked at Paris's smug face then punched Nathaniel in the stomach. Nathaniel lunged at Tariq, knocking him to the ground. Members of Tariq's family immediately began trying to pull the two friends apart. Paris felt a chill go up her spine as she looked up to see Tyrell's eyes boring through her.

"You're nothing but a gold-digging bitch," Tyrell spat at her, before running back toward the parking lot.

Paris stepped back from the tussle and tore her eyes away from Tyrell. Instinctively, her hand went to the necklace. While most of the trinkets she received held little value past the point of getting them, she loved the necklace. From a delicate gold chain hung a heart pendant with the words "Tariq's girl" inscribed on the front and her name on the back. It reminded Paris of a necklace a childhood friend received from her father. Paris envied the necklace and the sentiment in which it was given. Back then she'd longed for someone to love her enough to give her something so special. She didn't think Tariq loved her, but he definitely valued her presence in his life. The necklace was proof of that. There was no way she was giving it back.

If Tariq couldn't control his emotions, that wasn't her fault. The two exchanged a few punches before Tyrell came back on the scene with his father and a few male family members in tow. Paris watched in silence as the men separated the two friends. She felt a pair of eyes drilling holes through her. Tyrell looked at her as if she were the devil himself. She pulled Nathaniel's sport coat tighter around her shoulders and flipped Tyrell off. Who were they to judge her? Her heart tugged in sympathy for Tariq for a moment before Paris reminded herself that if she hadn't of hurt him, he would definitely have ended up hurting her. It's what all men would do if given the chance. She hadn't let Tariq get the best of her, and now he was angry. She brushed it off and composed herself before walking confidently off with Nathaniel.

She let her hips sway seductively and a swift glance over her shoulder proved her instincts correct. Tariq was still watching. She congratulated herself on maintaining control of the situation and gave Nathaniel a sidelong smile. He didn't know it, but there was no way he was going to get the best of her either. He was one opportunity away from ending up just like Tariq.

Paris continued her relationship with Nathaniel for two months after the fight between him and Tariq. Nathaniel supplied her and the twins with a new wardrobe. She deposited the money he'd given her, along with some she'd saved up from Tariq in a savings account. She was determined never to be a victim like her mother had been. Richard left Deanne with no money, lonely and bitter. Paris was no fool, she could learn from other's mistakes, and the lesson was clearly do it to them before they get the chance to do it to you.

Deanne began pressuring Paris about attending college at the end of Paris's senior year. Paris had no interest or intentions of going to college. The only thing she liked about school was being on the dance team. While Opal and Janay stressed over ACT and SAT scores, Paris had been busy perfecting her game on the opposite sex.

"Why don't you want to go to your prom, Paris? I had all these plans of getting you a beautiful dress and taking pictures. I know you've been seeing some boy around here," Deanne probed. She sat down on the edge of Paris's bed and looked thoughtfully at her.

Paris sat up in bed and shook her head.

"Nope. I told you, Momma, I don't really want a boyfriend," she insisted.

"I thought you were getting close with that Tyrell. You spent enough time working over there with him at his folks' dry cleaning business."

Again, Paris shook her head.

"I told you, Momma, we're just friends. I think they felt sorry for me," she said sadly. She hoped that would get Deanne off her trail.

"Paris, I hope you don't dislike boys because of what happened with your father and me," Deanne started hesitantly.

Uncomfortable with the conversation, Paris got up and began taking out her clothes for the next day.

"Paris Renee, I'm talking to you."

Paris slowly turned and looked at her mother. "I just don't have time for all that now. I don't have time to be crying over a boy. I see all my friends do it. And yeah, sometimes I heard you crying over Daddy late at night when you thought everyone was asleep. I don't want to deal with that," Paris said quietly.

Deanne shook her head dismally. "I hate you had to hear that, Paris. But that just means that your dad and I weren't meant to be together. That has nothing to do with you. You need to experience falling in love for yourself. It doesn't have to always end like that, Paris," Deanne said sadly. "You could still go to your prom. You'll regret it for the rest of your life if you don't go."

"I don't think so, Momma. I really don't want to go. I don't really get along with the boys at my school anyway. They are only after one thing, and it's so obvious."

Paris rejoined her mother on her tattered twin bed and folded her hands in her lap. Paris hated lying to her mother, but she'd gotten used to swallowing her guilt. She had told the truth about one thing. She didn't get along with most of the boys at her school. Since she hadn't given any of them the time of day, they'd been more than happy to hear Tyrell's news of her being a gold-digging whore. The only one who never said anything was JaJuan. He just looked at her as if he couldn't believe how she'd done him. To her knowledge, he'd never mentioned it to anyone else, and she was happy to keep it that way. She found she couldn't make eye contact with him for some reason, so she opted to avoid him completely.

"Have I told you, you've grown into a beautiful young lady, Paris? I'm so proud of you," Deanne said, breaking the silence in the room.

Paris leaned over and laid her head in her mother's lap. "I love you, Momma."

"I love you, too, baby." Deanne cradled her daughter's head in her lap. Paris shut her eyes tight to will back angry tears. She loved her mother so much. She knew if Deanne knew some of the things she had done, she would be hurt to the core. Besides the fact that she was hurting her mother, lately more and more people talked about her as if she was a bad person. Her reputation never recovered after the incident with Tariq and Nathaniel, and although Paris was an expert at covering her true feelings, lying on her mother's lap, she was unable to deny her pain.

She wondered why people couldn't see that she was trying to keep her heart protected. She remembered how her father's rejection hurt like it was yesterday. She could still see the pain in Deanne's eyes when the twins asked about their father. Paris didn't want that reality for herself. She swallowed sobs that would've told Deanne far more than Paris wanted to disclose. She just knew if she told her mother that she still hurt because her father didn't love her, it would only hurt Deanne more, and Paris didn't want that.

She looked up and gave Deanne a half-hearted smile. Things were much better the way they were. She would just have to find a way to be more discreet with her dealings with men. She didn't want to do anything that would hurt her mother and that included letting her see her daughter's pain. She was graduating in a few weeks and Paris knew she had to find a way to distance her lifestyle from her mother. She could always send the boys money and clothes from out of state. She would probably be a bigger help to her family out of town anyway. She knew Deanne still heard rumors about her, but chose not to address it. Staying in state would only result in Deanne being hurt when she realized much of the things she heard about her daughter were true.

The entire experience with JaJuan, Tariq and Nathaniel taught Paris that she needed to find a less personal way of getting what she wanted from men. Although for all practical purposes, she'd accomplished her goals in getting things from Tariq and Nathaniel, not to mention a few rides from JaJuan. The drama almost outweighed her profits.

When Paris was voted prettiest girl in the school, Opal and Janay were almost as shocked as Paris was.

"They don't even like Paris anymore," Janay complained.

After the initial shock, Paris shrugged the compliment off much like she had their previous interest. "Guys are fickle. You can't be sure of anything except the fact that they will use you up and leave you. That's why I always make sure I use them first," Paris advised her friends.

"How do you know so much about what guys will do? None that I know of have used you," Opal asked suspiciously.

"That's because I learned from my mom. Why stumble yourself if you can learn from somebody else's mistakes?"

Janay's speech about everyone's experiences being their own was lost on Paris. She hadn't listened to her girlfriends or anyone else for as long as she could remember. Besides, she'd already witnessed Janay's steady leave her for a girl that was sexually active and attended another school. Opal's high school sweetheart had taken her virginity and sullied her name after he gave the intimate details to the entire football team. They could tell her nothing on the subject of the opposite sex. She was going to be the predator, never the prey.

# CHAPTER NINE
# FLIPPIN' THE SCRIPT

Paris felt triumphant each time she collected a $1,000 from a customer. Her father had dismissed her entire existence for a measly $1,000. Now men eagerly paid that for a few hours of her time. It was ironic, and it fed a deep-seeded void festering inside her since the day her mother explained to her why she didn't have a father. One of her grandmother's favorite sayings was "let sleeping dogs lie" and that's exactly what Paris chose to do. She'd never mentioned the name Richard Dennison to her mother, her brothers or anyone else again. She resigned herself to finding a way to prove that she was worth much more than the insignificant grand her father paid to be rid of her.

Paris puckered her lips and blew an elderly black man a kiss, then gathered her sarong and positioned it around her taut twenty-six inch waist. She had just finished performing a private dance for him in the Champagne room, reserved exclusively for clients paying a grand and up. He was harmless, and Paris didn't mind dancing for him. Unlike most younger men, Harold never tried to touch or fondle her. He didn't even gawk at her in the vulgar way others did. He just peered at her through aged runny eyes, barely showing any signs of enjoyment as she wriggled and rolled her way out of everything except a pink g-string and stilettos. He was one of four customers she depended on to buy a private dance from her at least once a month.

Kenton received half of what she made, but she still made out nicely on those nights. While Mr. McCray mumbled through a thank you, Paris mentally checked the performance off her list. She had two more sets to do before the night was over, but she was feeling energetic and up for anything. She gave the man a kiss on his wrinkled cheek then headed to the dressing room to change.

"So have you decided what you want to do about the gig next week?" Kenton asked, falling in step with Paris. As usual, she was annoyed by Kenton's forwardness, but instead of snapping at him, she bit her lip.

"Yeah I'm gonna go ahead and do it," she answered nonchalantly.

She felt her stomach turn as she watched him rub his hands together anxiously like the greedy old scrooge from Charles Dickens's *A Christmas Carol.* Kenton's greed at her expense didn't sit well with her, but there was nothing she could do about it.

"Can I go ahead and get dressed by myself, Kenton?" Paris asked sarcastically, without bothering to turn and look at him.

"Oh yeah, sure. Hey, you all right, girl? You seem a little zoned out. Everything's okay, right?"

Paris put her hand on the dressing room door and pushed it back open. "I'm fine," she threw over her shoulder then pulled the door close behind her. Kenton's absence was the best thing about doing private shows. Although he got his cut of her earnings, he wasn't all up in her face. At one time, she had been able to tolerate him enough to have dinner and a little physical interaction occasionally with him. But after working at the club for a year, she began to see Kenton for the greedy little pimp he was and severed social ties with him. She let him know that their relationship was strictly business related. She knew that when it came down to making money, Kenton's greed could work to her favor, but she had no interest in dealing with him outside the club. Ever fearful of losing the money she brought to the club, he obliged and transitioned their relationship to a strictly professional one. Once, he'd tried to raise his percentage on Paris. She immediately threatened to leave the club. Surprised by her gall, he relented with the understanding that they would decide on a fixed rate. Now, he constantly pressured her into doing as many gigs as he could secure for her. She pulled her long brown hair into a maroon scrunchy then began wiping a cleansing pad across her face.

"Hey, girlfriend." Chocolate appeared from the other entrance to the dressing room, waving a wad of hundred dollar bills.

Paris smiled at Chocolate. "You got all that for an hour?"

Chocolate's mischievous smile tipped Paris off that there was more than she'd revealed. "You could say that. Boyfriend was all that though. I went ahead and let him eat me out for an extra $300," she whispered in a conspirator's tone.

Paris shook her head again. "Did you tell Kenton?"

"Fuck Kenton. Let somebody eat his kitty cat out for his own money. I swear he got one with his bitch ass."

Paris knew that Chocolate and Kenton had an off and on relationship, so Paris dismissed Chocolate's comments as retaliation from a lover's spat. There was no doubt in her mind that in the next day or so Chocolate would be back to singing Kenton's praises.

"I know that's right." Paris laughed. "I don't know though, girl. You may want to be careful about who you let up in that stuff. You'll probably see him every night this week," Paris joked.

Chocolate reached down and pulled up a skintight pair of inky blue capri pants. "That's fine with me as long as he visits the bank before the club." She stuffed the wad of money in a bulky green Dooney & Bourke handbag. "So what's up for tomorrow, girl? You know you need to go out with me. It's not often we get a Saturday off."

Paris pulled her midriff tee over 34C caramel colored cleavage. "I know. I hadn't thought about it though. I was kinda looking forward to just chilling at home."

"Girl, you're going out with me. We deserve a night out without having to shake our moneymakers. Let's see if we can't get somebody to shake theirs for us." Chocolate smiled mischievously.

"Please. I deal with these fools all week. I'm not trying to hear all this shit when I'm off the clock," she said nastily.

"We don't have to go out with them. I'm talking about us having a girls' night out. You know, going to the club, picking up some fine men, and not no clients either," Chocolate enthused.

"Girl, please. I don't care nothing about no men." Paris said smartly.

Chocolate blew out an irritated sigh. "Damn, maybe they're right. Maybe you do like girls," Chocolate muttered under her breath.

"Fuck you."

"You know that's what everybody here thinks," Chocolate said truthfully.

"Fuck these pathetic bitches, and I repeat, fuck you."

"You ain't got to get all like that, Paris, damn. You are so dramatic. It's no biggie if you do. Most folks in here are bi anyway."

"I don't like girls, and I'm not bi. But if I was, it still ain't anybody's business."

Chocolate put her hand on Paris's. "If you're not gay, then what's up Paris? As long as I've known you, you've been trippin with men like this, especially black men. What's up? Did you have a really bad heart-break or something that you can't get over?"

Paris digested Chocolate's question. Had she experienced heart-break that kept her from pursuing a healthy relationship? She decided she hadn't, but Deanne had one twenty-six years ago that she'd passed on to her daughter.

# CHAPTER TEN
# ARTIFICIAL SWEETNERS

Chocolate's prying pissed Paris off, but it served as a motivator at the private party they performed at the following week. Paris spent the remainder of her weekend re-hashing the conversation repeatedly in her head, until she was fuming on Tuesday when they arrived at the hotel where the party was scheduled. Having to do a private party that she hadn't wanted to do on her day off, had her teeth on edge. Their bodyguard, Cruz, led them up the elevator, then to the room. A white man with thinning brown hair and glasses opened the door, then spent the following five minutes welcoming and thanking them profusely for coming. The next ten minutes he went on and on about how beautiful and "exotic-looking" they were.

"Somebody better shut his ass up before he says the wrong thing and it's on," Chocolate warned in a hushed voice intended only for Paris and Cruz.

A hulk of a man, Cruz was a cutthroat Dominican who was usually their knight in shining armor and accompanied them to most private shows. He laughed gruffly at Chocolate's remark, then instructed them to wait by the door while he discussed the rules with the awaiting customers and accepted payment on behalf of Under the Cherry Moon.

"Are you ready for this?" Chocolate smoothed her wavy hair away from her face nervously with her hands.

Paris nodded. These private parties were always drama. There would be men who would do any and everything to try to push the boundaries. She chalked it up to her patience running thin, but lately she was having less and less tolerance for the dirty comments and groping that was sure to take place. While the money was good, she had to psyche herself up for the performances, and the least little thing could set her off.

Tonight she wanted to get in and out as quickly as she could.

Cruz returned and took his place by the door where he would remain until they were finished in approximately four hours. Paris and Chocolate walked over and let the man who opened the door introduce them to all his colleagues.

"I saw your show the last time I was in New Orleans, and I haven't gotten through one night's sleep without you in my dreams," he said. "This beautiful lady is Caramel, and this is her lovely friend Chocolate."

His exaggerated tone on the word friend alerted both dancers he was familiar with their duo act.

His eyes hungrily roamed over Paris's body, eager for a preliminary peek through her wrap dress.

"We're in for a sweet treat tonight," a hefty bald man exclaimed while devouring both dancers with his eyes, "Hello girls, I'm Paul."

Watching Paul's fat pink hands, Paris was sure he was about to completely rub the skin off them in anticipation.

Paris and Chocolate chatted with the men for thirty minutes, laughing infectiously at dumb jokes and stoking neglected egos, until finally, Paris couldn't take anymore and cued Cruz to start the beginning chords of Prince's "The Beautiful Ones."

At the drive-thru window of the Bank of New Orleans, Paris filled out her deposit slip, then placed the tube in the outgoing chute. To her, it was ludicrous that men worked long and hard, fifty and sixty hour weeks, just to give their money away to strangers who couldn't care less about them. She stuck her arm out of her window to retrieve the tube containing her deposit receipt and account balance. She was a few dollars short of thirty thousand dollars in this account and had twice that in her savings. Including her stocks, though only twenty-six, she was worth almost one hundred thousand more dollars than she was worth to her father at birth. She sucked her bottom lip in frustration.

She didn't want to acknowledge his presence or influence in her life today. But as hard as she tried, a little voice inside always said, *What would he think of me now? Wouldn't he be proud of me now? Wouldn't he be surprised to know his daughter makes this much money? To know his daughter was this pretty? To know his daughter had a bad-ass black Porsche? Would he like me now? Or would he still want to give me up for less than what I make in a few hours?*

After being needled all week, Paris decided she was tired of Chocolate's constant lecturing about her rudeness with customers and men in general. It wasn't any of Chocolate's or anyone else's business how she treated her customers. Sometimes it seemed the ruder she was the more some of her customers liked it. She was beginning to believe that men enjoyed fantasizing about women that they could never have. If that situation changed, they were off to chase the next unattainable goal. She laughed with Chocolate about the trick she played on little Mr. Married at the private show, but Chocolate hadn't been amused in the least. What Chocolate didn't know was that Paris played her little trick on many of her customers. She liked to think that was her way of getting even with them for the wrong they were doing against their wives and families. She hoped her actions were responsible for at least one wife getting a freakin' clue.

Chocolate warned what Kenton would do if he ever found out about her little tricks. But Paris thought she was being paranoid. There was no way for any of them to prove she'd left the lipstick marks on purpose. If the men were where they were supposed to be, they wouldn't have encountered any strange woman's lipstick stain on the insides of their collars.

She seriously thought about cutting off social ties with Chocolate. She had been cool for a season, but lately all of Chocolate's comments made her a lot less cool than Paris initially thought.

Her eyes perked when she identified Analise's phone number on her caller ID. Maybe she would invite Analise to visit for a weekend. Analise always had a way of cheering her up. She'd considered Analise her only real girlfriend before she moved to Atlanta to marry a ball player. Unlike Chocolate, Analise didn't remind Paris of things she was trying with all her might to forget. She picked up the phone and cheerfully exclaimed, "Hey Analise, girl"

"Hey girl." The lilt of her friend's southern accent made Paris's smile widen.

"How'd you know it was me?" Analise asked.

"Caller ID." Paris laughed.

"Who are you avoiding now days?" Analise joked.

"Grey and Harley, as usual." Paris cradled the phone between her ear and shoulder, then tucked her feet beneath her on her king-sized bed.

"What's Harley up to? And Grey, too, with his fine self."

"Not a damn thing but bugging the hell out of me. We have the same old lame conversation every time we talk. He just can't seem to get it through his head that I'm not quitting the club and turning into a kept woman. He says eventually he'll change my mind, I keep telling him not to hold his breath."

"Where's your man Dey then? I sure miss those hook-ups he sent you."

Paris laughed at her friend's reference. Once she'd asked Dey if he could send two pairs of Manolo Blahniks. Dey had asked which friend the shoes were for. When Paris said Analise, he sent the extra pair without making any fuss whatsoever. After that, on occasion he would send an extra pair of shoes or other trinkets for Analise. Their friendship had proved mutually rewarding, as Analise never failed to hook her up when her boyfriend was feeling generous.

"I haven't heard from him since he sent me this really cute bracelet a couple of weeks ago. You know how he is. He pops up every blue moon. He's so damn low-key I know he'd bore me for real if he was here more often."

"You know you need to settle down with Grey, Paris. I never understood why you won't. That man is fine, got money out the ass and he worships your dirty drawers." Analise laughed.

Paris's smile slowly faded. Everybody was meddling nowadays.

Suddenly the idea of seeing Analise didn't seem to be such a good idea anymore. "Don't you start, too," Paris said, getting out of her comfortable position and stretching her shapely brown legs out in front of her.

"I'm not, I'm not. I just called to give you my big news first."

Paris could hear the excitement seeping through Analise's voice. "What? What is it?" she probed, re-tucking her legs underneath her.

"Girl, I'm pregnant," Analise squealed happily.

Paris's brow wrinkled in bewilderment. "Pregnant?"

"Yes. I can't believe it. Can you? I was worried I wouldn't be able to get pregnant after all the abortions I had," Analise admitted in a hushed voice.

Paris was too stunned to speak. Her partner-in-crime was pregnant. Didn't Analise know that was the stupidest thing she could have ever done in a million years?

"Does Rick want the baby?" she asked doubtfully.

"Of course he does, we're married. I think he's more excited than I am."

"Hmm."

"What?"

"Well, are you sure this is a good idea? I mean you all haven't even been married two years yet. What if it doesn't work out? You'll end up raising that baby all by yourself," Paris advised carefully.

"Paris, we're not planning on getting divorced," Analise said as if she were talking to a child. "Besides even if we did, Rick would always take care of his child. And with all the money he makes, he'll be taking care of me, too."

Paris didn't respond. Why couldn't Analise understand how irresponsible it would be to bring a child into this world without knowing for sure that it would have a responsible father?

"Oh, before I forget, I called for another reason, too. I was wondering if you'd be interested in doing some modeling down here. The agency I work with is looking for print models for mostly headshots and stuff for magazine ads. I know you've told me no a couple of times before. But, hey, you can't strip at that club forever. I know you'd love it down here. You'll be married with a kid on the way like me before you know it."

Paris was once again speechless. Why did everyone keep telling her that she was getting older? Didn't they know she knew better than anyone? July second was circled on her calendar in a bold red marker with the number twenty-seven written inside the cellblock marked Tuesday. Of course she knew most strippers were forced out of the business by the time they were thirty, but she had another three years to go before that landmark. Maybe she could squeeze out a few more years even if she kept hitting the gym and the spa on a regular basis. But, more importantly, why was Analise assuming that she wanted the same life that she had?

She couldn't believe Analise was going to be a mother. Paris knew how hard it was to raise children without a man. She'd watched as Deanne attempted to provide for her children with a stepfather.

"So, what do you think about the modeling?" Analise pressed.

"I'll think about it okay? I'll call you next week."

"Can I get a congratulations?"

"I'm sorry. Sure, girl, congratulations. I just want everything to work out for you," Paris said softly.

She told Analise goodbye then hung up, rested her head on her silk pillow and closed her eyes. If she went to Atlanta, she would have to deal with Analise, Rick and their new baby. While that life might've been fine for Analise, Paris knew it would never work for her. She thought the cliché "It's better to have loved and lost than never loved at all," was pure bullshit. She would never allow herself to buy into the Prince Charming fallacy. The more she thought about it, the less excited she was about visiting Analise. She didn't want a constant reminder of the life she was never destined to lead.

Sunday afternoon, the doorbell chime shocked Paris. Angry that her peaceful afternoon was being threatened, Paris headed for the door. Her private community didn't allow solicitors, and she never invited company on a night she had to work. She peeked out her peephole and saw

Harley Cox, a dozen cream-colored roses in his hand. She debated acknowledging his presence at all, as she had to be at work in a few hours and relished her down time.

"Harley, what are you doing here?" she asked, swinging her front door wide open.

"I just came to give you these before you go to work tonight." He extended the flowers.

Paris gave him an exasperated smile, then took the flowers and put them in a vase on her table.

"I been missing you, girl." He pulled her into his arms in a lazy embrace.

Paris allowed him to give her a kiss on the lips then she pulled away and removed his arms from around her waist.

"So what's up? You're not going to give me a chance, baby girl?" He looked her over appreciatively.

Paris grimaced at his comment then turned her back to him. Harley had been pursuing her for the past two years relentlessly. Like Grey, he wasn't showing any signs of letting up any time soon.

"I know you're in your zone getting ready for work, so I won't hold you. Just tell me when I'm going to see you again, and I'm outta here," he said matter-of-factly.

She grimly realized he wouldn't leave without her agreeing to see him. "What about tomorrow afternoon?" She did a quick mental checklist to make sure she had nothing else planned for Sunday evening.

"That will work." He offered another lazy smile.

After a second kiss on the mouth, he opened the door and left without another word. Harley was the physical antithesis of Grey. With a baldhead, dark chocolate complexion, long lashes on expressive eyes and a sexy goatee, Harley defined sexy. He was six feet, five inches and two-hundred-twenty pounds of muscle with no flaws the naked eye could detect. Harley played for the New Orleans Saints. Although he handled her with kid gloves most of the time, Paris knew he was very self-centered. Harley had all the spontaneity and sensuality that Grey lacked, but Grey had the sensitivity and level-headedness that Harley lacked. In another lifetime, she would have married either of them, thinking that they were both pretty damn close to everything most women put on their checklist for a husband.

She could only imagine how appreciative Deanne would've been to meet a man like either one of them. But this was her life, not Deanne's, and now she had the best of both worlds. When she felt like the company of a man, she had at least three wonderful specimens to choose from. Would they be waiting on her forever? Of course not, but then she wasn't sweating them like that. If one of the three decided to move on, it was cool because charitable men were a dime a dozen at the club.

The more she thought about it, she realized there had been quite a few weeks since she'd heard from Dey. Harley and Grey's enthusiasm didn't fool her. She estimated that the minute she took either of them seriously would be the exact moment they would choose to fuck up.

She wondered how many other women Harley was involved with. There was no telling with his big baller athletic status and good looks. She knew his little black book had to be quite impressive.

Unfortunately, for his victims, Harley's positives didn't stop at good-looking, Harley was the most skilled and attentive lover a woman could wish for. She had to wean herself from sleeping with him to keep from becoming addicted to his technique. Harley's spontaneity, talents and switch button passion could make a woman lose her mind quicker than a hit of the purest cocaine. After their first encounter, she forced herself to kick him out of her condo. She immediately took a bath, washed his intoxicating cologne off her, re-gained focus, then put herself on a self-imposed Harley schedule. It wouldn't be wise to get too used to Harley Cox. She needed to handle him with a long-handled spoon she'd decided, recalling the old adage her grandmother was notorious for quoting.

Thinking about the last time they made love in his convertible Jag sent chills down her spine. She experienced a tingling sensation from the memory, but pushed it out of her mind. The fact that he was a great lover just attested to the fact that he'd slept with too many women, she reasoned. There was no way a man could be that skilled and talented without putting in a lot of practice.

Harley picked her up at two o'clock on Sunday afternoon with a picnic basket in the trunk of his XK-8 Jaguar convertible.

"You look nice," he commented, taking in her sundress and sandals appreciatively.

She knew that the sunny yellow of her dress was a striking contrast to her rich caramel skin tone. She thanked him politely, but remained silent on the drive to the river. Harley was taking her out on his boat, which was why he had packed them a lunch prior to picking her up.

"I don't know what's wrong with you," he said, smiling at her once they were on the boat and floating slowly.

She cocked her head and squinted at him. "What do you mean?"

"Come on now." He extended his arms. "What more could a woman want than this?"

"Aren't we the confident one?" She turned her attention back to her sandwich and glass of wine.

"I'm serious, Paris." He leaned over the table and clasped his hands in front of him. "I want to be with you."

"Harley, please. What's up with all the pressure?" she asked, mocking his attempt at a romantic conversation.

He took a bite of his tuna salad sandwich. "I know what I want. I've known for a while. I don't know why you won't take me seriously."

"What about what I want?" She sucked a bit of tuna off her thumb and looked expectantly at him.

"That's a good question. What do you want, Paris? Are you with Grey? Is that it?" He drew in an irritated breath and looked out over the peaceful waters.

Paris exhaled loudly, exaggerating her boredom with the topic of conversation. "No, I am not with Grey. I'm with myself, and that's what I want right now. Why is that so hard for everyone to understand?"

"So old Grey's been trying to get you on lockdown? I know it's not that young rapper dude is it? Dey, right? My homeboy said he saw you all up on dude at his video shoot a couple of months ago. Dude was telling everybody his girl was this fine stripper down at Under the Cherry Moon."

"Harley, I don't talk about you with Grey or the rapper dude, and

I won't talk about them with you. Furthermore, I don't ask you about any of the little groupies I see you out with all the time," she remarked laughing.

Harley didn't seem tickled. "It's because you don't care. I just want to know what's up with you and them busters so I will know if I need to back off."

"You can back off if you want to back off, but I am not with anyone, and I am not going to be until I'm ready," she said sassily, staring him directly in the eye.

Harley finally broke the gaze and looked away. "Why are you so against settling down?" he asked softly.

Paris laughed. "You aren't trying to settle down, Harley Cox. Why would you? You got the world by the tail." She smiled, enjoying needling him.

Harley shook his head. "I just wish I could understand why you keep everybody at bay. I mean, you must've been hurt before, but everybody's been hurt. Life goes on."

Paris's eyes flashed in anger, then narrowed at his intrusion. "Harley, I think our afternoon is just about over. Pull this boat over or steer it back or something. You are really tripping."

"Come on, don't be like that. For once, don't take out Miss Bad Ass. Just talk to me," he said, attempting to pull her in his arms.

"Harley, get your got-damn hands off me, turn this boat around and take me home! And don't come knocking on my door with this bullshit anymore. If you can't handle things the way they are, then you need to move on."

"I'm getting tired of your smart-ass mouth. You need to chill with all the cursing." He threw his wine glass, and it cracked against the side of the boat, splattering glass over Paris's ankles.

"Turn the damn boat around, Harley. Take me the fuck home."

"I ain't playing with you. Shut your fucking mouth. I'll take you home." He stood and motioned the driver. "One day somebody's gonna knock the shit out of you because of that smart-ass mouth of yours," he said, shoving past her to the staircase leading downstairs.

"Why don't you try it?" A satisfying smile settled around her lips, declaring a triumphant standoff.

"I don't know why I keep fucking with you," he threw over his shoulder.

"Whatever." She rolled her eyes and put her leftovers in the trash, then focused her attention on the waves lapping against the side of the boat. Harley drove like a maniac on the way to her condo and all but threw her out before burning rubber down the road.

"I need to leave his crazy ass alone," she admitted to herself once she was safely inside her home. Harley hadn't raised his hand to hit her, but he'd come damn close enough. She wasn't afraid of him, just didn't care for all the drama. She didn't need him yelling at her and throwing shit like he was inclined to do when he didn't get his way. It was probably high time she cleaned house and got a new set of suitors, she mused.

After her final set Saturday night, Paris was exhausted and anxious to get out of the club. She grabbed her duffel bag and headed toward the dressing room door when Jezebel sauntered into her path.

"So, Paris, have you seen the latest *Essence*?" Jezebel asked.

The smile pulling at Jezebel's scarlet mouth raised Paris's alarms. "Did you need something?" Paris asked in a clipped voice.

"Oh no, no. I just wondered if you saw your friend in the spread they did on the hottest new couples. What's the rapper's name you date sometimes?" Jezebel's heavy Spanish accent tried to relay innocence, but Paris knew better. "Is it gay or something like that?" Jezebel pressed on.

Paris stopped in her tracks and shifted her weight to her left hip. "You must be trying to give me a reason to knock the shit out of you," Paris threatened calmly.

Jezebel widened her eyes in innocence. "Paris, there's no need for all that ghetto hostility. It's not even like that. I was just wondering if you saw this." She thrust the glossy magazine in Paris's face.

Paris reluctantly took the magazine, forcing her face to remain emotionless as she took in the picture of Dey and a mocha-colored young woman holding hands. The caption underneath stated the picture was from the party where they first met. A second picture of the couple was placed directly under the first. This one showed the woman dressed in a bridal gown holding Dey's hand as the two of them jumped over a broom. Paris read the caption under the wedding photo.

*In a simple, elegant ceremony with fifty of the couple's closest friends, Deontay Whitsen and Brione Vann were joined in holy matrimony. Known to his fans as Dey, the hardcore rapper claims he knew the minute he saw Brione, she would be his wife. The couple plans to honeymoon over the summer in Africa.*

Aware Jezebel was studying her face for signs of betrayal, Paris would die before she gave her the satisfaction.

"I knew he was getting married. In fact, I encouraged him to propose. She's a sweet lady." Paris placed the magazine in Jezebel's hand.

Jezebel opened her mouth to speak but stumbled around for a response. It was obvious she hadn't expected Paris's quick response. Paris turned to walk away then thought better of it.

"Oh and Jezzie." Paris moved into the girls face. "If you ever come at me like that again, Kenton will have to pull me off your cheap-looking, Mexican jumping bean ass. You'll end up giving me the rest of your clients, and once they come this way, they won't be back. Believe that bitch."

# CHAPTER ELEVEN
# TASTE MY ICE CREAM

Maybe she did need to move to Atlanta. Things were definitely getting out of control in New Orleans. Since going out with Harley last week, Paris decided to start avoiding his calls as well as Grey's. Grey had somehow worked up the nerve to come to the club and wait for her after her last set backstage. This infuriated her, because she knew how Grey felt about her dancing. She definitely wasn't crazy about his disapproving eyes judging her from the audience. She had told him that he was not to come backstage again under any circumstances and left him sulking in the hallway.

Chocolate questioned her about the situation after running into Grey. Paris tried to explain to Chocolate that she wasn't leading Grey on. She seriously considered cutting Grey and Harley off for real at this point. It was becoming more of an annoyance instead of a chance for occasional fun.

She told herself she wasn't bothered by the news of Dey's marriage to his squeaky clean new sweetheart, but she was annoyed that he hadn't even told her. Why did she have to open up a magazine and find a picture of him in front of a preacher in a tuxedo? After denying she was bothered, she reminded herself that she should've expected that from him. She knew men were trifling and quick to backstab, so she shouldn't even trip. Dey's behavior was exactly why she vowed never to marry or be involved in a committed relationship. She couldn't imagine how she would have felt if she actually had feelings for Dey. Paris chuckled to herself, thinking about how disappointed his wife would be when she discovered his smoking put a major kink in his sexual performance. She wouldn't be surprised if in a few weeks, after Africa of course, she received another call or care package from Mr. Deontay Whitsen.

Paris hadn't liked her name when she was in elementary school. Her mother had given her and her brothers very unusual names, and they were often the butt of jokes. In first grade, she'd asked her mother why she named her after someplace she'd never been.

"PJ laughed at me today in class. He said I wasn't French, so my name shouldn't be Paris," the sniveling six-year-old cried.

Deanne pulled her onto her lap and ran her fingers lovingly over Paris's long black braids.

"When I was a little girl, that was the one goal I had. I thought Paris, France sounded like such a beautiful place. I loved how the name of the city sounded rolling off my tongue. When I a child, someone read me a story about Josephine Baker in Paris, France. I remember hearing about all the wonderful foods, perfumes and clothes they had there, and thought that would be the most exciting thing that could ever happen to me. When the doctor handed you to me, I knew being your mother was the best thing that could've ever happened to me. I already had my Paris."

Observing her mother closely, Paris could see every single lost dream in her mother's eyes. Dreams that were replaced by three little sepia-skinned, brown-eyed children. Paris wondered what her mother's life would've been like if she'd never gotten mixed up with Richard and had three children. She realized how much her mother had given up in order to raise the three of them on her own. Deanne never regained control of her life. Instead, she was content with the goal of raising Paris and her brothers to the best of her ability.

Although she didn't have a father, she had a mother who put her children first and tried to give them all the love she had to give. It was the last time Paris regretted her name. It was also the reason Paris didn't like being called by her given name while dancing. That day she realized her mother had blessed her with a name that bespoke of her love and dedication to her daughter. Many days Paris felt like she didn't measure up to the aspirations Deanne had for her daughter when she'd named her after her dreams deferred.

Before Caramel, she'd been called Indigo and before that Dreams. Neither name had the staying power that "Caramel" had. Since working at Under the Cherry Moon, she'd developed a connection with her stage name. When she applied for her license plate, Chocolate warned her that the plate would all but eliminate her anonymity outside the club. In spite of the warning, Paris put the plate on the front of the flashy Porsche. Paris did three private shows before the end of the month and made a total of $3,200 dollars and fifteen cents from them. Analise finally pressured her into a verbal commitment to make the trip to Atlanta, just to visit with a local photographer to take some professional pictures.

Paris decided not to drive her Porsche this time, not wanting to put too much wear and tear on the car. She managed to put Analise off for a bit with her offer. Her flight wouldn't leave for another three months. The only reason she'd actually booked it so soon was to get Analise's determined ass off her back. She was looking forward to the trip for a few reasons, one named Harley and the other Grey. It would do her good to get away and not have to deal with them for a while, or this client at the club that was starting to freak her out.

She knew his first name was Jay, but she didn't know his last name. He'd visited the club every night for the past week and a half. That in itself wouldn't have been such a big deal if he hadn't ordered at least four lap dances from her each night. Paris thought if she had to look at his shifty eyes one more time, she'd scream. It looked as if she'd be screaming tonight, because she could've sworn she spotted him earlier in the front row.

She traced her eyes carefully in black kohl pencil, then lined her lips in raspberry. She didn't feel like doing the next set, which was a duo act with Chocolate. They only did the duo act on Saturday nights. Many customers came just to see that particular show. She never understood why men were so fascinated by the idea of two women. It was a silly notion since most of them could barely give one woman an orgasm before falling off into a drug-induced sleep.

She had gotten so used to performing that sometimes she forgot how risqué the show actually was. When Kenton first approached them with the idea, she had been dead set against it. Chocolate didn't think it was a big deal, which worried Paris. It wasn't that she thought Chocolate was bisexual, but rather that there wasn't much Chocolate would not do for the right amount of money. Once a customer asked Chocolate if she would perform oral sex on Paris for an exorbitant amount of money back in his hotel room. Chocolate approached Paris with the offer, stressing the dollar amount they would both receive. Paris had told Chocolate hell naw and to never approach her with shit like that again.

Kenton had convinced Paris that men who frequented strip bars lived for this type of entertainment, and they would only have to do it once a week for fifteen minutes. The act was infamously known as the Gentlemen's Sunday. It involved Chocolate and Caramel smearing whipped cream and cherries on each other's bodies and adeptly removing them. The first few times Paris found it was extremely degrading, but after she counted her tips for that night, she'd pushed that thought to the back of her mind. It didn't last that long, and after all, she and Chocolate were friends. She wasn't turned on by it, but if customers were, and they were willing to pay ridiculously to think she was, so be it.

Each time they performed this particular set, the two of them were bombarded with questions about their sexuality over raised eyebrows and hopeful mischievous smiles. The first few times, both dancers were vocal with curious clients about the act being merely an illusion, but Kenton insisted their negative comments about the show were bad for business and convinced them to keep quiet on their sexual preferences.

"I'm not asking you to lie and say you're bi, but just don't say that you're not. Let them keep that fantasy in their head. That's how you have to look at it. It's their fantasy. It's got nothing to do with you personally," he'd reasoned after Paris had gone off on one customer.

"You ready to get this over with?" Paris asked Chocolate, checking the nozzle on her whipped cream bottle.

"Yeah, girl, I need to cut out of here early tonight. My baby isn't feeling well, and I want to pick her up a little early," she said, placing a strand of chestnut colored weave directly over her left eye.

Paris nodded her head in understanding, but inside she wondered what the hell was wrong with Chocolate. How must she feel being down here with three young children at home? Mommy couldn't be there to hold her sick baby's hand because she was down at the strip club spraying whipped cream all over another woman. There was something sick about that scenario. That was another reason Paris was never going to have children. It was enough that she was too ashamed to tell her own mother about what she did for a living. She never wanted to deal with explaining that to a child, certainly not a child that called her mother.

# *CHAPTER TWELVE*
# *PLAYING WITH FIRE*

Paris dropped her purse on her nightstand and collapsed onto her bed. Exhausted, she had just finished a bachelor party for a newly drafted Atlanta Hawks forward. The groom hadn't been the problem; he was twenty-two years old and a bit awkward. It probably hadn't dawned on him that he was a millionaire yet. Some sister caught him right at the cusp of stardom, Paris thought, smiling to herself.

A short while later, the phone rang, forcing her drooping eyelids to suddenly fly back open. She looked at her caller ID and identified Harley's number.

"Fuck off, Harley," she mumbled, cutting her eyes at the violently ringing phone.

She'd spent the last three hours with a bunch of rowdy, oversexed black men and there was no way she was going to pick up the phone and engage in conversation with anyone with testosterone right now. *Those men had such nerve,* she thought angrily. She knew at least half of their trifling asses from other parties and as regulars at the club. Realizing sleep wasn't in her immediate future, she surrendered and made her way out of bed.

She dug her feet into her thick cream-colored carpeting and wriggled them around in its softness. *Maybe a bath will make me feel better.* Gathering the last bit of strength in her, she switched through the condo to her bathroom. She unclasped her pink demi-cup bra for the second time that evening and walked out of her matching g-string underwear. Reaching for the marble nozzle in her ceramic tub, she turned the hot water up as hard as it would go. Next, she picked up a box of bath beads that were supposed to pop and fizz on your skin, soothing and relaxing your muscles. Once the tub was filled to capacity, she eased herself in slowly, as to not send any water cascading over the sides. Gathering her hair off her neck, she twisted it into an untidy knot atop her head.

Paris slid down in the tub until her neck was fully immersed, leaning her head back against the rim. Once again, she closed her eyes and tried to summon peace. It didn't work. She kept getting mental images from the bachelor party. Maybe she was burnt-out on parties, and needed to put that on hold for a while. Perhaps it was time to take a much-needed hiatus. The chants of "take that shit off" and "ooh babies" from the overly enthusiastic men seemed imprinted on her psyche. She couldn't shake it.

Paris opened her eyes to escape the images and voices and absently began studying the design on her body soap. She'd left her signature lipstick print on three of the men that she knew were married. She got less and less pleasure from doing that now. It didn't seem as if any of their wives were ever any bit wiser. She'd done several things to customers over the years that should've caused their storybook lives to take a turn, but her clues always seemed to go unmarked by their wives. The husbands always ended right back at Under the Cherry Moon the next week or the next month, crisp and freshly earned dollars in hand. Paris knew her attempts to get back at the men were immature and petty, but couldn't help feeling a deep resentment for them. It seemed that men would rather be anywhere or doing anything rather than being at home with their families.

"I know what you're saying, but dude was really upset," Kenton insisted.

"I can't believe you're bringing this bullshit to me," Paris said incredulously.

Kenton shook his head. "Paris, I'm just saying be careful. We don't need no pissed off niggas running around here starting shit. I'm not trying to be having this type of drama here," he said angrily.

Paris rolled almond shaped eyes at Kenton and sighed dramatically. "So what are you saying?"

Kenton looked at her widened eyes and seemed to lose some of his edge. "Nothing. Just be more careful," he muttered then headed toward his office in the back of the club.

Paris rolled her eyes a second time. A part of her was thrilled that one of her ploys had finally paid off. One of the men she'd left her lipstick print on called Kenton, furious when his wife discovered the shirt. He'd insisted that Paris had done it on purpose and demanded Kenton do something about it. Fortunately, for him, he'd been able to tell his wife that lipstick stains from strippers were a common hazard at bachelor parties. His wife bought the story, but he'd been furious that a stripper tried to play him that way.

*If only his wife could've seen him begging me for a taste*, Paris thought smugly. *There was no way he would've been able to get out of that shit.*

Chocolate had been sweating her hard about doing it at the last party they worked. Although Chocolate hadn't gone with her to the party where it happened, she knew Kenton would ask her eventually since they were usually together. Paris hoped he'd let this ride but she wasn't sure. To an extent, she had Kenton wrapped around her finger, but there were two things Kenton put before his lust for the female persuasion: his club and his money. She'd seen him kick out numerous beautiful dancers over things much less than this. She opened the back door latch and stepped out into the parking lot. She'd let Kenton cool off tonight then talk to him tomorrow. Maybe they'd have dinner. Maybe she'd even let him come home with her. It had been over six months since she'd last been intimate with someone.

She'd been with Kenton before, when she first started dancing. She was sure if she had let him, he would have been happy to have a relationship with her until the next new dancer came along. Paris wasn't having it. She let him know from the jump she wasn't into anything except getting her G-spot hit that night and a few nights after that. It hadn't been a bad little fling. Kenton was average looking with a creamy brown complexion and a muscular build. He was thirty-eight years old and had been in this business for over fifteen years. He didn't take any mess from anyone, and to Paris that was attractive.

She fished around in her purse for her keys to deactivate her alarm. Her eyes caught a white stripe accentuated by the midnight black sleekness of her Porsche. The words "slut" and "bitch" were painted across the driver side door of her car. She clutched her chest in surprise. She quickly walked around to the passenger side of her car, and the same words were written there. She swiped a finger across the paint to see if the words would come off. They wouldn't. It appeared they had been written in shoe polish. Her eyes whipped around her surroundings in the desolate parking lot quickly, making sure the culprit was nowhere in sight. She reached down in her purse and fingered her .35 pistol. Its porcelain handle felt eerie in her fingers as she clutched it nervously. She made her way back to the club.

"Let me take you home," Kenton said, rubbing Paris's arms.

She shook her head. "That's not necessary. I'm fine. I'll just catch a cab."

Kenton shook his head emphatically. "Not tonight, Paris. I'm going to make sure you're in the house tonight. Bring Miss Bad Ass back tomorrow." He looked at her curiously. "You know you're still shaking?"

Paris sucked her teeth irritably. She didn't want to let some creep freak her out like this. *Men prey upon fear. They can only do what you let them do.* Still, she had to admit the message written so boldly across her car had startled her.

"Do you really think it was the guy from the bachelor party?" she asked quietly.

Kenton nodded solemnly. "Yeah, I do."

She wrapped her arms around herself and watched as the wrecker hoisted her car up onto the flatbed. She'd called a roadside service and had a truck come and tow her car to Sonny's body shop. She knew Sonny would be just as upset as she was. After convincing her to buy the car and financing much of it, Sonny always treated the car as if it were his baby. Paris found it amusing that Sonny was oftentimes more interested in the car than he was in her. This, of course, was fine with her considering she didn't consider Sonny a priority unless the car was involved.

"Are you okay?" Kenton asked again.

"Please," she said, dropping her hands and picking up her purse. "It takes more than that to scare Paris Renee Jackson."

Kenton just shook his head, then opened the door to the club. She waited while he turned off the lights, locked up and prepared to drive her home.

Kenton instructed Paris to take the following night off. Realizing she needed to rest and get her mind right, she didn't put up an argument. Worrying about the freak that vandalized her car wouldn't do her much good on the stage. Friday afternoon, Chocolate stopped by.

"Girl, you really think that guy did that because you left that smudge on his shirt?"

Paris shrugged. "Kenton thinks so. I don't know. It could be some pissed off customer or anybody. I mean, hell, it could be someone that's visiting the club's website and has never even been inside the club."

"I don't know, it just seems like it's probably somebody that's been around here to know what car you drive and all."

"The car has my name on it. It ain't that hard to make the connection," Paris snapped. Chocolate's inability to think for herself irritated Paris to no end.

"I told you not to put that shit on your car in the first place. You just giving niggas another avenue to get at you outside the club. You should get that plate taken off."

"I ain't taking shit off my car. I had that plate custom made and it goes with the car. It's not coming off," Paris said stubbornly.

Chocolate pursed her lips and rolled her eyes at her friend. "Did you pay for the shit?"

"Hell no, Sonny did," Paris said quickly.

"Have you noticed anybody acting weird? What about somebody you used to go out with?"

Paris shook her head. She wouldn't tell Chocolate or anyone else about the threatening letter she'd received two days ago at the club.

Addressed to Caramel, the letter contained the same offensive words that were written across her Porsche in shoe polish.

She hadn't thought anything was suspicious when she saw the cream envelope setting against the mirror at her station. She often got letters, cards and even gifts from admiring customers.

"Be careful girl," Chocolate advised. "You know there're some sick-os out there for real."

"Girl, please. I won't start tripping over some shoe polish on my car. That's some bitch shit anyway. Females usually do shit like that. You know what I mean?"

"Oh snap, you don't think it was a woman do you?" Chocolate leaned across Paris's coffee table. "I hope nobody's wife is flippin' out."

"I don't know, and I don't care as long as they don't come nowhere near me. If they do, you know I carry Pearl with me at all times." Paris motioned as if she were pulling the trigger on a gun. Pearl was Paris's nickname for the gun she'd bought for her twenty-fifth birthday.

"Girl, I pity the fool that messes with your evil ass." Chocolate laughed.

"Quit calling me evil," Paris said, smiling. "Anyway I think this is as good a time as any for me to get away from here for awhile. I told Analise that I would come down there in a few months and take some pictures for this agent that she has. She's trying to get me to move down there. Maybe I should just go down there a little earlier." Paris took a sip from her water bottle.

Chocolate bucked her eyes. "You can't be leaving me up here." She reached out for Paris's hand across the table. "I can't stay at that stank club without my girl with me. Them new girls get on my nerves, and that's the truth."

Paris jerked her hand away playfully. "I didn't tell her I was moving. I told her I would think about it, and I am. It may be time for me to make a move."

"Well check on stuff for me, too. If you can model, so can I." Chocolate smoothed her wavy tresses away from her face.

Paris smirked at her comment. Another reason she didn't have many female friends was because of the ever-present feminine vice—jealousy. Paris assured her she would check on getting her a modeling job, too. She would've said anything just to get Chocolate to leave. She appreciated her concern, but she had an inkling Chocolate's interest was more for gossip's sake than genuine concern. Of course, word had gotten out about her car being vandalized, even though it'd been repainted good as new a day later.

True to his word, Sonny had dropped everything and had two of his men work on Paris's car. He even gave her a discounted price of one hundred dollars and she in turn would give him a couple of free dances whenever he came into the club. Paris had a feeling that he'd be coming in to the club soon to collect, but she was okay with that. Sonny was an old, harmless man.

She reached into the drawer under her coffee table and pulled out the letter. The message "Slut bitch you ain't shit" in bold black print jolted her to the core. Paris looked at the words once more, then crumpled the paper and tossed it in the trash. For some reason that didn't feel good enough, so she retrieved the paper from the trash and tore it into tiny pieces, then threw it away again.

"I'm tired that's all," Paris assured Analise over the telephone. Analise's call had brought a smile to her face. Although her goals were very different from Paris's, she respected Analise's ability to stay focused in the midst of all the drama that took place in the club.

"You just need to take a break from all the private parties," Analise assured Paris.

Obviously shaken, Analise listened as Paris told her about the psycho's note addressed to her at the club. Paris denied knowing why the maniac had chosen her instead of one of the other girls at the club. Analise was a chicken, and Paris stopped telling her about little tricks she'd done to her customers a long time ago. Paris took a bite of an apple and chewed pensively before responding.

"I don't know, Analise. I'm just tripping," Paris said. "Bill's got to get paid, so I got to do what I got to do. It's not that bad once it's over."

"You know what? Honestly, I don't even know how I did it that long."

"What do you mean?"

She just knew Analise wasn't trying to front on her. She remembered Analise being all about getting paid back when she in New Orleans. This new married Analise might be pulling the wool over her own eyes, but Paris wasn't fooled for a second.

"I just don't think I could ever go back to dancing. It all seems like a bad dream."

"Please, if you hadn't been rescued, you'd be right along with me," Paris remarked, determined to give her friend a dose of reality.

"There was no way I was going to be working there as long as you have. You're better than I am, girl. For me, dancing was just a tool to get what I wanted. This was the plan all along. I was just waiting on the right man."

"Don't you mean the right sucker?" Paris laughed.

She had to admit; Analise had her husband's nose wide open. Paris could remember the first time he'd requested a private dance from Analise. He'd returned to the club every night for two weeks before he got the nerve to ask for a private dance. After the set, Analise had pocketed five hundred dollars in excess of what her normal fee would've been.

"Ole boy's in love," Kenton teased. "The next thing you know, he'll be in here singing on his knees with an engagement ring."

Paris smiled at Kenton's off-beat humor, but she remembered the look in Analise's eyes. Analise had known he was the one from the moment she slid her g-string clad bottom on his expensively tailored lap.

"He's not a sucker. I love that man. I'm a good wife," Analise insisted defensively.

"Whatever. I'm not trying to marry none of these weak ass pieces of shit that come in the club. If they're in the club now, they'll be in the club after they're married."

"Now, girl, you know I'm not having that. He knows better," Analise remarked wisely.

"Oh so you're Sherlock Holmes now? I guess you could just feel it if he stepped out on you," Paris teased.

"No, but I tell you what. If he does slip up and step out, my alimony payment will be more than enough to keep me straight for the rest of my life."

"He didn't ask you for a pre-nuptial agreement?"

"Girl, please." Analise laughed.

Paris joined in the laughter. "No pre-nup? I told you that Negro was a sucker, but I can't hate. You worked it girlfriend."

"You need to quit trippin' and get out here so we can get you hooked up."

"I keep telling you, I'm not trying to be tied down to no sorry ass Negro. They get on my nerves after a couple of dates anyway, and that's the halfway decent ones. I can't be sitting around waiting for him to fuck up. Then I'd have to kill his ass."

It was Analise's turn to laugh at Paris. "Let me let your old evil ass off the phone, and let me know when you're ready to stop shakin' ya ass."

Paris experienced a stab of irritation at Analise calling her evil. Chocolate called her evil all the time, but Paris chalked it up to Chocolate not having the ability to think for herself. Kenton was forever calling her evil as well, but she told herself it was because he wanted her eating out of the palm of his hand like the other dancers. Analise was one of the only people she respected, and it didn't sit well with her for Analise to agree with Kenton and Chocolate. Before she allowed herself to get too introspective, she decided to get off the phone. Maybe Analise was getting soft on her after all.

"Yeah, yeah," Paris mumbled. "I'll talk to you later."

A shiver ran up her spine as she stood up to throw her half-eaten apple away. She couldn't imagine some Negro lying up in her house demanding she cook and clean for him while he ran the streets. More importantly, she couldn't imagine going through labor with some Negro's children just so he could up and leave her with mouths to feed and only one income. Nope, that life wasn't for her. Analise could have it. She just needed to get a couple of consistent Sugar Daddies that would pay her bills for her, then she could cut the private parties totally out. Lately she hadn't felt like entertaining anyone, so she'd all but discontinued her usual payers. A few customers would help her out with bills occasionally, but she didn't have to have sex with them. They just enjoyed her company. She just didn't have the stomach to lie up and have sex with some nasty old man to get her bills paid or to fund her weekly facials and trips to the beauty shop. Analise told her there were at least three of her husband's teammates that were sweating her about meeting her "shorty" from New Orleans. Paris would get down there eventually and see what they were working with.

"Them niggas'll end up working my last nerve, and I'll be ready to kick Analise's ass," she said out loud.

Yet, a part of her felt it may be worth the trip, if only to get away from the drama at the club. Perhaps by the time she returned to the club, the asshole leaving her the notes would be long gone.

"Hey, Miss Paris," a bubbly, albeit male voice, greeted her as she entered her health club.

"Hey yourself, Clark." She smiled at the thin, young man behind the receptionist desk.

"You're looking good as always," he said, snapping slender fingers.

"That's you, that's you," Paris replied good-naturedly.

Clark had been the receptionist at the club since she became a member. He was the only man in the place that hadn't tried to hit on her in one way or another, and she was convinced it was because he was gay. Deanne would've given her a tongue lashing if she knew Paris was socializing with Clark's "type". Paris knew her mother would be horrified if she knew what type of person her daughter had become.

Working out was like a breath of fresh air to Paris, because she could escape what she had become. Her condo, her car and her wardrobe were constant reminders of what she did for a living. Belles and Beaux offered her a brief getaway to another life. It allowed her to entertain what if's, even if it were for only ninety minutes or so at a time. As of late, Paris found herself wishing she could extend the time of escape well past ninety minutes.

Clark always made her laugh, and he was a genuinely nice person, which was more than she could say about most heterosexual men.

"You doing aerobics today?" Clark questioned.

Paris shook her head. "Don't feel like being sociable today," she said bluntly.

"I hear you, girl." He handed her a key to a locker and a towel.

She changed into her workout gear then locked her clothes and purse away. She decided to head to the treadmill and run. Running had always been a wonderful stress reliever for her. She had received another threatening letter last night before performing. The letter had been a replica of the first letter with the same thick childish handwriting. She talked to Kenton about the letter and asked him if he had figured out who the man was that had called about the lipstick smudge. The man hadn't left his name. Kenton had tried unsuccessfully to get a listing of the men who attended that bachelor party, and there was no way she could get a restraining order without having a name. She'd just have to wait until the bastard got the balls to show his face, she mused.

She increased the speed on her treadmill, nodding briefly at the young man getting on the treadmill parallel hers. Headphones in place, Paris focused on the clock in front of her and the soothing pat her ponytail made on each of her shoulders as she ran. Left, right, left, right. She watched her red and silver DKNY tennis shoes hit against the tread. An hour and fifteen minutes later, Paris was oblivious to the sweat drizzling down her neck and shoulders. Her Maxwell CD had repeated itself at least twice, but she was back on her favorite cut, "Maybe You." She felt someone staring at her and looked across at the guy that had gotten on the machine next to hers. His lips moved, but she couldn't hear him. She removed her headphones and slowed her machine down to an easy walking pace.

"I was trying to keep up with you and all. Didn't want to let a girl outlast me, but you are serious about your run. You must be a track star or something," the young man teased while flashing a smile Colgate would've been proud of.

Paris looked him up and down. His slender six-foot frame was a beautiful honey-brown color, and he had the most adorable twinkling brown eyes. His hair was cut low into a fade with crisp waves melting against the back of his head. Sensuously full lips that naturally curled into a mischievous smile framed beautiful teeth. Paris couldn't help but admit that she found him adorable.

"I didn't realize I'd been on so long. I hope no one else was waiting for a treadmill." She wiped her face with her gym-issued towel.

"I don't think so, I haven't noticed anyone. I'm Marcus. Marcus Rogers." He extended his arm. Paris made a point of putting both her hands on the bar of her machine so she wouldn't have to shake his hand.

"I'm Paris."

"Like France?" He quickly removed his outstretched hand.

"Naw like Texas," she said sarcastically.

He looked puzzled for a second, then chuckled good-naturedly. "I guess you get that a lot." He cut his machine off and walked over to stand next to hers. "I just joined the gym this week. It's pretty nice, not too crowded."

Paris shrugged her shoulders then reached down to cut off her machine. "It's alright."

Actually, she loved the peace and quiet at this health club. It was fifteen minutes from New Orleans and did not have a very big membership. Paris's main reason for joining was the odds of running into one of her clients were smaller. She didn't need any customers coming up bugging her or asking about her show. For some reason, when men put a buck in your g-string, they thought that gave them the right to approach you anywhere at anytime.

"Can I buy you a drink at the café before you call it a night?" he asked.

Paris stepped off her machine and looked him full in the eyes. "No thank you, Marcus. Marcus Rogers," she mimicked before turning and heading toward the women's locker room, leaving him staring after her swinging ponytail.

She paused in front of the locker room door and turned her head to see if he was still watching. He was. She grimaced, refusing to admit that his smile gave her goosebumps. In another lifetime, she may have jumped at the chance to go get that drink with him.

She started her Camry and put the car in reverse. She took a deep breath and closed her eyes, the memory of his warm brown eyes materializing behind her lids. She opened her eyes and backed the car out of the parking lot, determined not to take yet another backward glance.

# *CHAPTER THIRTEEN*
# *IN THE HOT SEAT*

Paris placed a six-pack of yogurt in her empty shopping basket then paused to look at the selection of orange juice.

"Hey there, Ms. Paris."

Harley's voice startled her.

"Hello," she said warily.

Harley was hard to read, and she couldn't recall the mood he'd been in the last time they spoke.

"What're you doing out this late shopping for groceries?" he asked. "Come to think of it, I never pictured you in a grocery store, period."

Paris rolled her eyes. "And just how am I supposed to eat if I never grace a supermarket? And since you're asking questions, what are you doing in here shopping? Isn't there someone on staff to do that for you?"

Harley looked thoughtful for a second, then flashed his signature wicked grin. "Naw, baby, I'm a one-man-show," he joked. "Seriously, I was yearning for some chips and just felt like getting out and driving. I guess I just figured you found some poor lonely soul to take you out whenever you got hungry."

Paris sucked her lip irritably at his sarcasm. "Whatever, Harley. I'll see you later." She pivoted on her heel and started toward the check-out.

"What? Are you mad? I'm just playing witchu, girl." He laughed as he placed a hand on her left shoulder and pulled her around. Paris narrowed her eyes and stared at his hand on her jacket until he removed his hand.

"Damn, you always got that guard up don't you?" he questioned.

"Is there something I can help you with?"

"No, no. I just was going to ask if you were all right. I heard some pervert has been messing with you at the club."

"And where did you hear this?" She switched her basket to the opposite hand and rested it on her hip.

"That's not the point."

"It is the point. You know I don't like folks all up in my business," she remarked snidely.

"That ain't no shit you should want to keep to yourself. Niggas is crazy nowadays. You know that."

Paris looked Harley directly in his eyes then sighed. "You know I'm not scared of none of the weak-ass punks at that club. Somebody's just blowing smoke, that's all. I'm not sweatin' it. So, are you going to tell me who told you?"

Harley shook his head and laughed. "You know your girl Chocolate got loose lips."

Paris could've kicked herself. It should've been obvious Chocolate would tell Harley's teammate Raymond. Paris knew Chocolate had been sleeping with Raymond for about seven months. Even though Raymond had no problem throwing money at Chocolate, Paris knew he had no intentions of taking her anywhere but to his hotel room. Raymond was a second-string wide receiver for the Saints and was just as fine as he was charming. Paris told Chocolate not to take the Negro seriously because she knew he only sported white women on his arm during the daytime while he was content to sleep with sistahs at night. As usual, Chocolate took offense to Paris's warning and immediately deferred to her relationship with Harley. Her dumb ass couldn't see the difference, so Paris quit trying to snatch the wool off her fake eyes.

"I should've known. I forgot her chicken-headed ass was sprung on your buddy."

"Come on now. That's your girl. Don't talk about her like that. Ray's got game. I can't lie. That nigga's got women everywhere sprung. It ain't just Chocolate."

Paris shifted her feet irritably, the chill from standing in the freezer aisle for over fifteen minutes had transformed into goose bumps erupting over her arms and legs.

"She's not that much my girl or she wouldn't be out telling Negroes my business. I need to be getting to the house." Paris changed the subject, already tired of thinking about Chocolate's stupidity.

"Alright, let me walk you out to your car." Harley reached over and took her basket from her.

"It's about time. I know you saw me switching that from hand to hand five minutes ago," Paris said, shoving the basket at him.

"Hell, you're so independent I thought you wanted to carry it yourself."

"Whatever, Cox," Paris threw over her shoulder as she led him to the checkout.

Harley ended up buying her groceries and giving her money to go to the salon the next day. They'd spent another thirty minutes in her car discussing the same old song and dance. Paris was upfront with him, letting him know she felt he only wanted her because he couldn't have her, but he wasn't trying to hear it. After she spent ten minutes assuring him it wasn't because of Grey or anyone else, then another five rejecting his sexual advances, he finally let her go.

Considering how Paris had to put up with Harley, she figured she deserved every bit of cash he gave her and then some. She ran fingers through her freshly touched-up tresses and smiled to herself. It was a good thing she didn't have to foot her own bill at the salon. She'd be out of over four hundred bucks a month. She didn't always rely on the same person, but she never considered taking her own checkbook out for daily expenses. Besides, it was all a part of the package Harley and all her other "sponsors" enjoyed. Paris remembered the turning point in her adolescence when she'd began concentrating on her looks. It had taken a while, but slowly she'd begun to see potential when she looked in the mirror.

The year she'd tried out for the dance squad had truly been a construction year. Paris recalled sitting on her bedroom floor with a freshly purchased tub of off-brand relaxer. She'd jimmied the door shut so

Ivan and Sharp couldn't disturb her, and waited until Deanne was off to her weekend job so she'd have a clear block of time in which to work. Reaching in her jeans pocket, she pulled out the sheets she'd torn from a friend's *Black Hair* magazine. The magazine suggested going to a salon to get a relaxer, but had helpful tips for someone applying one to their own hair. Paris took her hair out of the two braids her mother had told her to put in the day before.

Pushing up the sleeves of her rugby, Paris shut her eyes and said a quick prayer before scooping the creamy white solution and placing it on her crinkled hair. She started at the roots and pulled the odorous mixture all the way through her hair. Once she'd covered her entire head, she began pressing the kinks out starting at the root. One hour and fifteen minutes later, she'd blow-dried her straight hair and was looking in the mirror with pride. Unfortunately, she had forgotten to lock the bathroom door. Ivan burst in just as she was modeling with her hair piled high on top of her head.

"Oooh, Paris, what did you do to your hair?" he asked wide-eyed.

"Nuthin'," she said, moving out of the mirror. "Don't you see me in here?"

"I got to go to the bathroom. You've been in here forever. I can't hold it anymore," Ivan squealed. He pressed his legs together and hunched over.

"Oh, go on to the bathroom. I wish we had two bathrooms," Paris grunted.

She quickly disappeared around the corner to her bedroom and smiled again at her brand new reflection in the mirror. The transformation was definitely worth all the trouble she was going to get in when Deanne realized she'd disobeyed and permed her hair.

Paris snapped out of her reverie when her cell phone beeped. She slid her hand in her oversized designer bag and retrieved the slender silver phone. She made a face when she recognized Kenton's number flashing in the caller ID box.

"What's up?" she asked.

"Hey, I was thinking, why don't you come in a little earlier tonight?"

"Why would I do that?" she asked, laughing incredulously.

"I'm saying, I don't want nobody trying to get at you before you get in the club," he said nonchalantly.

"What's going on, Kenton? Did something else happen?" Silence. She took the phone away from her head to make sure she hadn't lost her connection. "Kenton, are you there?"

"Yeah I'm here. Look, we got another letter for you here. It was lying on the bar addressed to Caramel. It's no big deal. I'm sure it's just somebody trippin' for a minute. I'm saying let's just do stuff a little different 'till this is over."

"I told you I'm not running from nobody," she said with confidence she didn't feel. "I'll be there when I get there."

"Paris, just come in later then. I don't want some idiot trying to rush up on you. What are you doing now?"

"I just got my hair done. I'm cool. I told you I'm not scared, Kenton." Feeling someone was watching her, she quickly looked over her shoulder, but no one was there. "I'll come in later then."

"Just call up to the office when you get in the parking lot. I'll have Cruz come get you."

Paris ended her conversation with Kenton and clicked the tiny phone off. She pulled her Porsche into her condo complex and pretended she didn't see her neighbors giving her disapproving looks as she pulled into her parking space. She was grateful for the extra time she now had to get ready. After being out during the day, it took her more time to wind down for the impending evening.

Inside, she headed straight to her bathroom to start her bath water. Then it was on to her bedroom to lay out the different costumes she would wear tonight. Paris pulled out a Budweiser set that consisted of blue hot pants with a Lycra half-shirt with the beer logo imprinted on the front. She went back into her walk-in closet and began sifting through various costumes. She pulled out a black leather skin-tight corset with a matching black g-string. She had to remember to wear this one last, as it made red marks on her skin from being too tight. She pulled out her black garter and thigh highs to match, then collapsed on the bed.

She felt like calling in and telling Kenton she didn't feel like working tonight. The tediousness of the entire night loomed ahead, and she dreaded its arrival. She reminded herself that she was in control, and fear was the first step to losing that control. Placing her feet firmly on the ground, she pushed herself up and toward the bathroom. Shaking bath beads into the tub, she dipped her foot in to check the temperature. The warm water was welcoming, and she slipped down in it until she was immersed, except for her head.

Paris closed her eyes and inhaled, enjoying the soft scent of jasmine the beads gave off. The smell triggered the memory of a lewd comment a customer made after he recognized the smell of jasmine on her. Her eyes flew open and instantly, the feeling of peace evaporated from the room. Some nights, she closed her eyes and fantasized taking out her gun and blowing away every asshole in the club. The nasty comments and rude looks were enough to make any woman hate the male species. If she concentrated hard enough, she could imagine their pathetic faces begging as she aimed the gun at them. They wouldn't have anything demeaning to say to her then, she was sure.

She'd make them explain why they abandoned their families and spent money on women who cared nothing about them. She'd get revenge for every scorned wife who was oblivious that half her husband's check was being tucked into another woman's g-string. She'd get even for the brides who were busy fantasizing about exchanging vows with their soul mate while he had sex with a dancer his friends prepaid hours earlier. And last but not least, she'd get even for all the children who went to bed missing a father who would never come home because he had more important things to do with women who excited him much more than their mother, even after she'd given him everything she had and then some. Paris felt herself slowly relax. She opened her eyes and reached for the liquid soap. It was time to prepare for another night at Under the Cherry Moon.

# *CHAPTER FOURTEEN*
# *MEETING A NEW FRIEND*

After her car was vandalized a second time, Paris began driving her Camry again. When she purchased the Porsche, she'd seriously considered trading the Camry in, but decided against it after she realized that the small amount they would give her for it would not put a sizable dent in the cost of her Porsche. It was actually nice driving the older, roomier car. The biggest perk was, she didn't get all the honks and obscene gestures she got when driving the Porsche. She knew much of that was due to her vanity plate.

She reluctantly admitted to Kenton that the threats continued to come. Kenton suggested she go to Atlanta a little before schedule, but she was dead set against it.

"The day I start letting these niggas scare me is the day I quit dancing period, and I'm not ready to do that," she said stubbornly.

Kenton let the discussion go, as she knew he would. She was his bread and butter. He didn't really want to take the chance of her leaving Under the Cherry Moon. Paris learned early on that men always had an ulterior motive, especially when they acted considerately.

Grey continued to call her nonstop since the day she'd asked him to leave. She didn't dare tell him about the notes and her car, or he wouldn't leave her side. Harley, on the other hand, seemed to have disappeared. Paris was convinced this was his way of giving her time to sweat. In their last conversation, he'd told her he was going to give her exactly what she wanted and leave her alone.

"Then we'll see if that's really what you want," he'd threatened.

Paris wanted to laugh in his face but thought better off it. *If that Negro only knew.* The only person impressed with Harley Cox like that was Harley Cox. It surely wasn't Paris Renee Jackson. She didn't get down like that over any man. She rested her back against the free weight machine and pulled the fifteen-pound weight.

An isolated part of Paris was not disappointed when she felt a light tap on her shoulder. She knew it was Marcus before she turned around to find him looking intently at her. It had been almost two weeks since he'd first introduced himself. She had been slightly disappointed not to see him the last few times she'd been at the gym.

"You know you're not doing that right," he said.

Trying to ignore his disarming dimples and her attraction for him, Paris scowled. "I've been doing it like this for over six months. It's been working fine."

Marcus smiled at her then reached out to adjust her arm. "You're putting stress on your elbow doing it like that. Doesn't that feel better?"

Paris hesitantly watched his slender brown fingers positioning her arm. She attempted to lift the weight again. "Yeah I guess it does. You're right."

"Don't worry about thanking me. I'll let you buy me that drink I got turned down on last time," he teased.

Paris looked him full in the eyes as if he were irritating her. Marcus seemed oblivious to her attitude and continued giving her his signature mischievous smile. Finally, she couldn't help but return his smile. This was the first time a man refused to react to her dismissive attitude. There didn't seem to be anything short of cussing at him that would take the smile off Marcus's face. She was convinced he was aware of the fact that his dimples and charming ways made women unable to refuse him. His charm was probably a calculated move on his part she reminded herself.

Regardless of Paris's reservations, she found herself actually enjoying talking with him over a protein shake at the club's café. He had recently moved to New Orleans from Killeen, Texas and was still trying to get accustomed to the unique Louisiana culture.

"There's so much history here. I hadn't been here before flying in for this job interview, but I'd seen pictures of Mardi Gras and had a few college buddies that were from the area. It's not really what I expected," he said.

In spite of herself, Paris returned his smile. "I've been here for mmm... about four years. I'm originally from Mississippi."

Marcus looked as if he was waiting for her to elaborate on her past, but she didn't. "You're either very quiet or I've already struck out miserably," Marcus said cautiously, although his eyes were twinkling into hers.

Paris shook her head. "I usually don't respond well to being picked up when I'm trying to get a workout in," she said sassily.

"When fate sends you an opportunity, you have to reach out and grab it or you may not get another chance."

"Fate, huh?" Paris scoffed. She certainly wasn't a believer of fate. Everything in her life was and always had been extremely deliberate.

His eyes held hers momentarily, then he glanced down at his empty cup. "I need to get home, but I would like to talk to you again. Something tells me I shouldn't even ask for your number, but I will give you mine. Give me a call if you believe in fate." He pushed a small white business card across the table at her.

Paris arched an eyebrow at him but smiled. "I don't believe in much of anything, Mr. Rogers," she said quietly.

Undaunted, he grinned at her. "We'll have to see what we can do about changing that."

With that, he winked at her and was gone. Paris picked the card up and quickly read it. He was a certified public accountant for a large firm in New Orleans. Marcus E. Rogers. She read the name aloud, liking the way it sounded, and then smiled to herself. If only things were different with her, maybe. *No.* She reminded herself there was no such thing as maybe and there certainly wasn't any such thing as fate. Paris finished her shake, then got up and slowly made her way over to the trash. She pitched her empty cup inside followed by the small white business card.

Paris was almost an hour late to work the following Saturday. She was relieved there hadn't been another letter that week. It was already hard enough to convince herself work was worth it, but the thought of performing in front of some sicko that was threatening her added unimaginable stress. She had planned on heading straight to Kenton's private office and telling him that she wasn't feeling well. Kenton surprised her by meeting her in mid-route to his office.

"Hey, baby doll, I got good news. I don't want you onstage tonight," he informed her, placing both hands squarely on her shoulders.

"What do you mean you don't want me onstage?" she asked, afraid she was acting like a punk. "Kenton if you think I'm going to hide out until those letters stop, I told you to forget it. Besides, I haven't gotten one this week, maybe he's finished."

Kenton shook his head. "It's not that. I got a request for a private dance for you. This cat is really coming out the pocket," he said eagerly.

Paris watched in disgust as Kenton rubbed his greedy little hands together.

"I really don't feel like doing anything like that tonight."

Kenton looked closely at her. "Paris, this dude is going to pay $1,000 per hour for you. All you gotta do is dance for him. That's all. Nothing more, nothing less. I gave him the Cherry room. It's all set up. The stage is lit up and everything. Look at it this way, at least doing this you know that crazy nigga won't be fucking with you or anything. Plus, I told him he had to pay for a minimum of three hours because you would be missing a Saturday night, which is your biggest night."

Paris narrowed her eyes at Kenton, and he immediately stopped rubbing his hands.

"How much is your cut Kenton?" she asked nastily.

His face fell. "Come on now, Paris. You ain't got to be like that. You know it's not even like that."

"How much?" she asked, walking down the hall toward her dressing room.

Kenton picked up his stride in order to keep up with her. "It's sixty percent, just like it always is at the club," he said.

Paris rolled her eyes. It was just like she thought. Kenton did get sixty percent of all her in-club earnings, but when she did private showings, he only got forty. By scheduling this private show in the club, he was able to up his percentage.

"Who is this guy? And where do you get off scheduling something like that without talking to me first?" Paris angrily stormed back toward the dressing room. She was tired of Kenton pimping her out on his terms.

Kenton caught up and got in front of her. "Look, Paris, don't trip out like this with me okay? I really thought you'd prefer this. I know you been worrying about that psycho, even though you won't admit it."

Paris turned her head and sucked her lip. *Am I becoming that transparent, or is he bullshitting me?*

"I'm not gonna front," Kenton continued. "I don't know who the guy is, but it can't be the one writing the letters, believe me. Plus, I got Cruz for you. He'll be there the entire time, right outside the door."

Paris silently stared at the wall in front of her.

"All right, we'll do forty percent, just like all your other private shows away from the club," Kenton offered.

Paris's eyes met his. "Fine," she snapped. "But don't do this shit to me anymore. Especially not when shit is crazy like it is now. I don't need anymore surprises."

On her way to the Cherry room, Paris realized that the customer didn't have any specific requests as to what she should wear or what performance he wanted. She opted for her red silk robe, complete with matching red string bikini and red stiletto heels. Her dark brown hair fell in loose curls around her face, and she lined her lips with dark berry pencil then filled them in with scarlet lipstick. She outlined her eyes in smoky black and added fake lashes for drama. Confident that her customer would be pleased, she made her way to the small blue painted room entitled the Cherry Room. Cruz was already waiting by the door for her.

"Who is this guy?" she whispered.

Cruz shrugged heavily muscled shoulders. "He was already here when I got here. Cho brought him in then left. If you need me, you know the password," he said gruffly.

Paris granted him a quick smile, then reached for the door. The room was completely dark except for the lights lining the stage. The door she entered put her directly on stage. She squinted to see a figure sitting out in the dark.

"Is anybody there?" she questioned in a sultry voice then slowly sauntered to the edge of the stage, letting her hips sway as she walked. "Are you there?"

"It's me, Paris," a familiar voice answered.

Paris gulped involuntarily, almost choking on her own breath. A shadow stepped out of the darkness. It was Grey.

"What in the fuck do you think you are doing?" she demanded angrily.

"This is the only way I can get you to talk to me," Grey said stubbornly.

She furiously balled her fists. She wanted to take them and smash them into Grey's pathetic face. She could just feel her knuckles cracking against his chiseled high cheekbones. *Knowing his wimpy ass, he'd probably start crying,* Paris thought angrily. She fought the urge and, instead, stared directly in his eyes until he lowered his head.

"How dare you come in here and try to play me like this just because I don't want to go out with you," she bit out.

Grey sat stock still, apparently unmoved by her tone. "I tried reasoning with you. I know you're better than this. I could take you away from all this. You wouldn't have to be a stripper, dancing for men for money. But no. You want this life. You choose this life. So now, I choose to treat you like a stripper. It occurred to me that maybe that's where I've gone wrong this whole time, trying to treat you like something you're not," he said with an unfamiliar nasty edge in his voice.

"You can go straight to hell, Grey," Paris threatened from between clenched teeth. "I'm not dancing for your sorry ass."

"Oh you are going to dance, Paris. Kenton already took my money. Good money by the way. I'm going to get all $3,000 dollars worth or I'll sue the club," he said smugly. "I paid Kenton cash for you on Tuesday, so I would suggest you check that smart ass mouth of yours and start doing what you do best, taking off your clothes."

For once Paris's shock outweighed her anger. This couldn't be the pathetically sweet Grey who brought her food and constantly asked to take her out. This couldn't be the faithful Grey who pleaded with her to stop stripping and let him take care of her more times than she cared to remember. The old Grey had never so much as breathed "no" to her, let alone disrespect her like he was doing now. Somewhere along the line, she had let Grey get out of hand, but she couldn't figure out when it happened. For a fleeting moment, she wondered if Grey could be her stalker. She looked into his grayish blue eyes then threw that theory out the window. Underneath the angry front, she could smell his desperation.

"Grey, you need to ask Kenton for your money back, and then call me when you can act like you got some gotdamn sense," she said, attempting to regain control of the situation.

Grey shook his head no. "I told you once that you would be mine, and if this is the only way I can get you to spend time with me, then so be it."

Paris sucked, stalling, raking her brain to find a way out, but came up empty-handed. "You don't want me to be with you, Grey. You want to own me, and you will never be able to do that, not for all the money in the world. You want to treat me like a stripper okay," she said sweetly, "I can treat you just like a customer."

She glanced at the clock. "You have two hours and thirty minutes. Is there any song you'd like me to start with?"

Grey exhaled in relief, but shook his head no. She knew turning the situation around would get to him, but it was his own weak-ass fault. He looked totally emasculated sitting with his head down, hands resting primly in his lap. She pivoted on her heel and went backstage to turn the music on.

"Don't you ever book me to dance for that bastard again!" Paris exploded into Kenton's office in the middle of what appeared to be a close encounter between himself and another dancer. Sundae excused herself, quickly standing up and pulling her bra top down over her uncooperative silicone 36DD's.

"What the hell is wrong with you?" Kenton asked.

Paris could read his anxiety over not finishing what he and Sundae started.

"What the hell is wrong with you?" Paris shot back.

"Who was the guy anyway? He wasn't the stalker was he?"

"I guess if it was I wouldn't be standing here in front of you now would I? My ass would probably be cut up or dead somewhere."

"Just chill, Paris, alright. Now who was the guy in the room you all up tight about?"

"It was Grey's punk ass," Paris spat.

Kenton sniggled, letting her know he remembered who Grey was to her. "So the pretty boy is stepping it up a bit," he remarked snidely.

"Fuck him. He better not come anywhere near me outside of here. I'm warning you. I'm not dancing for his ass anymore. Get him somebody else. I'm sick of his bitch ass."

"So Grey's money isn't green anymore?" Kenton asked. He adjusted his slacks, then collapsed in the leather chair behind his desk.

"I don't need this shit," Paris fumed. She threw her hands up and started for the door.

"Paris, sit down," Kenton yelled suddenly.

"Who in the hell do you think you're screaming at?" Paris asked incredulously.

"Please," he added simply, extending an arm to the chair facing his desk. He sighed then got up and poured them both a shot of brandy from a crystal canister behind his desk.

"Here, drink this. You need to calm down. I'm not used to you flipping out like this, but because of everything that's been going on with this maniac harassing you, I'm gonna excuse all this drama, this time."

Kenton left off with that as his attempt at an apology for yelling at her. Paris eyed him suspiciously, but gratefully sipped on the drink he offered her.

"Okay, so tell me what's the deal with Grey."

Paris finished her drink. "I broke things off with him a couple of weeks ago. Ever since then he's been wilding out. He's calling the house every day, damn near all day long. Begging, pleading, working my nerves. I told him I wasn't feeling him anymore and quit accepting his calls, so that's when he gets the idea to come up in here and buy me for the entire fucking night."

Kenton made a face then calmly leaned forward and refilled her glass. "Your mouth really doesn't become you, Paris. A nigga doesn't want to hear that shit from a female. I hope you're not out there talking like that to customers."

Paris rolled her eyes. "As long as I'm makin' money, what does it matter what I say to the men up in here? I'm not here to talk about my *fucking* vocabulary. I'm here to let you know that I'm not getting played like that anymore."

Kenton calmly took a sip of his brandy. "Did you tell him why you didn't want to see him anymore?"

"I don't owe him shit. I don't answer to Grey. That's the problem. He wants to control me, and I'm not having it. I'm just sick of his whining ass. He was smothering me to death."

Kenton clicked his tongue against the roof of his mouth in disapproval. "That's why I tell you all to keep everything professional. Keep it in the club. You should've made his soft ass keep coming here to see you, and this mess never would have happened. Y'all gonna learn to stop sleeping with clients. It's bad business."

"Spare me the speech, okay. At the time I started spending time with him, it was in my best interest."

"And it's in the club's best interest that we keep his money coming in on the regular." Kenton looked up to see Paris swelling with anger all over again "Look, don't flip out on me again. I hear what you're saying. At least until all this bullshit is over with, we won't let him book you or anything like that. I think we should revisit this topic, once you've calmed down and are thinking rationally again."

"We can revisit all you want, Kenton. I'm not dancing for Grey here or anywhere else," Paris insisted stubbornly.

Kenton nodded at her and motioned to refill her glass.

"No, I'm cool."

"You haven't gotten any more threats or anything have you?"

Paris wanted to throw up at Kenton's phony attempt at concern. She shook her head. He was so full of shit there should have been a stink cloud surrounding his trifling ass at all times. Satisfied she'd accomplished her goal for the moment, she asked him if he wanted her to send Sundae back to his office.

"Would you do that for me?" he asked, licking his lips. Paris left his office in disgust; she'd had enough of pathetic men for one night.

# *CHAPTER FIFTEEN VENTURING OUT OF YOUR COMFORT ZONE*

"Paris, I know you probably hate me, and you have every right to. I don't know what came over me. I just wanted to see you. You won't talk to me. You keep blowing me off like I'm a nobody. I just wanted you to listen to me. I wasn't trying to disrespect you. I can't imagine why you'd think that, sweetheart. Paris, you know I love you. I want to marry you. That's right, sweetheart. Why don't we just get married? You know that's all I've ever wanted. I've just been trying to show you how wonderful it would be if the two of us were together. I know you can't imagine it, but trust me. I would take care of you for the rest of my life, the rest of your life. Just let me prove it to you, Paris. The world would be yours. It's not right for you to be doing that for every man that comes in that club. You're too…"

Beep.

Grey's persistent whining prattled on, disregarding the beep signaling the answering machine cutting off. Paris shook her head in disbelief. Grey was completely sickening to her now. She couldn't believe she'd actually enjoyed being with him at one time. Her answering machine switched to message number four, and she wasn't surprised to hear Grey's anguished voice pick up where he'd left off.

"Baby just let me explain. I can't tell you how sorry I am. I'm so sorry, Paris. Don't hate me. I didn't know what else to do. You left me no choice. I don't know why you're doing this to me. I just need to talk to you. Call me. Please, Paris, just call me and let me apologize to you. I'll try you again later," he sniffled.

Paris quickly pressed delete then retrieve to get the next message. She felt a warm flush as Ivan's voice filled the room. He was just calling to see how she was doing. It had been a while since he had heard from her, and he and Sharp were getting worried. Paris pursed her lips at the recorder. Ivan knew good and well Sharp hadn't said he was worried about her. Although she knew Sharp loved her, he wasn't apt to show emotion to anyone. Actually, Paris had always thought she and Sharp had that in common.

Ivan was always telling her and Deanne that he loved them, but Paris could count the times on her fingers that she had ever uttered those words without Ivan or Deanne's prompting. Growing up, Sharp and Paris had dealt with their poverty and the rejection from their father by internalizing much of their hurt and disappointment. Ivan, on the other hand, always wanted to talk about everything. He had even told Paris that he forgave Richard for "doing whatever it was he had to do."

"Don't you ever just want to sit down with him and ask him why?" Ivan would muse aloud. "He must've had a reason. It wasn't right, but there must be a reason. Maybe he didn't have bad intentions

Paris would roll her eyes and Sharp would tell Ivan how much of a fool he must be to believe that. The three of them had that conversation more times than Paris cared to count, but Ivan's sensitivity made her love him all the more. Although he was twenty-three and all grown up now, there was still evidence of that sweet little boy that held their family of four together. Paris thought it was lucky for Sharp that Ivan was down at the college complex in Atlanta with him. If not for Ivan, Sharp was sure to get into trouble. Sharp acted first and thought later. Ivan had always been the consistent voice of reason. Paris hated to think of the day when another woman would figure that out about Ivan and exploit it. She never worried about Sharp being used or being fooled. She was sure he could hold his own in that department. She knew for a fact Sharp felt the same about her.

"Paris Jackson, fate deals us a third opportunity."

The somewhat familiar voice stunned Paris, and she almost tripped and fell on the treadmill. She glared angrily over at Marcus who was walking slowly on the treadmill adjacent hers.

"So shall we take fate up on her third and possibly final offer?" he questioned hopefully.

Trying to find a distraction to focus on, Paris turned her head away. Her eyes searched for anything but that smile of his. She'd never met a man with a smile that was so hypnotizing.

"Paris?"

She turned and concentrated on his eyes. "What do you mean take fate up on her offer?"

"I mean I just joined a new church and they are having a fellowship picnic this Saturday around noon. Why don't you go with me? It will be a safe first date and that way fate won't be upset with you for passing up perfectly good opportunities thrown your way. Oh and I won't have to show up alone," he added, laughing lightly.

Paris almost laughed aloud. She'd never in all her twenty-six years dreamed of being asked to go to a church, especially not by a man.

"What church do you go to?" Paris asked.

"Believer's Voice of Victory. It's not far from here. About twenty minutes away."

She breathed a sigh of relief it wasn't in New Orleans. She would never want to take the chance of running into a customer at church with his family. *Am I actually considering this?* Even entertaining this was ridiculous, and yet she was actually flattered that a man would look at her and want to take her to church.

"Will you go?" Marcus pressed.

"This Saturday?"

"Yes, Paris," he answered gently. "You can meet me there if that would make you more comfortable. I don't know anyone there yet, and I really don't feel like people giving me that pity conversation." Her brows furrowed. He continued, "You know when you go someplace and you're new and alone, how everyone tries so hard to make you feel comfortable?"

Paris laughed and nodded. "When I was younger, I never stood up in new churches when they would ask for first time visitors. I couldn't stand that complimentary conversation," she admitted. She didn't add the fact that she hadn't darkened a church pew since leaving Deanne's house eight years ago.

Marcus smiled, and she immediately felt uncomfortable.

"I was just about finished here," she said nervously.

"Do you need the address of the church?" he asked, cocking his head to a side.

She shook her head no. "I'll look it up."

"You're not going to stand me up are you, Paris Jackson?"

"No I don't give pity dates or stand folks up. I would've just told you no, again," she said smartly.

He chuckled. "I have no doubt about that. No doubt at all."

Paris studied her heart-shaped face in her vanity mirror. Her large almond shaped eyes were clear and had an eagerness in them that was new. Her naturally pouty lips were tilting on their own like she had a secret to smile about. Well, she did have a secret in a way. She, Paris Jackson, aka Caramel, was going to a church picnic. The best part about everything was that Marcus knew absolutely nothing about Caramel. He hadn't asked about her occupation or where she lived. She decided for now she'd keep quiet about everything.

Usually Paris told guys what she did up front because she knew the two reactions she was bound to get. Either the truth would disgust them and they would no longer want anything serious with her or it would turn them into Captain Save-A-Ho who wanted a trophy stripper on his arm to show off in front of his boys and to shower with gifts. They really didn't care anything about the person she was inside. Paris didn't have time for either reaction; they both equaled "don't give a shit about Paris".

She knew other women often felt sorry for strippers or escorts because of how men looked at them, but Paris thought she had the better end of the deal. Most of the women pitying her had men that didn't give a shit about them and were doing any and everything they could behind their backs. She would much rather know upfront where she stood, and she did. She always did.

Her smile drooped as she found her thoughts wandering to which reaction Marcus would have after he learned what she did for a living. He was a church-going man, so he would probably choose reaction number one. She started to apply eyeliner, but after a second thought, closed the tube and returned it to her makeup case. She didn't want to look anything Caramel today. She wanted to just be Paris. She brushed on a little loose powder instead and added a light lip-gloss. For a finishing touch, she swept her lashes with a single stroke of mascara. She parted her hair on one side then tucked it behind her ears. She looked in amazement at her reflection. Instead of twenty-six, she looked closer to eighteen.

She hadn't been out of her house without her full face on, except at the health club, since she'd started working at Under the Cherry Moon. Kenton constantly stressed how important it was for all his star dancers to always look the part whether they were in a grocery store, a library or performing at a bachelor party. He didn't want the image his customers had being tarnished by one of the girls being spotted in rollers and house shoes. Paris smiled at her fresh-faced reflection in the mirror. For a split-second, she wished she was able to look like this all the time, just be herself. She hoped Marcus liked this side of her. Her spirits lowered with the knowledge that it was only a matter of time before found out about her job.

Before Paris could open the door to her Camry, Marcus was at her side taking her hand and helping her out of the car.

"Paris, you look beautiful."

His eyes took in her chocolate linen suit and sandals. Unable to do anything else, Paris simply returned his smile. She didn't think she'd ever heard a man sound so sincere with those words in her life. He led her up the concrete steps that led to the enormous church and through the impressive sanctuary. The picnic was on the two acres behind the church, and there looked to be at least one hundred people already there.

"I brought us a blanket," Marcus said, leading them over to a secluded spot that had a large blue quilt spread out.

Again, Paris smiled at him and politely at the churchgoers they passed on their way to the blanket.

"I went ahead and made our plates. I hope you don't mind. I didn't know how much would be left by the time you got here."

"That's fine. That was very sweet," she mumbled.

They sat down and Marcus passed her a paper plate with barbecued beef and chicken. There were also baked beans, potato salad and a piece of Texas toast on the plate.

"So," he began after they sat in silence for a few minutes, "tell me all about Paris."

"What do you want to know?" Paris asked cautiously, her bright eyes on guard.

"Well first off you can tell me how old you are," he said teasingly.

"I'm very legal," Paris joked, "I'm twenty-six."

Marcus's eyes widened in surprise. "I would've guessed twenty-one. I was hoping you were older though."

Paris smiled and took a small bite of barbecued beef. For some reason, she was feeling strangely uncomfortable on this date. She'd never felt like this before. She usually needed to be the one in control of the situation, but with Marcus, there didn't seem to be a need. *He's just like all the rest,* she reminded herself as she listened to him tell her he was twenty-six also.

"So what do you do?"

His question hung in the air like an ominously heavy rain cloud. Paris almost choked on her lemonade.

"Are you okay?" he asked.

He offered her a napkin and patted her lightly on the back. She nodded, letting him know she was fine.

"I-I'm a choreographer," she stammered.

After the lie was out, she immediately regretted it. She'd never lied about her job to a man before, but here she was on church grounds lying. She couldn't very well tell Marcus she was a stripper could she? *It wasn't a total lie,* she reasoned. She did choreograph routines for new girls just starting at the club. She peered over her drink, trying to see if

Marcus had bought her lie. It felt so ridiculous coming out of her mouth that she was certain he wouldn't believe it. But it appeared he swallowed it, lock, stock and barrel. He was nodding as if he were impressed.

"That must be a fun job."

"So you're an accountant?" she asked, eager to get the conversation off herself.

She didn't want him to ask her any more questions, as she knew lies had a way of snowballing until you had a huge pile of shit on your hands.

*You are an absolute idiot,* she reprimanded herself on the way home after the date. She hadn't been herself all afternoon, laughing and joking along with Marcus, blushing at his jokes. This was crazy and certainly out of character. She didn't need this in her life right now with all that was going on. Besides, she was certain she and Marcus weren't looking for the same type of relationship. He'd introduced her to members of his congregation as his friend. She'd spent the entire afternoon with her fingers crossed, hoping she didn't run into anyone that was familiar with Paris as Caramel from Under the Cherry Moon. Marcus had thanked her for meeting him and asked if he could call her. Wanting to get away from his church friends and his hypnotizing smile, she'd relented, giving him her home number.

Her mind wandered to the others that were calling her house. Grey still hadn't given up and was steadily leaving messages night and day. She figured it was only a matter of time before he showed up either at her condo or at the club. Harley had called her cell phone a couple of times, but hadn't left a message. She knew from prior experience he would be making a personal visit soon, hoping absence and his body in a tank top would've made her heart grow fonder. She looked at her gold bangle watch—4:35 P.M. She had two and a half hours before she was due at the club. What an ending to the perfect date, she mused. She was going to have to get rid of Marcus before she became unfocused. She decided to let the answering machine catch his calls, just like it caught Grey's and Harley's calls.

# *CHAPTER SIXTEEN MISS BAD AZZ TURNS CHICKEN*

"Anywhere" by the group 112 was blasting from the speakers at Under the Cherry Moon. Paris, Chocolate and Mary Jane were twirling, writhing and percolating all over the stage. Paris dramatically pushed her tresses out of her face then dramatically licked her lips, letting her tongue sensually outline her bottom lip. She rolled her head back, allowing her hair to fan out then settle haphazardly around her face. Chocolate's legs were entwined around one of the poles on stage. Mary Jane was lying on the floor with her legs spread eagle.

Paris winked then flicked her tongue suggestively at a customer that beckoned to her with a fifty-dollar bill in his mouth. She ran her fingers over her breasts, squeezing them in between her fingers. Her hips rolled in tune with the music as she hypnotically removed her white string bikini top and threw it out to the audience. She then got down on all fours and crawled across the floor to the bottom of the stage, accepting another customer's money in her g-string. She opened and closed her legs in time with the music, concentrating on how much longer the song had to play instead of the dollars being waved in her face.

"Let me lick some of that sweet caramel. I'll lick it all night long."

The voice belonged to an elderly man in a Kangol who slyly reached out to place a liver-spotted hand on the inside of her thigh. Paris's eyes widened in unadulterated fear, but she relaxed when Cruz stepped up to the old man and whispered something in his ear. She had one more set to do tonight, and then she'd be finished. She took the money she'd been given and placed it in her jar onstage. She went over to one of the poles and swung around it, arching her back so that her hair tumbled down her back and her exposed breasts pointed toward the lighted ceiling.

She was doing a good job of tuning out the barking and rude comments of the customers. She had less than a minute to go with this song and then she would get a break. Fifteen minutes was all she needed. She caught a glimpse of Mary Jane in white hot pants and matching heels with her legs open gesturing toward her honey pot. Chocolate had her behind toward the audience and was rolling and bouncing her ass in perfect lazy eights to the audience's delights.

"If you want it we can do it in the black 500 with the top down," the rapper taunted on the single.

Paris strained to hear the last notes of the song then half ran back to the dressing room after the set was over. She was nearly out of breath when she got there. She quickly sat down and stared at her reflection in the lighted mirror. She was angry and ashamed at the tangible fear widening her pupils. Her eyes caught a bouquet of red roses on the corner of her cubicle. Probably Kenton making a peace offering she guessed, picking up the flowers and sniffing them. Or they could be from Grey she reasoned, picking up the small white card and using a fingernail to open it; she pulled the card out and flipped it open. *Slut bitch. You ain't shit.* The fear in her eyes seized her heart, and she fell to the floor. She'd thought for sure this was over.

"Girl what's wrong?" Chocolate asked running over to kneel beside her on the floor.

She carefully extracted the crumpled card from Paris's trembling fingers.

"Go get Kenton," Chocolate ordered Mary Jane.

The girl took one look at Paris's petrified face and ran down the hallway, heels clacking, her hands cupping her naked breasts.

"Chocolate and Tenisha are going to take you home. Go home and get some rest. I'm going to check on some things, and I'll call you later on tonight," Kenton said firmly.

Paris shook her head emphatically. "This asshole is not going to see me running home; letting my friends drive me home. No, I'm staying here until the night's over," she said stubbornly, crossing her arms over her chest.

Kenton shook his head at her. Paris could tell he was frustrated, but she didn't care. She had to do this for herself. She didn't run from anything, and she wasn't going to let some man turn her into a victim. *You can only be a victim if you allow yourself to be one,* she reminded herself, vainly attempting to calm her rattled nerves.

"Will you talk some sense into your stubborn ass girl before she gets her ass killed?" Kenton asked Chocolate.

He stalked out of the room, angrily calling for Tenisha.

"When are you going to Atlanta?" Chocolate asked, pressing her back against the wall so she could sit down next to Paris.

"I'm supposed to go in about six weeks or so, but I'm still not sure." Paris whispered. "I'm not leaving early though, so don't even try it."

Chocolate rubbed Paris's hair, trying to smooth it out of her face. "I've never seen you scared before," she said softly.

"I'm not scared," Paris snapped. "This just caught me off-guard. With everything that Grey's been pulling lately and Kenton tripping with me, I just didn't expect this, that's all." She shook her head violently, oblivious to a tear that was taking her makeup down a path on her face with it.

Chocolate was quiet for a moment. "It's okay to be scared, Paris, and it's okay to feel. You can't keep this front up forever, sweetheart."

She put her arm around Paris's shoulder, and for the first time since she'd met Paris, Paris let her hug her without a fight.

"I can't talk to you right now," Paris said quickly.

"I just want to know when I can see you again," Marcus insisted.

Paris swore she could hear his smile over the phone. "Marcus, there is just too much going on in my life right now, and I don't want to lead you on. I think it would be best if we just let things end as they did last Saturday," Paris said reluctantly.

Marcus's silence caused her to begin rethinking her decision. If the situation were different, perhaps she could replace Grey and Harley with Marcus. She enjoyed his conversation much more than she did theirs, and although he wasn't as financially secure as her other suitors, he was definitely doing well. Perhaps he could be persuaded to pay some of her bills. She shut her eyes, resenting the temptation to bring Marcus into her complicated lifestyle. In truth, she didn't want that from him. She didn't even want to think about him in that way. This was the main reason why she needed to end this now.

"It's not you. It's me. I just don't need anything extra going on right now," she said, trying her hardest to sound firm, but gentle.

She wasn't sure why she was going out of her way to shield Marcus's feelings. If he were anyone else, she'd have severed the ties without worrying about being harsh.

She didn't want to feel sympathetic toward anyone that had a penis between his legs right now. She couldn't allow herself to feel anything for any man besides Sharp and Ivan, and she definitely needed to stop entertaining pursuing any type of relationship with Marcus.

"You need a friend, Paris. I can sense that. I want to be your friend," Marcus explained simply. "I'm not trying to push you into anything you don't want. I just want to get to know you."

*What part of no does this fool not understand?* She did not take kindly to repeating herself, so she didn't. She would let Marcus work this out for himself. She hoped he figured it out before she had to talk to him the way she did Grey and the others.

"How about we work out together? I usually go to the gym around eight in the evenings. I just want to see you again. We don't have to go out if you don't want."

Paris exhaled loud enough for Marcus to hear it on his end of the phone line. Instead of getting upset, he gave her his signature chuckle.

"Paris, why are you making this so difficult?" he asked in a lazy voice.

In spite of herself, she felt her exterior melting. "I told you, Marcus. This just isn't a good time."

"Okay, well if you ever do want to see me, I'm there at eight every night."

"I've really got to go."

"All right I guess I'll talk to you later, but Paris…"

"Yes."

"I told you I am a strong believer in fate. If you take a chance, you may learn to believe in it, too."

Paris hung up the phone and turned her ringer off. She couldn't handle all of this at once. *What is happening to me?* She had more drama in her life now than she ever had. True to form, Harley had shown up earlier that day, looking as fine as ever in a basketball jersey and matching shorts.

"What do you want, Harley?" she had asked. She was too exhausted to give him the attitude she wanted to.

"Why you coming at me like that when you ain't seen me in over a month?" he asked, feigning hurt.

Paris rolled her eyes. "Harley, I'm really getting tired of these games, so if you need something, please let me know. If not, I'll holler at you later," she said, walking to the door and opening it.

Harley went over and closed the door. "What's up with you, Paris? Why you treatin' me like this? I tried to give you some space because that's what you said you wanted. You know I want to be with you. Why you always playing games and shit?"

Paris narrowed her eyes at him until she could barely see. "I ain't the one playing games, and you know it," she spat.

"Okay you're not playing games huh? You know I want to be with you right?" he challenged.

"Have you ever thought that I don't want to be with your black ass?" she asked angrily.

"Oh, so it's like that now huh?"

"Yeah it's like that," Paris said, her eyes shooting daggers into his.

"You weren't saying all that a few months ago when I had you all up on me in my car," he said nastily.

"Get the fuck out of my house, Harley!"

She knew it would only be a matter of time before Harley gave up. He didn't take rejection well. It wasn't good for the image he had of himself.

"Bet, Paris. But don't come running back to me after your old ass can't strip no more, 'cause I ain't gonna want you then. You missed your chance, baby."

He pushed past her and stalked out to his new Benz. His tires screeched so loudly when he pulled away, she'd thought his tires were on fire.

Trying to massage away the migraine that was slowly entering above her eyes, Paris rubbed the temples of her head. Maybe she should just spend a few days by herself with no phone calls or impromptu visits. She didn't have to be back to work until Wednesday, which meant she had two days off without anything to do. Kenton knew better than to call her with any more private parties. She decided to call her mother, since she was planning on turning off her phone until time to return to work. Deanne answered on the first ring.

"Hey, Momma," she said, smiling at the sound of her mother's voice

"Paris! What are you doing, sweetheart?"

She could tell her mother was happy to hear from her also. "Nothing I'm just relaxing a little bit."

"Did you go to church this morning?" Deanne probed.

Paris shook her head; she'd anticipated her mother's question before Deanne opened her mouth to speak. "No, Momma, I haven't really found a church up here. It's a lot different than back home."

"Well maybe you just need to look a little harder. One day you are going to realize that you need God in your life. You've been down there four years. You know that's more than enough time to have made a commitment to a church home. You need fellowship, Paris. Especially since you're down there without any family."

"I know, Momma. I go visit different churches every now and then. I haven't felt a connection with any one church. I need to feel a connection before I make a commitment, but I hear you," Paris made a half-hearted attempt to pacify her mother. The truth was, she was certain she'd feel an overwhelming sense of shame if she participated in worship services.

"Ivan told me you are planning a trip down there in a few weeks. That will be nice. You all haven't seen each other since Christmas."

"Yeah, I am actually looking forward to seeing them and checking out any chicks they got down there."

"Don't be meddling in their little romances," Deanne joked. "And speaking of romances, haven't you met someone yet? I'm sure there must be some nice men down there. I don't want you to end up alone like me, Paris."

Although her mother's voice was light-hearted, Paris knew she was only half-joking. With her mother's question, the first thought that popped into her head was to tell her about Marcus. He would be exactly what Deanne would want for her daughter. A church-going man that was successful, good-looking, and best of all, he actually made her laugh. But there was no sense in telling Deanne about someone that Paris was never going to see again. She was sure Marcus had given up on her after she brushed him off on the phone. Plus, she didn't plan on going anywhere near the gym at eight o'clock in the evening.

"No, Momma, not yet. I'm only twenty-six. I've got plenty of time. Besides, it isn't the end of the world not to be involved. You're not doing too badly."

"I know, sweetheart. I'm fine, but when I was your age, I wasn't alone. I had my chance at relationships, and I chose not to get involved again. You haven't even given one a try yet. I worry about you."

"I'm fine. I'm perfectly happy being by myself. I'm trying to get my life together. I don't have time to be putting up with crap from some man."

Deanne clucked her tongue against the roof of her mouth softly. "Paris, all men aren't bad."

"Humph," Paris muttered. She didn't believe that for a second, and she didn't think Deanne did either. Hadn't she learned firsthand with Deanne what men were capable of? Paris invoked mental pictures of clientele shoving dollars at her, objectifying her, their eyes reducing her to a piece of ass and a pair of firm breasts. Frustrated, she attempted to purge the club from her thoughts. Talking to her mother always filled her with a burdensome sense of guilt and shame. She acknowledged it was becoming harder and harder to shake off those feelings once she hung up the phone from talking to her mother. Anxious for a way to get out of the conversation and back to some much-needed solitude, Paris began twitching her foot.

"How's your job going?" Deanne asked.

"It's okay. Same old same."

"I still wish you would take some classes or something. You know you don't need to be working that night shift. Who is up calling some center at two o'clock in the morning anyway?"

"People do call. If something is wrong with their service or something. It pays the bills though. It's alright."

In the beginning, she'd planned to tell Deanne about her job, but the more time passed she realized she just couldn't do it. She made up an excuse to get off the phone with her mother then quickly hung up the phone. She turned off the ringer on her downstairs phones, but determined to have uninterrupted solitude, completely unplugged the cordless in her bedroom.

"Peace and quiet at last."

She checked the locks and made sure her alarm system was on, then trekked upstairs to her bedroom. She took off her knit shorts set and laid across her bed, face-down in her lace bra and panties. She had told herself repeatedly that she wasn't afraid of this psycho that was stalking her. She fed Kenton and Chocolate that line, but inside each note shook her more and more.

*What is this psycho thinking? Is he just writing the notes to scare me, or is he planning on doing something else?* She raked her brain trying to come up with an explanation that would ease the growing tension behind her temples. She knew most men were all talk, but was forced to admit there were some that were dangerous and psychotic. She couldn't count the number of specials she'd watched where prostitutes and strippers were abused or victims in homicides. She would always turn the channel when they reenacted the crimes; she couldn't stomach it. Her thoughts always traveled to the five-year-old Paris watching her mother being violently hit by a man she'd tried to date. Paris squeezed her eyes shut to block out the horrific memory and pushed herself up off the bed. A warm bath and a glass of brandy would calm her down.

The combination could possibly calm her nerves to the point where she could actually fall off to sleep.

Paris spent Monday drinking tequila and stuffing herself on pepperoni pizza with extra pepperoni and light cheese. The sound of her answering machine picking up calls annoyed her, so she hid out in her bedroom upstairs, sitting Indian style on her comforter and watching talk shows. One of the shows did a series entitled "My family doesn't know about my sexy job." Her first reaction was to flip the channel, but curiosity won her over. She tuned in to hear the reactions of the families. A blonde-haired woman with huge hair and lips filled with to capacity with collagen, explained to an unsympathetic audience her situation.

She complained that her husband did not make enough money to support her, so she decided stripping would be a good way to help pay the bills. Not only did her husband have no clue, but her parents thought she'd been attending night school the entire time and were babysitting her three-year-old twins. Paris digested the "boos" and "hisses" of the audience as the woman told her husband who walked off the stage after she dropped the bomb on him. The woman didn't look like she cared that her husband was upset. She just kept on licking her puffy lips and tossing platinum blonde curls over her shoulder.

Paris scowled at the television. Looking at the woman, she could understand why the audience was treating her so cold. This was the stereotypical image immediately conjured up when people heard the word stripper. Paris looked at herself in her full-length mirror. She certainly didn't fit that description right now. Her dark brown hair that usually hung to the middle of her back was piled on top of her head in a messy ponytail. She had on an over-sized Southern University T-shirt and cotton shorts. Her caramel skin looked naked to her without her M.A.C. and Fashion Fair makeup.

Entranced, she watched as another stripper took a seat next to the talk show host. This one was an African American and had a ridiculous waist-length auburn weave. Her toasted almond complexion was hidden behind layers of makeup that were at least two shades darker than it should have been. Her lips were heavily outlined, as were her eyes that looked as if they were about to close due to the fake lashes and layers upon layers of cheap mascara that were clumped on top of them.

*Is that how my Caramel character looks?* She opened her smaller closet and retrieved one of her costumes from work. She compared the skimpy white panties and bra to the get-up the woman named Desire wore on television. Paris threw the outfit on the floor and then revisited her reflection in her bedroom mirror. *I want to be Paris Renee Jackson again.* She sighed. *But it's been so long. Can I find the real me?* She thought about when she chose the course her life would go—when she'd tried out for the dance team her senior year in high school. *It's been so long.*

# *CHAPTER SEVENTEEN DAMSEL IN DISTRESS MEETS A KNIGHT UNDER A CHERRY MOON*

The tough exterior that would become Caramel had been born the day she tried out to make the dance team. No, she hadn't called herself that then. And no, she hadn't actually had to strip then, but that was where the attitude was born. After making the dance team, Paris knew she had an automatic key to the male weakness. She would anxiously await the team's half-time performances, taking extra care to perfect her hair and makeup. Finally, she was getting attention from men, older men. The ones she'd always been in awe of but felt so rejected by. She began getting offers from small clubs in the area just before graduation. It started with one older man coming to a school-wide celebration and approaching her after the squad had performed to Jasmine Guy's "Try Me."

"Paris, isn't it?" a bald man asked, tapping her on the shoulder.

"Yes," she turned around and flashed him her performer's smile.

"You are a great dancer. The whole group is good. But you, you have real talent."

Paris flushed at his compliments. "Thanks," she said shyly.

"Not only are you a great dancer, but you're fine, too."

Paris was aware he could barely get his sentence out straight for leering at her eighteen-year-old breasts barely covered by a black and blue midriff. The man told her his name was Leroy and insinuated that he would have a job waiting for her once she graduated. He gave her $200 dollars and made her promise not to forget him when she graduated in May. Paris took the money and kept the promise.

The first club she danced in was called "The Clique" and met the qualifications of the common low-budget hole-in-the-wall. At first she didn't dance, just served drinks on a platter in a pair of extremely uncomfortable hot pants that were the source of numerous lewd comments by the patrons. After serving drinks in too tight shorts for a year, Paris started calculating her tips and comparing them to the tips the dancers made. She also noticed that none of the dancers were particularly attractive, nor were any of them skilled at their craft. Instead of synchronized routines, the girls just jiggled around, sometimes on beat, sometimes offbeat to the music. The temptation was too great. She knew that if only she could get up there, she would blow the other dancers out of the water.

The owner of the club who had approached her while she was in high school hooked her up with a couple of the other dancers. The three of them shared an apartment that he paid the rent on as part of their compensation. If she was going to be locked into working at a club because the owner was paying her rent, she might as well be making as much money as possible. With her mother convinced she was living with some friends From school working at a department store in New Orleans, Paris approached the owner, got his approval and began her career as a stripper.

He made her do a performance for himself and several other members of the staff before he allowed her onstage for the first time. Paris had been right in her assumptions, and the men were thoroughly impressed. The owner told her he wanted her to strip from the first time he saw her, but he thought it was important for it to be her choice.

"That's the stuff dreams are made of," one of his partners commented.

His beady eyes devoured Paris's twenty-year-old body as if it were a piece of homemade sweet potato pie. The men looked at each other and smiled. The owner dubbed her "Dreams" and concocted a theme intro consisting of whimsical music while the deejay informed the crowd that their dreams were about to come true.

With more tips rolling in than both of her roommates combined, Paris began feeling more and more confident onstage. She was also painfully aware that she wasn't seeing anything more in her weekly paycheck than her roommates were. She figured that since she was turning this little club out, it was time she move on to bigger and better things. She had never been caught up in being a headliner, because titles didn't pay bills.

She wanted to find a more reputable club with clients who had more reputable pockets. She began listening more closely to clients talking about other strip clubs in the area. She graced a few big spenders with her smile and a few extra minutes of table dances and received the name of two club owners that were looking for dancers. After calling both clubs on her night off, Paris learned the hiring process was much more complicated than at The Clique.

She started working on two new sexy routines. After she perfected them both, she decided to try them out on the customers at The Clique. Again, Paris had hit pay-dirt. The men loved the routines and even the other dancers began asking her to help choreograph their performances. Paris declined on their offers and didn't tell anyone she was planning to leave. It wouldn't do to be thrown out of her apartment before getting on with another club.

One Saturday she called in sick at The Clique and borrowed her roommate's car. Clad in a pair of skintight acid-washed jeans with a skimpy tank top, she headed across town for "Club Indulgence." Paris's dangerously curvaceous 5'6" frame, coupled with her saucy attitude, was enough to get her past the bouncers and ushered into the back room where she was given an opportunity to audition privately for a spot. Once inside, she quickly changed into a lace black garter belt set she'd spent over two hundred dollars on from Victoria's Secret. She fluffed her hair, letting it hang wild and unruly around her shoulders and down her back. Three-inch high black t-strap heels completed her transformation from fresh-faced twenty-two-year-old into an experienced seductress.

Five black men and one white man all at least fifteen years her senior sat around a rectangular table waiting for her to entertain them. One of the men motioned for the music to start, but Paris held up her hand to stop them. She confidently walked over to their table and handed them a silver compact disc. The CD was quickly slipped into a handheld boom-box sitting on top of the table. The evil grin of a predator spread across the face of the owner as the initial strains of

Monifah's "Suga" filled the room.

"Damn, baby girl is not playing is she?"

Paris ignored the comment and focused on performing. The hypnotic music seduced her own limbs as she slid into the perfect splits. Paris knew she had every man on the judge's panel under her spell as she slid across the lighted floor, making sure she visually connected with each man at the table. The owner beckoned her to come to the table, and she quickly accepted the challenge. She sauntered over to him, not missing a beat, and slowly straddled his lap, never breaking eye contact. Paris began rolling her pelvis hard and slow across his groin; he broke eye contact and laughed nervously. Brown eyes sparkling in triumph, she silently congratulated herself on accomplishing her goal. It had been like taking candy from a baby, not anywhere near as hard as she'd thought it would be.

The girls at this club were certainly beautiful, but she was packing a lot more than beauty. Paris had learned while dancing in high school that her large almond shaped-eyes and pouty lips could hypnotize just about any male that looked her way.

Paris wasn't surprised in the least when the offer to dance at Club Indulgence was made as soon as she finished with her performance. With the help of owners Mack and Ty, she found a small efficiency apartment and began life on her own.

She'd worked at the club for three months when Kenton James walked into the club one fateful night. One of the dancers told the rest of the girls he was a former club owner from Atlanta looking to bring an upscale gentlemen's club to New Orleans. Paris didn't let on that she heard the conversation, but made sure she spotted where he was seated.

The atmosphere at Club Indulgence was much more competitive than at The Clique. As one of the youngest dancers, Paris stayed out of the way of the more seasoned girls and all the gossip and drama they enjoyed. Most of the dancers were bi-sexual and into performing all types of extras with customers. Paris definitely wasn't feeling that.

One particular night, she was one of the last to go onstage. Paris was waiting with one other girl in the back for her cue. Mack told the two of them there was going to be a short delay; they needed to sit tight for a while. He would let them know when it was time for them to go onstage.

"That's cool with me," Paris said gratefully. She sat down, slipped her stilettos off and relaxed against the wall. She wasn't feeling this last set anyway.

"Me, too. I'll keep Paris company," the other dancer said sweetly.

Paris's ears perked up at her words. The girls name was Alize. Paris had brushed off sexual advances from her offstage a couple of times. Alize was thirty-two years old, 5'11" and had Paris by at least twenty pounds. Paris scowled at the girl behind her back. She didn't want this bitch tripping with her tonight. Just as Paris got up to check on the progress onstage, Alize cornered her.

"Hey where you going, Dreams?" she questioned softly.

"Quit playing, Alize. I'm not in the mood for this bullshit tonight."

She hoped her tone alerted Alize that just because she was the youngest, didn't mean she was the average naïve chickenhead. The older woman had a reputation for turning young girls out, but Paris wanted her to know she was not about to be added to her list of gullible conquests.

"Aw, girl, you don't know what you could be in the mood for. You need to stop tripping and let an older woman show you a thing or two. I know you don't got a man, so you must be needing a little help," Alize purred.

Paris didn't flinch as Alize moved within an inch of her mouth and began caressing the side of her face.

"You just don't know how good I could make you feel."

The feel of Alize's hand on her breast shocked Paris out of her standoff. Bright variations of red flashed in her head as her breath became ragged.

"Bitch, don't you ever put your hands on me!"

Before she realized it, she'd pushed Alize off her and down on the dressing room floor. For a second Paris panicked as she recognized the fury starting to boil in Alize's eyes. Paris's heart raced a mile and minute because she knew if Alize got up off the floor, she would try her hardest to knock her head in. Desperately searching for something to defend herself with and hoping someone would interrupt what promised to be a fight, Paris scanned the dressing room. Unable to find anything handy, she settled for one of her scarlet spiked heels and braced herself for assault.

"You stupid, little ho. I'm going to whup your ass, then take what I wanted in the first place," Alize growled.

Her arm snaked out and grabbed the side of Paris's sarong and panties, ripping them both. Paris closed her eyes and brought the shoe down on Alize's head as hard as she could. The sharp heel made a cracking sound as it connected with Alize's cheekbone. Paris heard the woman's bloodcurdling screams then she saw blood pouring down her face. She was relieved the screams brought Mack, Ty and a barrage of other people rushing into the room just as Alize was gathering the strength to charge her again.

Ty restrained Alize, but some of her loyal friends began reaching for Paris. Paris looked around for an ally, but couldn't find one. What she did find was the sympathetic eyes of Kenton James who had obviously been chatting with Mack and Ty. A dancer named Chardonnay grabbed a handful of Paris's hair. Paris struck her arm with the bloody shoe.

The second attack caused the men to have to struggle to grab several other girls, all clawing for the 5'6" one hundred twenty-five pound Paris. She cast a pleading look at Kenton, who seemed to be the only one feeling her right now. Ty yelled for someone to take the shoe away from her. Kenton took his jacket off and covered her with it, somehow managing to escort her through the middle of the mayhem.

"Damn, baby girl, you were about to get your ass kilt in there. What the hell did she do to you?" he asked.

Paris couldn't get her breath to speak, but was grateful for the quick save. Kenton made a mad dash for his plushed-out Tahoe, half-carrying her the entire way. He opened the door and threw her in the front seat then got in the driver side and peeled out of the parking lot.

Once they were safely on the highway, Kenton began laughing a deep hearty laugh.

"What's so funny?" she demanded.

"You. You got a lot of spunk, I'll give you that. I've been watching you for the past two nights. You're good, girl. I was going to approach you tonight with an offer, but I like that it happened this way."

Trying to figure out his aim, Paris stared across the seat at him.

"So I guess seeing an Amazon almost kicking my little ass just worked out good for you," she remarked sarcastically.

Again, Kenton laughed. "Well, I look at it this way. Now you're in my debt. I got a little more leverage than I would've had if I'd just approached you out of the blue."

"Is that so?" Paris questioned, cocking a perfectly arched eyebrow at him.

He held out his free hand while his other handled the steering wheel. "Kenton James, I'm the owner of a new club; Under the Cherry Moon."

Paris shook his hand limply, but didn't respond. It was obvious he already knew her stage name and that was all he needed to know for right now. She was busy worrying about how she would get her car from the club, never mind the fact that Alize was not going to let up until she had another opportunity to beat the shit out of her.

"Like I said, I've been watching you. I like what I see. You bad as hell, and that's on the real. I want you to work for me. My stuff is a lot different from Club Indulgence. We don't fuck with you, so my girls gonna make big-time money, more than you'll ever make there. Besides, the way I see it, your little ass ain't gonna be able to go back to Club Indulgence and keep your health. There ain't no damn way."

Kenton's comment irritated her, but she knew he was right. Alize had serious pull at Club Indulgence, and it was obvious from the way nobody jumped to her defense that battle lines had been drawn. Kenton's plans were making a lot of sense to her. Why was she shaking her behind for men who weren't coming off more than a few dollars a night? This could be the break she'd been looking for.

"Why they call you Dreams?" Kenton asked.

"The manager at The Clique gave me that name."

"That shit don't stick. I get what he was trying to say, but it don't grab you or nuthin'."

Paris rolled her eyes at her reflection in the passenger window. Men always wanted to transform a woman into their interpretation of what she should be. She wasn't trippin' over a name. Kenton leaned back in his seat and looked her up and down.

"Don't you need to keep your eyes on the road? I ain't trying to escape death back there to end up getting in a car accident with you."

"You got a smart-ass mouth. You need to be telling a nigga thank you," Kenton advised.

"You're right," Paris acknowledged. "Thanks for getting me out of there."

"You're welcome." He nodded, then began his appraisal of her again. "Add butterscotch to chocolate and you get caramel. That's you, baby, smooth and sexy just like caramel."

Paris looked strangely at him for a minute then smiled in spite of her bad mood.

"Not bad," she agreed.

"You damn right, it ain't bad. You're getting ready to make the both of us a lot of money, Caramel," Kenton said wisely. "You listening?"

Paris nodded slowly. "I'm listening."

# *CHAPTER EIGHTEEN TURNING UP THE HEAT*

By Tuesday evening, Paris was restless to the point of losing her mind. She'd watched television and slept the entire weekend, but still didn't feel rested or think her mind was straight enough to go back to work, but there was no choice. She refused to stay holed up in her condo anymore.

Her eyes looked clear and bright and her migraine was gone. She glanced at the clock on her bedroom wall—7:15. She opened the drawer with her workout gear in it and stared at her sports bras and biker shorts. Fifteen minutes later, she was in her Camry and heading toward the health club.

"Paris," Marcus's eyes mirrored his surprise. "I was starting to give up on fate."

Paris smiled faintly. She didn't know what had come over her. All she knew was something had pushed her into her workout clothes and over the freeway to Belles and Beaux.

"I thought you said you started your workout at eight." She gestured toward his sports bag and water bottle. "It looks like you're leaving."

He shifted his bag to his left shoulder. "I told you I had just about given up. Didn't want to be sitting up in here waiting on you forever like a big punk," he said, flashing a half-smile.

Paris's eyes quickly ran from his Grant Hill jersey, down to his long sinewy legs encased in the new Jerry Stackhouse Nikes.

"Well I guess if you're on your way out..." She bit her bottom lip in an attempt to calm her nerves. She'd never been nervous around a man before. She'd always been the one in control, smiling to herself, watching men struggle and stutter out lines trying to pick her up. But here she was with the roles reversed, and she didn't like it at all.

Marcus tilted his head to the side and peered down at her. "Have you eaten?"

Thinking of the entire medium pepperoni pizza she'd inhaled the day before, Paris flushed. "No, not today."

"You haven't eaten anything today?"

She shook her head no. He reached out and took her hand in his.

"Come on, Miss Paris. I know just the place. Is your car locked?"

Paris nodded her head yes, then returned his smile. He led her over to a cream Escalade with charcoal tinted windows. He opened the passenger door for her and she got in.

"Thank you," she said politely.

He slid into the driver's seat and clicked the car stereo on. Paris was pleasantly surprised to hear jazz flood the car. "I'm really glad you came." He steered lazily, as his left hand rested on the window ledge.

Paris nodded, but didn't respond. She wasn't used to being out with someone like Marcus. Everyone she encountered knew she was a stripper, and the conversation inevitably turned to the club. They rode in silence until fifteen minutes later when Marcus pulled up in front of a restaurant with the words Delta Café on a huge lighted overhead sign. Worried someone would recognize her from the club, Paris felt uneasy.

After they were seated, she calmed, noting that their booth was secluded enough that the chances of someone seeing them were very slim. The menu consisted of everything from jambalaya to hamburgers. Marcus told her they had the best old-fashioned ice cream shakes around. They both decided to order one: hers strawberry, his chocolate. The waitress returned with Paris's shrimp *etouffee* and his lobster tails.

"So tell me more about Paris." He focused his soft brown eyes on her face.

Paris glanced over at him through lowered lashes. "What do you want to know?"

"Okay, I can see you're going to make it hard on me. Well how long have you been dancing?"

Paris's heart turned over at his question. Why did this have to come up so early in the conversation? She'd decided in the car ride over that she would tell the truth once they got to the restaurant. However, she didn't want it to lead the conversation though. She wasn't sure if they'd have much more to talk about once she revealed she was a stripper.

"Since I was in high school," she said, trying hard to sound nonchalant.

"My sister did a stint with an ice skating show. You know, one of those Disney on ice shows. She had a good time. You must really love dance to have chosen it as a career." He took a sip of his drink. "I'll have to get you to dance for me," he said with a sly twinkle in his eyes.

Paris swallowed too quickly and began to cough.

"I…I didn't mean…I meant I'll have to take you dancing," Marcus corrected himself quickly.

Her eyes skirted across the table from his plate to hers. *This is ridiculous. I need to just come out and say it.*

"I'm sorry. I didn't mean to offend you," he offered apologetically.

Paris shook her head. "That's okay. How long have you been a CPA?"

She could've kicked herself. She'd let the opportunity pass to tell him the truth tonight. She couldn't very well bring it up after they ate dinner. *Oh yeah, you remember when you joked about getting me to dance for you? That's actually what I do for a living. I dance for men naked.*

He told her he'd just passed his exam, and this was his first job as a CPA. He had a younger brother and an older sister. His parents had been accountants, and he looked up to them growing up. She told him about Sharp and Ivan and a little about her childhood, omitting the important parts. He asked her about her parents, and she nonchalantly told him they separated when she was young. She adeptly changed the subject when he asked if that bothered her growing up.

Oblivious to her standoffish attitude, Marcus had her laughing comfortably before they finished their meal. She found herself unable to distance herself during the conversation. There was a warmth about him that seemed to draw her in. She hoped he found her attractive, but wasn't sure. Unlike most men, he hadn't spent the entire evening complimenting her. After thinking about it, she realized he hadn't complimented her at all since the church picnic. Paris's face clouded over as she wondered if he was only interested in her as a friend.

"Is something wrong?" Marcus asked.

She shook her head no and forced a smile back on her lips. Even though she didn't want a relationship with Marcus, for some reason she wanted him to like her. And in order for him to like her, he had to find her attractive. *Maybe I should have worn something more revealing.* She had on a Nike T-shirt and matching shorts. Her sports bra and biker shorts were underneath, but maybe she should have taken that off. She had planned to change in the locker room. She hadn't counted on running into Marcus before she got in the club. Paris didn't realize she was chewing on her bottom lip until she looked up and saw Marcus's eyes riveted on her mouth. She immediately covered her mouth with her hand nervously.

"I probably should get you back to your car." He reached out and touched her hand briefly.

"Yeah I have to go to work tomorrow. I probably should get back," she agreed.

"I'm really glad you decided to come," he said, his eyes holding hers until she looked away.

Paris nodded and stood up motioning for him to take her arm. She became uncomfortable with the anxious feelings closing in on her. Once they arrived at the club, she quickly opened the passenger door, to prevent him from opening it for her.

He walked her over to her maroon Camry. "I hope you had a good time," he said, leaning down slightly.

Paris looked up at him and smiled. "I did, thank you."

"You don't talk a lot," Marcus said thoughtfully.

"I talked," she rebutted playfully.

He shook his head. "There's so much I want to know about Paris Jackson." He reached for her hand. "Can I see you again?"

Paris studied her tennis shoes and chewed on her lip. *I should just tell him and put myself out of this misery.* A gust of wind whistled by, blowing the tips of her ponytail against his chest. Marcus picked up a few strands of her hair and rubbed them between his fingers. Paris inhaled sharply. She felt his fingers running along her cheekbone, then he tilted her chin upward so that she was forced to look at him.

"I've been wondering what it would be like to kiss you all night," he whispered huskily

Paris closed her eyes as his lips brushed against hers faintly at first and then more firmly. She put a hand to his chest to push him away, but her hand didn't budge. Instead, it lay limply on his chest.

"Can I see you again?" he asked hoarsely, drawing away from her parted lips.

She attempted to turn her head, but his hand firmly held her chin. She nodded. "Yes."

He kissed her again on the forehead and gave her a long hug. "You be careful getting home, okay?"

She nodded, keeping her eyes on the car keys in her hand. He closed her car door once she'd gotten in and stood there until she pulled off. She avoided looking at her reflection in the mirror until she'd gotten off the highway on the exit leading to her home. She glanced quickly at her reflection and was surprised to see tears peeking out from the corners of her eyes.

After arriving home from work Wednesday night, Paris was anxious to check her messages. At the sound of Marcus's voice, she sat down close to the machine and held her hand over her heart in a vain attempt to slow its frantic beating. Once again, he'd told her how much he'd enjoyed having dinner with her and said he looked forward to seeing her again. Her smile disappeared and heart dropped instantly as the voice switched to Grey's pleading voice, telling her he was going crazy.

He claimed to be checking to see if she was okay. He said it wasn't like her not to call him back for so long a period of time. *He should've thought about that before he tried to humiliate me at the club.* She deleted all four of the messages he'd left, then listened to one from Michael. He was the owner of a dry cleaners and insisted on doing all of her dry cleaning free of charge. He was informing her that her clothes were ready, and he had tickets to a comedy show if she'd like to go. That is if she wasn't busy. *Please.* She rolled her eyes. She wondered if his wife knew about the extra tickets to the comedy show.

Performing hadn't been that hard tonight. There hadn't been any notes or surprises, just the same old customers with a few new ones too scared to approach the dancers, but gawking with lusty eyes all the same. Chocolate and Kenton had exchanged looks whenever they didn't think she was looking. Chocolate had mouthed, "Is she okay?" to Kenton at least twice, oblivious that Paris could see her in the mirror. She hadn't felt like going off on them. She understood where they were coming from, especially considering what had happened the last time she was at the club.

After their set, Mary Jane cautiously asked her how she was doing. Paris told her she was certain the crazy ass leaving the notes had forgotten about her by now. He was probably just pissed because of the lipstick stain, but he'd get over it. After all, hadn't they told her there hadn't been anything strange going on during her days off?

Paris stepped out of her work clothes and slid her pampered naked body between pink satin sheets. She cuddled up with her pillow and dreamt a dream of what ifs. What if things were different, and she could be with Marcus? What if she weren't a stripper? What if all men weren't dogs? What if her father had never left? What if…

The doorbell being pushed repeatedly woke Paris from a particularly blissful sleep. She glanced at the clock and pulled her cotton robe around her, hastily tied the belt and hurried down the stairs two at a time. "It's barely seven o'clock in the morning. Who could be ringing my doorbell like a fool at this hour except Grey" she mumbled groggily. If it was Grey, she would call the police. She'd had enough of his bullshit.

She placed one hand on her door and peered through her peephole. Shocked by who was at her door, she turned off her alarm system, unlatched the deadbolt and opened the door.

"Can I help you officer?" she asked, pushing sleep-tousled hair out of her face.

A beefy white police officer and an older white woman she recognized as one of her neighbors were standing in her doorway. They both looked her up and down before speaking. Paris followed their eyes to her exposed cleavage then pulled her robe tighter around her.

"Can I help you?" she repeated, narrowing her eyes at both of them.

"Ma'am, do you know who did this to your property?" the officer asked, clucking his tongue at her attempts to cover herself.

She looked at him as if he were crazy. Realizing she had no idea what he was talking about, he gestured toward her door. She gasped. Across her door the words "slut bitch" were painted in white shoe polish.

"Oh my God," she gasped. She pushed past the officer and the old woman to survey the rest of her property.

"Do you know who did this?" the officer repeated, this time clearing his throat in an effort to regain her attention.

Unable to speak, she shook her head no.

"We are a private community, and we've never had this type of trouble before," the woman sniffed, glancing down her nose at Paris. "It would have to be someone that she gave her passcode to."

"No, I don't know who did this," Paris said to the police officer then narrowed her eyes on the old white woman. "For all I know, it could be one of my jealous neighbors." The woman seemed to shrink two sizes. Paris couldn't think of anyone she'd given her passcode to besides Harley and Grey. Dey might've had it at one time, but he hardly ever came to her place. When he was in town, she usually met him somewhere.

"I have gotten several notes just like this one at the place where I work. And my car has been vandalized twice in the past few weeks."

The officer scribbled something down on his notepad. "Where do you work, ma'am?" he inquired.

Taking in the woman's renewed condescending expression made Paris grimace.

"She's a stripper," the woman spat.

The officer raised his eyebrows and gave Paris another once over.

"I work at Under the Cherry Moon," she admitted, matching the woman's condescending stare.

"This neighborhood is full of upstanding, moral citizens who make honest livings. Her kind doesn't belong here."

Paris chose to remain silent instead of strangling the old bitty. Truth be told, Paris didn't like the neighborhood too much herself now.

The officer shifted his weight to his right foot and glared between the two of them.

"Do you own this property?" he asked Paris.

"Yes."

"Still, we don't want her kind causing problems for the rest of us. Isn't there anything we can do to keep this from happening again?" the woman asked, motioning with her hand toward Paris's door.

"Mrs. Hofer, I appreciate you calling us on this matter. I'll speak with Ms. Jackson and see if we can't find a way to get this resolved. We don't want anyone in this community feeling threatened, including Ms. Jackson. Do you mind if I ask you a few questions?" he asked Paris.

"No. Please come in," Paris said, leading him into her living room.

She closed the door in Mrs. Hofer's prune face with a thud.

"I need to talk to you right now," Paris said, closing the door to Kenton's office. Kenton looked up from his phone conversation and motioned for Paris to sit. She sat and crossed her legs slowly. Her fuchsia sundress inched its way up her thighs, revealing toned caramel thighs.

"Now," she mouthed firmly. Kenton nodded but put a finger to his lips. Paris focused on him until he shifted uncomfortably in his leather chair, and reluctantly ended his call.

"He knows where I live, Kenton."

Kenton leaned forward in his chair. "What are you talking about?"

"He knows where I live," Paris repeated.

"How do you know?"

"He was at my house. Wrote on my door. He wrote the same thing on my car. The same thing in the notes," Paris said, uncrossing and crossing her legs. She became enraged as she saw Kenton's eye following her legs. Here she was scared shitless, and all he cared about was getting into her pants. "Can't you find out who was at that bachelor party? This doesn't make any sense. I only danced for about five guys that night. There's got to be a way to know who's doing that or at least narrow it down," she said irritably.

Kenton redirected his eyes from her legs to her face. "I've been trying to get a hold of Kevin to see if we can get a list of the names that were at the party, but he's been out-of-pocket. There's no one else that could have done this? Don't you live in a gated community? Maybe it's one of the fellas you get down with."

Paris shook her head no. "There's no way it's someone I know. There are only two, maybe three people who I've given my passcode too, and it couldn't be one of them. It's got to be this guy complaining about the lipstick stain."

Kenton leaned back in his chair and nodded thoughtfully. "He did sound pretty upset about his wife threatening to leave him."

"It's his own fucking fault," Paris snapped spitefully. "I know somebody knows who this punk is."

Kenton shook his head. "Maybe you should stay at my place for a few nights."

Paris rolled her eyes. "No thanks, Kenton. I'd sooner stay at a hotel. I filed a police report."

"When did you do this?" he asked, squirming in his seat.

"One of my neighbors did after they saw the message he wrote on my door. I know you're not trippin' over me filing a report."

"I just wish you had talked to me first, is all. You know I like to keep the club's business out of the papers. It's bad for business," he said slowly.

Paris scowled at him. *This motherfucker has some nerve.* He was busy staring up her dress, but was upset because she called the police on an issue of her own safety.

"So what do you want to do? Are you coming in tonight?" he asked.

"I don't know."

Paris chewed on her bottom lip. She didn't want this asshole to know she was scared. If she didn't show up after his latest stint, he would know that he was getting to her. Besides, the police officer told her they were going to put an extra security guard at the fence that led to her gated community.

"On second thought, yeah I'll see you in a few hours. I'll be fine," she said, getting up and leaving Kenton's office without a backwards glance.

Paris relaxed her hands in the shallow bowl the nail technician placed in front of her. Chocolate suggested they go get manicures and pedicures to get Paris's mind off her stalker. Acknowledging she didn't necessarily feel like going home alone with all this on her brain, Paris agreed. If she could figure out who the stalker was, she would feel much better. As the situation stood, she felt completely helpless and vulnerable.

"Why don't you come up with a list of possible people it could be," Chocolate suggested.

"I'm telling you, Chocolate, I don't have any idea who it could be," Paris reiterated.

"So let's just put everybody's name in the hat. I mean it could be anybody. Nobody should be ruled out right now. Who all have you been seeing?"

Annoyed with Chocolate's theory, Paris shifted her stance. There was no way anyone she knew or was dating could be doing the stalking.

"I told you, I don't know who it is. I haven't seen Dey in months. Not since he up and married ole girl. Harley and I got into it, so I ain't seen his ass in weeks either."

"He was pretty pissed off at you. He told Rodney that he almost went off on you and that you had a smart-ass mouth."

Paris sucked her teeth. "Harley wouldn't do no bitch-ass shit like this," she spat. "He wouldn't let himself get on a woman's tip like that, believe me. His ego is much too inflated for that."

"Well what about Dey or Grey?" Chocolate asked. "Didn't you say Grey had been trippin' lately?"

Again, Paris blew her words off lightly. "You know Grey. There's no way his weak ass would come at me like this. And Dey couldn't focus on anything this long but a bag of weed. Besides, he's a straight shootin' married man now. No, it's got to be one of the niggas that I got at one of the parties." After looking at the non-existent possibilities, her conviction was even stronger that the perpetrator was one of the pathetic assholes she'd imprinted with her signature lipstick stain at a party.

Chocolate's eyes widened at Paris's admission of doing her little trick on so many men. "Let's hope not girl. I don't even want to think about what could pop off if that's what this is about. You don't play with men's families. I learned that shit a long time ago. Niggas will straight go off."

A heavyset woman seated on Paris's left shifted loudly and made a scoffing noise at Chocolate's inappropriate language. Paris turned cold eyes on her, sending her the message to mind her own business. The woman sniffed disdainfully before turning to whisper to the woman seated to the left of her.

Satisfied the lady had been sufficiently checked, Paris returned her attention to Chocolate's unsolicited words of wisdom.

"What about the old dude that works on your car? Didn't you say he asked about spending more time with you?"

"Why would he fuck up my car just to fix it? Plus he's not like that. He's a pussycat. He did ask me to go to his fraternity ball with him, but he was cool when I told him no. He ended up taking his wife. He knew he was gonna get hung up about that anyway. He was just asking to hear himself talk."

"Maybe he wanted you to need him for something," Chocolate reasoned.

"Naw, he's too scared his wife would find out if he took it to that level. He's paranoid about me getting mad and calling her."

"So you haven't noticed any of your clients acting strange? Richie, Leroy, DeWayne, none of them been trippin' out witchu?" Chocolate admired the berry-colored polish being applied to her left hand, then looked expectantly at Paris.

Paris shook her head adamantly. "I told you it has to be somebody from a party."

"Will you please stop doing that shit? I've been telling you that shit was going to get out of hand. I don't even know why you trippin' like this. What do you care what their wife knows so long as you get your money?"

The Korean woman doing Chocolate's nails gave her a disapproving glance, letting her know their conversation was too loud.

Paris took the hint and lowered her voice to respond. "Save it, Chocolate. The shit isn't happening to you, so you don't need to be worried about it."

"The hell it isn't. I don't want to see nobody trippin' with you, but on the other hand, if some psycho is after you, what makes you think he won't go after one of us if he can't get to you?"

Paris narrowed her eyes on Chocolate, but she did feel slightly guilty about putting Chocolate and the other girls in this predicament. She didn't want anyone else to be penalized or hurt because of the games she played on clients. She never considered the ramifications of her actions might lead to the other dancers at the club.

"It's not going to come to that. I'm telling you, this guy is bluffing. You know crazy customers are a dime a dozen," Paris attempted to calm Chocolate's worries.

"I know there were plenty of psycho niggas that came in the club where I used to dance, that's why I came over here," Chocolate said. "The customers up in here don't be trippin' out like that. Most of 'em got too much to lose. I mean, I'm witchu. I hope he's blowing shit out his ass, but if he's not—" Chocolate stopped short of finishing her sentence.

"You go dry now." Chocolate was directed to the front of the salon to sit under the nail dryer.

"I'll be over there, girl." Chocolate gestured.

Paris nodded solemnly. She was doing her best not to let Chocolate or anyone else know she was growing more and more anxious with the whole situation. If she let on that she was afraid, it would fuel everyone's fear, and that wouldn't be good for anyone. News of her fear would make its way back to the perpetrator, and that would serve as a coveted reward for his actions. She stuck her chin out defiantly. There was no way she would show this rattled her. There was no proof this wacko was acting on something she'd done, and even if he were reacting, it was his fault for being in the wrong place at the wrong time, she reaffirmed. She shook the blame off, cleared her conscious and joined Chocolate at the front of the salon.

# *CHAPTER NINETEEN DINNER AND A DATE*

In spite of the craziness escalating around her, Paris enjoyed spending time with Marcus. She'd been out with Marcus four times since they had dinner at the Delta Café. She knew she was on dangerous ground, but she couldn't help herself. Marcus made her laugh, and that was something no other man had been able to do. When she was around him, it was like all the drama she was going through didn't exist. The latest incident with this stalker had her wanting to get out of the house as often as possible. Besides making her laugh, Marcus also made her pulse race. She hadn't been intimate with a man since going to an ESPN appreciation dinner with Harley six months ago. She'd enjoyed herself, and after drinking a few glasses of Hypnotiq with Harley and his friends, she was feeling a little generous and very racy. They were all over each other before they made it to Harley's black convertible Bentley. After pulling away from the party, Harley pulled over on the side of the highway and turned the engine off. With minimal kissing substituting foreplay, Harley had pulled her onto his lap, pushed her mini skirt up and pressed his fingers inside her, hitting just the right spot. She'd climaxed all over his fingers, giving him the perfect opportunity to push himself into her.

Paris had never wanted anything more than that with Harley or anyone else, and that was all she knew. She had only slept with eight men. While two of them had been willing to have intercourse with her without all the extras, the other six had tried their hardest to reach out to her emotionally. She wasn't having it. Grey had been one of the unfortunate six, and she had made it abundantly clear to him the entire time, she wasn't interested in him like that. No one had forced her to challenge the boundaries she put around herself until now. Marcus kissed her and she melted. Where she'd never let men kiss her much before, she yearned for Marcus's kisses.

She knew part of the attraction she had for Marcus was his being totally in the dark about her lifestyle. All her other sex partners had known she danced for money and had put their own stereotypical expectations on intimacy with her. Harley assumed that she liked rough sex. Poor Grey was so worked up about sleeping with a "bad girl" that he had just about spilled himself when she'd removed her panties. Paris was sure she didn't live up to any of their expectations. She was no sexual expert, nor did she want to be whipped or tied up. Most men assumed she had an overactive sex life that consisted of everything from other women to S&M. It was much easier to go without it. Before the last time with Harley, she'd slept with Grey a few times, and that had been it for the year. At this point, she didn't feel like explaining why she was a celibate stripper.

She lit one of the pink taper candles on the table and rechecked dinner. Everything was set. She had finally asked Marcus over to her house, and she was preparing dinner for the two of them. After driving to the nearest bookstore, she'd picked up a cookbook and finally decided on fettuccini Alfredo. The salad and wine were waiting, as were the store bought croissants.

At 6:45, Marcus called from the gate. She gave him her passcode, and directed him to her unit. She rushed to check her reflection in one of the rectangular glass cut mirrors in her dining room. Her hair was parted on one side and brushed behind her ears. It hung in soft curls down her back. She wore a silver halter-top with an asymmetrical black skirt that skimmed one knee but went much shorter on the opposite leg. Sexy black sandals completed the outfit. She was a little nervous because she'd never dressed this way in front of Marcus. On their previous dates, she'd gone out of her way to look as little like her character Caramel as possible. He'd given her compliments, but never referenced her figure, and she was beginning to wonder if he was attracted to her again. She'd refrained from the heavy make-up, opting for face powder and a light plum blush and raisin lip-gloss. Exactly five minutes later, her doorbell rang.

She closed her eyes, inhaled, then slowly exhaled and opened the door. He stood hesitantly in the doorway, not moving or speaking for a moment. The teasing smile Paris had begun to expect from him was absent as well. *He doesn't like it. I must look cheap.*

"You-uh, you look nice, Paris," he said, handing her a beautiful bouquet of irises.

She smiled then opened the door wider, inviting him in. "I made fettuccini Alfredo," she said shyly.

"Sounds good. You have a nice place." He looked around her expansive living room.

Paris smiled a thank you over at him. She tried to look objectively around the condo. It was done in earth tones of cream, burgundy, rich sienna and cocoa browns. It was a home she would have labeled a dream when she was younger, but now it was a constant reminder of the profession she'd chosen. All of her success and possessions were because she danced naked and allowed men to degrade her for money. The heavy price tag extracted the novelty out of owning her own condo in an upscale neighborhood, and brand new Porsche at age twenty-six. When all was said and done, the reflection in the mirror she saw was nothing more than a stripper. Granted, a well-paid stripper, but a stripper nonetheless.

Marcus seemed to notice her somber expression and walked over to her. "Is everything okay? Why don't you take a break? Go ahead and sit down. I can finish bringing out the food." He rubbed her shoulders.

Searching for a sign of what he saw in her, Paris looked into his soft brown eyes. She knew no man was this genuine and attentive without some ulterior motive.

"You look tired," he said, leading Paris over to a glass high backed chair and urging her to sit.

She watched in amazement as he disappeared into her kitchen then reappeared with the dish of fettuccini and a large serving ladle.

"Is there anything else we need?"

Paris shook her head no. Marcus winked at her across the table.

"Paris?"

She looked expectantly at him.

"Why are you so quiet? What's going on in that head of yours?"

His tone was firm yet genuine.

"I—uh… It's nothing. I have been under a lot of stress from work."

He took a sip of wine. "You want to talk about it?"

"No, no I don't feel like thinking about it right now. Is everything okay?" she asked, uncertainty plain in her voice.

"Everything is beautiful, including you. I didn't know you could cook. That's too good to be true," he said jokingly.

Paris blushed. Eventually Marcus got her to relax, and she enjoyed their dinner. She'd bought strawberries, homemade vanilla ice cream and pound cake for dessert. Marcus decided he wanted a sundae, but he wanted to share it with her. She disappeared into the kitchen to make the double sundae.

"I like lots of strawberries," Marcus called out.

"Me too." She laughed.

"Aw, no, then I better help you. I don't want you trying to hog all of the strawberries," he said coming up behind her.

She scooped a heap of strawberries onto the huge sundae. "Is that enough?" she asked, playfully poking him in the chest. She fed him a spoonful of ice cream and strawberries.

"You didn't get any whipped cream on there," he teased. "You're supposed to get a spoonful of everything," he mumbled through a mouthful of ice cream and strawberries.

Paris couldn't help but laugh as he struggled to swallow the huge scoop of ice cream.

He reached into the drawer and got a tablespoon in order to return the favor. "Close your eyes," he instructed.

"No way."

"Come on. Close your eyes. You can trust me,"

Putting her hands over her eyes, Paris reluctantly obeyed.

"Now open your mouth," he said.

She opened her mouth, and he fed her ice cream, strawberries and whipped cream all in one bite.

"See, that's how you give someone a taste of something. You see how I got everything all on the spoon?" he joked.

"Okay, okay give me another chance?" she purred slyly.

Marcus looked suspiciously at her.

"Trust me."

He closed his eyes, and she smeared a huge dollop of whipped cream all over his lips.

"See, I knew you couldn't be trusted. Ice cream sundaes are something that shouldn't be played with," he admonished, feigning indignation.

Paris laughed, then put her finger to his lips, swiping some of the whipped cream off. She looked coyly up at him while sucking the whipped cream off her finger.

He pulled her into his arms then kissed her lightly on the lips, smearing whipped cream across her top lip.

"Why'd you do that?" she asked.

He smiled wickedly at her then leaned in and expertly licked the top of her lip before slipping his tongue into her mouth. Paris dropped the spoon she was holding, and it clattered loudly as it hit the floor. She tried to pull away to retrieve the spoon, but he held her firmly in his arms, gently sucking on her full bottom lip. His mouth tasted so good on hers she gave up and concentrated on exploring his mouth. Marcus gently entangled his fingers in her hair, holding her head as he kissed her deeply. She slid her arms around his neck and allowed her tongue to tease then follow with his. Her heartbeat accelerated quickly until it slammed against her ribcage at a hundred beats per minute. She could feel a stirring in the pit of her stomach.

She couldn't remember a kiss ever feeling like this. Marcus caressed her face softly then ran his fingers through her hair and over her exposed shoulders. A chill ran down her spine as he lightly dragged his fingertips over her back and shoulders. He moaned her name in her ear, which caused her to tremble from her fingertips to her knees. In an effort to gain perspective, Paris recalled the last time she'd been intimate with a man in her mind. It had been with Harley and that paled miserably in comparison to this.

Paris's fingertips trembled as she allowed her hands to explore the muscles in his chest. Marcus picked her up and pushed her back on the kitchen counter in one fluid motion, barely missing the leftover whipped cream and strawberries still littering the counter. Paris's breath caught in her throat as his hands firmly wandered up her thighs, his kisses all the while getting deeper and more demanding. She wanted nothing more than to feel him inside her, kissing her like this, saying her name, telling her…

"Marcus," she breathed faintly.

"I know, I know. We can't do this. Can we?" he murmured in her ear. "You feel so good Paris," he moaned.

She closed her eyes and tried to gather her thoughts. She couldn't sleep with Marcus like this. She hadn't told him anything about herself. He didn't know who she was. Besides that, the way Marcus was making her feel scared the shit out of her. She couldn't sleep with him when she felt so vulnerable.

"I can't." She finally got the energy to say. Reluctantly, she pulled away, his eyes focusing on her parted lips. He kissed her again then pulled away and helped her down. She stood in front of him with the top of her head pressed into his chest. His fingers played lightly with her tousled hair.

"I should go. I don't want to, but I should," he said hoarsely.

Pressing her head harder against him, Paris nodded limply. She didn't want him to go, but she knew if he stayed she would take him by the arm and lead him upstairs to her bedroom. She was fascinated by how gentle he was with her. *Could he possibly be that gentle inside of me?*

"I'll call you later," he said.

"Okay," she agreed weakly.

Neither of them moved an inch. Thinking that too much movement would cause her to renege on her decision, Paris was almost afraid to blink.

Eyes glazed over with lust-filled emotion, Marcus lifted her face to look at him, but was silent. It looked as if he were in turmoil over his decision to leave her. *He just wants some*, she reminded herself. She shouldn't read anything more into his passion-filled eyes. Didn't her customers look at her that way when they were stuffing dollars in her panties? Hadn't Grey looked at her that way before he'd humiliated her at the club that night? She was sure her father had looked at Deanne this way before getting her knocked up and leaving her alone with three kids. Still something in Marcus's eyes was different. *A wolf in sheep's clothing*, she reminded herself. *A wolf in sheep's clothing.*

"That shit is just plain stupid, Paris!" Kenton yelled angrily.

Paris sucked her lip and stared defiantly back at Kenton's angry face. "Come on now, Kenton. Anyone of us could've accidentally done that at a party. When did we become liable for our client's dirty laundry?" Chocolate piped up, attempting to take the heat off her friend.

Kenton's eyes blazed through Chocolate. "So are you saying it was your lipstick that showed up on old dude's collar?" Kenton asked.

"No," Chocolate answered.

"This is between me and Paris. Keep your ass out of it unless you want to be all the way up in it." Kenton's threat was plain in his tone and the cold eyes he directed on Chocolate.

Chocolate glanced sadly over at Paris, but didn't raise her gaze to meet Kenton's.

*Her ass has always been a damn coward*, Paris thought angrily. Chocolate's submissiveness enraged her almost as much as Kenton's greed.

"She's right you know. Why am I responsible for some sorry ass not washing the lipstick off his shirt?" Paris challenged.

"Bullshit, Paris. This shit is coming up too often. I ain't stupid. You're doing this shit on purpose!"

Paris rolled her eyes at him dramatically. "That's it," she said sarcastically. "I was just so angry because I wasn't going to be the lucky bride that I wanted to mess this guy's shit up. Do you think he's the one stalking me?"

"I don't know if he is or isn't, but whoever this mofo is, he's pissed off. I ain't letting no nigga tell me who to let dance in my club, but I ain't trying to lose customers either," Kenton spat angrily.

"Fuck him," Paris said evenly.

"No, Paris, fuck you. You need to watch this shit. You do your thang here and it's all good, but I can't be having this drama. If you're not smart enough to see that you gonna get yourself killed, I'm sure as hell smart enough to know this shit is bad for business. If you can't keep your business straight, you gonna have to move on."

Kenton slammed the dressing room door as he left Chocolate, Mary Jane and Paris standing there. Paris sat on the stool in front of her mirror and began brushing her hair.

"Girl you have got to slow down," Chocolate said softly.

Mary Jane's wide eyes mirrored Chocolate's advice.

"For real, Paris," Chocolate persisted. "This dude who called up here was crazy. He's probably the one stalking you. He told Kenton he lost everything because of that shit you did at the bachelor party. His wife had given him one last chance."

Paris's eyes met Chocolate's in the mirror. "Well I guess that nigga blew it then. That shit is ain't my fault. If he had one last chance, he should have kept his ass at home," Paris remarked flippantly.

"You gonna mess around and end up dead," Chocolate advised.

"I told you, I'm not letting no pathetic client scare me, and I meant it. He's just tripping. Kenton should've handled it anyway. He sure knows how to handle you."

Chocolate flinched then left the room in a huff. Mary Jane followed silently behind.

*Just like a freakin hand puppet*, Paris thought, watching Mary Jane leave the room. She couldn't believe Kenton had come at her like that in front of Chocolate and Mary Jane. He should've had the call traced and caught the psycho since he was so convinced this was the guy responsible for the letters and vandalizing her car. She threw her comb, brush and lip-gloss in her bag then prepared to leave.

She didn't want to end up leaving by herself tonight. She kept telling herself she wasn't scared, but just wanted to be prepared. If the psycho decided to sprout a pair of balls tonight, it wouldn't do to end up alone and unprepared. For a brief moment, her thoughts flittered to her evening with Marcus a few nights back. She couldn't imagine how different her life would be if she could revel in the new experience of falling for someone. For the first time since she began stripping, she was being forced to face what she had given up when she chose this life. There would be no falling in love for her, no budding romance to cherish.

Ashamed of the reasons behind her thoughts, she reminded herself to stay focused. It wasn't smart to be daydreaming about Marcus when there was someone out there threatening her life. She rechecked her bag for Pearl, then headed for the backdoor exit.

# *CHAPTER TWENTY EVERYBODY GOT ISSUES*

"He sounds too good to be true, Paris. Girl, I am so happy for you," Analise exclaimed.

"He is too good to be true, and I don't know what you're so happy about. You said the same thing about Grey, Harley, Dey and I can't even count how many others."

"All right, all right. I get your point, but it just sounds like something's different about him. It sounds like you really like him. I've never heard you sound like this before," Analise countered defensively.

"It's not like that, Analise. I swear I don't know why I tell you anything. You're always trying to get me hitched up with the latest nigga to come around."

"I just want you to be as happy as I am. What's so bad about getting married?"

"Nothing for you. It's just not for me," Paris said bluntly.

She immediately lost interest in the rest of her conversation with Analise. She was due to fly to Atlanta in a few weeks, and Analise was much more excited than she was. It would be a relief to get away from Under the Cherry Moon for a bit. Maybe this whole stalker thing would cool off by then. *Out of sight, out of mind,* she reasoned, trying to calm her nerves. For all she knew, this idiot was showing up at the club every night watching her dance. Perhaps if she was absent for a month, he'd think Kenton fired her and move on, maybe lose interest.

She also looked forward to seeing Sharp and Ivan. She'd talked to Ivan and was surprised Sharp hadn't told him about her job. Ivan wore his heart on his sleeve, and if he knew, she would have been able to detect it in his voice. Instead, he'd asked about her job at the call center and even suggested she try enrolling in school part-time. Going to school was the last thing on Paris's mind, but she told Ivan she'd think about it.

She would also be more than happy to get away from Grey's pathetic ass for a while. He was still calling and even showing up at the club when she worked. He'd shown up every day last week, giving her exorbitant tips. Tips that she promptly mailed to his office the next day. This had gone on for the last two weeks. Grey continued pleading with her to keep the money.

"You deserve it. You're so beautiful."

His repentant voice sickened her over the answering machine after she'd sent his money back a third time. Paris began to wonder if Grey was the stalker, but she knew this had started long before Grey went crazy. Plus, conservative, bored, stuck-up-my-ass Grey would never use language like that, even if he were threatening someone.

Analise confirmed her flight information again before they got off the phone. Analise had been a true friend to her, and Paris knew she was a genuine person. Analise had never gotten on her nerves before, and she suspected her friend's marriage and fairy book lifestyle was the unspoken cause of her annoyance. Paris wished she'd never told her about Marcus. Now their conversations would no doubt end up circling around to Marcus Rogers and why Paris wouldn't give him a legitimate chance. She didn't need to hear Analise's urging because truthfully, she was fighting with herself about that very same thing. She sighed, hearing Analise's favorite question. *But what if he's the one, Paris*?

While getting a fill at the salon the following day, Paris indulged herself on thoughts of Marcus Rogers. One part of her saw nothing wrong with riding the wave out with Marcus. She'd never been heartbroken by anyone besides her father, and she surely wasn't about to start now. She could have fun with Marcus, and as soon as he fucked up in the least, she could send him packing. But an unfamiliar voice told her that ending might not prove as easy an option with Marcus. If he disappointed her, it would hurt too much. And he would no doubt disappoint her; of this she was sure.

She knew that once she told Marcus she was a stripper, he would either dump her immediately or treat her differently. She'd gotten to know him well enough to know that he expected women to respect themselves. He had a great deal of admiration for his mother, and Paris could tell from his stories that she was nothing like his mother. She saw she was setting herself up for rejection, but he made her feel so good. He made her feel like a lady, as if perhaps she was valuable beyond her T&A. And although she had proof from the way he responded to her that he was attracted to her, something told her he wanted more. Maybe just maybe, he was attracted to more than just her physical beauty. Paris played with the phone cord absently. *What could he be attracted to about me if it isn't my looks? That's all I've ever been able to get men interested in, so what is so different about Marcus?* She knew she wasn't particularly brilliant or cultured like he was. *What does he see in me?* She wondered. *Maybe he knows the truth about me already. Maybe he is just interested in fucking me; perhaps it's the mystery that keeps him interested.*

Whatever it was, it was sure to fade as soon as he knew the truth, and she planned on telling him as soon as she got back from Atlanta. She had told him earlier on the phone that she was planning a trip to Atlanta and would be staying for about a month. He was at work, so he'd had to get off the phone before they were finished discussing it, but she could tell he was taken by surprise.

"I thought things were going well between the two of us," he'd remarked.

"This trip has been planned for a while," she said matter-of-factly, ignoring his open-ended statement.

"Paris? I don't know what to say or what to think."

Usually Marcus was full of energy, and his teasing ways were what attracted her to him so much, but that was absent from his voice now.

"Can I come by tonight?" he asked hopefully.

"I have to work late tonight," she said quickly.

"Have lunch with me tomorrow."

She'd hesitantly agreed and said her goodbye's, reclicked the talk button on her phone, then dialed Kenton.

"I'm on my way. I'm leaving here in ten minutes," she said coldly.

"Alright, sweetheart," Kenton said.

They hung up simultaneously. Kenton had made her promise to call him when she was on her way in to the club. She'd received two more notes since the incident on her property, both via the club's mail. It was as if the stalker wanted her to know that he hadn't forgotten about her. An officer she'd once done a private party for had shown up at the club three nights in a row, following her police report. He claimed he was making sure she stayed safe, but Paris knew it was a way for him to watch booty on the clock. Regardless of his motives, Kenton had not been happy about having the law on the premises at all times. Occasionally he stretched the rules and allowed customers to pay for extra treatment from some willing dancers, and having the police on the grounds was messing his money up. He'd finally gotten the officer to just stop by periodically. He told him he would personally make sure Paris was safe going to and from work.

Paris started driving her Porsche again on a regular basis. She figured that if the stalker could send messages to her, she could return the favor. Her message: *I ain't scared of you.* She drove the car with the top down everywhere except her dates with Marcus because there was no way to explain her vanity plate, and there wasn't a reasonable explanation how she could afford such a luxury car being a choreographer. She'd told him her mother helped her with the condo payment, and although he didn't seem suspicious, she didn't see a way to throw a Porsche into that story.

She slid into the driver's seat and gunned the engine. She'd missed her baby. The Camry was nice, yet nothing turned her on more than the feeling of being in control.

Readying for her lunch date, Paris looked wistfully at her driver's license photo staring up at her from her palm. She was hoping for good news from Analise's agent. Analise had promised that it was mostly just a formality. She was certain Paris would be able to do some part-time modeling in Atlanta. Paris reminded her that she was only 5'6", but Analise insisted height wasn't a priority in print modeling.

Paris didn't really see herself as a model, but then she didn't have the faintest idea what she could do otherwise. She grimaced at the image staring at her from her palm. *What can I do if not dance or entertain men? Humph, is that my only form of value?* She laughed bitterly, remembering the lie she'd told Marcus. She'd half-expected him to call her a liar right there on the spot. Her associates would if they heard her tell someone she was a dance choreographer. She could almost hear Kenton's surefire laughter and sarcastic remarks. She pushed herself up from the sofa and headed toward the stairs. *Should I tell Marcus about myself today over lunch?* That would be a definite way to get him off her back, if that was what she really wanted. She shook her head miserably. She couldn't bear to see his facial expression when he realized she was just a nasty-ass stripper. All the admiration mirrored in his eyes would quickly transform to disgust and scorn. He'd probably be just like Harley and Grey, then be angry she didn't give it up on their first date. She closed her eyes and exhaled. *All right, girlfriend, how are we gonna get out of this one?*

Paris shifted uncomfortably in the iron-backed chair. Marcus had just excused himself to return a phone call. *That's probably his girlfriend*, she thought with relief. If Marcus had a girlfriend, then the whole situation she'd worked up was trivial. It didn't matter that she was being dishonest with him if he were being dishonest with her.

"Sorry about that," he said as he returned. "That was one of my clients."

He proceeded to tell Paris about one of his clients that was in major trouble with the IRS. Paris bit down hard on her bottom lip. *So much for that theory*. As much as she wanted to believe Marcus was being dishonest, she knew he wasn't. For the first time in her life, she could look into a man's eyes and tell that he was not bullshitting her.

"I'm sorry. I must be boring you to death. I can see you zoning out over there."

Paris shook her head. "No. No, I'm sorry. I just have a lot on my mind right now, that's all. That's what I need to talk to you about."

Marcus put his fork down and gave her his full attention.

"I…Marcus I am going through a lot right now. This trip to Atlanta has been planned for a while. I thought there was a chance I wasn't going, but now I know I have to get away for a while. I hope you understand when I say this has nothing to do with you. If I'd known I was going to meet someone like you, things might've been different, but as it is right now, I need to go for awhile."

Paris took a quick gulp of water and swallowed too fast. *Where the hell did that come from?* She hadn't planned on saying that. She wasn't used to her heart stepping up and taking over where her brain usually won out.

"Where does that leave us when you get back, or are you coming back?" Marcus asked, looking into her face.

Paris studied the sweat trickling down her glass of Perrier. "I don't know," she said solemnly. "Maybe it wasn't fate after all."

Marcus looked strangely at her. "Whatever you're going through, Paris, it's apparent to me that you need a friend, a real friend. I want to be that, but you've got to level with me. It's not about us having a relationship or anything like that. I believe that there is some divine purpose behind us meeting. I imagine you probably have a lot of guys trying to get with you, and that's not what I'm about."

"I know that, Marcus, or at least I know you're not like most guys, but you can't begin… I don't really think anyone can help me at this point in my life but myself." She twirled her straw in her glass.

"Will you let me be your friend?" He leaned forward and touched her hand lightly.

Paris let the tip of her tongue trace her upper lip. "We can be friends, but I've got to take this trip, and I am not sure when I'll be back."

"How can so much pain be behind such beautiful eyes? It's there all the time, Paris. I don't think I've ever seen your smile reach your eyes." Marcus pushed a strand of hair out of her eyes.

Paris lowered her gaze and brought her glass to her lips. Even after gulping the cold liquid, her mouth still felt dry. *Will you care about my pain or want to be my friend after you know my secret?* She couldn't remember how many times she'd heard Kenton tell other dancers to leave their problems at home.

"These customers come here for one reason and one reason only," he'd said. "Men want to fuck strippers. They don't want to hear your problems or listen to your sob stories. You are a pair of juicy titties and a fat ass, and that's it. Don't bring that drama here. Leave that up to their wives and girlfriends."

Paris turned her head from the memories of Kenton's harsh but truthful words. *I don't have a problem anyway.* Once Marcus found out the truth, he would drop her faster than a hot potato.

"Whatever is wrong, it can't be that bad. You're young, beautiful, smart and you've done very well for yourself at a young age. Most women would trade places with you in a second."

Paris smiled sadly at his observations of her. *If only you knew how I've done so well for myself. I doubt any woman in her right mind would trade places with me. Surely, the price would be too high for most women,* she acknowledged sadly.

"Come to church with me on Sunday," Marcus said hopefully. "You're not leaving before then are you?"

Paris shook her head. "I'm not sure about church."

Marcus dropped his head and stared at his napkin in silence. "What do you want me to do, Paris?" he asked, discouraged. "I think you know that I really want to spend some more time with you, getting to know you better. Do you want me to give you some space?"

"I do need space, but it's not what you think. There's just a lot going on right now. I'm leaving in a few weeks, and I think I just need some time to work some things through by myself. It has nothing to do with you. If things were different, then maybe," she let her voice trail off as she didn't know the ending to the sentence she'd started.

"Maybe they will be different soon?" he questioned hopefully.

"Maybe," Paris agreed, disheartened. "Maybe."

"I'm just saying, Caramel," Jezebel whined, "this psycho could come in here trying to get at you and hurt everybody in here."

"Kenton, you better get Mamasita here straight," Paris warned.

Kenton's eyes stared at the bouquet of dead roses addressed to Caramel. "This motherfucker is really trippin'," he said slowly. "Maybe you should just take some more time off. I mean, weren't you planning to anyway?"

As usual, Chocolate attempted to intercept the direction of the conversation, acting as the voice of reason. "It's not that I'm afraid for the club, but Paris, I am scared for you. Kenton, can't you beef up security around here or something?"

"For real, Kenton. It don't make no sense for somebody to be walking up in here like that," Mary Jane agreed.

"I thought I had. I don't know how this fool is got in here. It has to be someone who knows the setup back here and knows how to get in and out without being noticed. It must be someone one of you brought back here before. I done told y'all to keep your shit straight," Kenton answered angrily.

"Ain't nobody brought no psycho back here," Paris snapped. "Besides, whoever it is, he's not trying to get anyone else. He's just trying to get to me. If he was really gonna do something he'd—"

"Paris don't even try that," Chocolate interrupted. "This nigga done tore your car up, and painted all over your front door. He keeps leaving shit for you here at the club. The next step is he's gonna come after you. You need to wake up."

Paris turned her back to the conversation and inhaled deeply. *What is this guy doing?* Paris hadn't told Chocolate or Kenton that she'd had to get her home number changed. She'd been getting prank calls. Instead of trying to figure out if it was this psycho or one of her other suitors, she'd just changed her number. The only person she'd told had been Marcus, and he was so unsuspecting he'd assumed a caller had gotten her number mixed up with someone else's.

"You don't have any old angry ex-boyfriends do you?" he'd asked.

Paris had stared at him blankly until he assured her he was just joking.

"Paris it's your call," Kenton said solemnly, placing a hand on her exposed shoulders.

"Isn't that sweet of you Kenton," Paris said dramatically.

She'd known he wouldn't tell her to take off. Kenton would never volunteer to lose money.

"I do want you to have a bodyguard with you at all times though," Kenton continued, "Cruz and I were talking, and he said he'll do it. We're gonna hire another guy to help him out at the club until all this is taken care of. He'll take you to work and wherever else you need to go for the next two weeks or until we find this muthafucka."

Paris felt her left eye twitching and mentally chastised herself. It wouldn't do her any good to admit she was afraid now. *Is stripping really worth all of this?* For the second time in her twenty-six years, Paris questioned why she'd never had a plan B.

# *CHAPTER TWENTY-ONE WHEN IT ALL FALLS DOWN*

Kenton finally convinced Paris that she needed to take the threats seriously. He offered help on his own terms, which meant assigning one of his club bodyguards to her instead of further involving the police. Paris relented after he reminded her of a case three years ago where a regular at a nearby club killed one of the strippers.

Cruz was getting on her last nerve. He actually thought he was entitled to a piece, just because he'd volunteered to be her personal bodyguard. *Just like a man, always thinking with his little head, no matter that his client is scared for her life.* She rolled her eyes in disgust at his hulking frame. The phone rang and Cruz looked over at her.

"You want me to get that?" he asked gruffly.

"I think I can handle it," Paris retorted sarcastically.

"Hello."

"Hello, Paris."

Marcus's voice was like a warm whisper settling around her body.

"Hey, Marcus," she said nervously.

She smirked at Cruz's nosy glance and replaced her antique phone with the cordless.

"Is everything thing alright?" he questioned.

"Yeah, I just needed to change phones. I'm on my way upstairs."

Once upstairs, she closed her bedroom door softly and sat down on the bed. "Sooo, what are you doing?"

"Honestly?" Marcus asked.

Paris could hear him returning her smile through his silky voice. She closed her eyes and pictured his dimple peeking through his left cheek. "Of course, aren't friends always honest with each other?"

Marcus chuckled. "You have a point. Well, friend, since you put it that way. Honestly, I can't stop thinking about this beautiful girl I recently had the pleasure of meeting. I told myself it was stupid to sit here daydreaming when I could just call her up and hear her voice."

Paris swallowed at his admittance. She started to speak but couldn't think of anything to say. If she were going to be honest, she would tell him that she thought about him a lot also. But then, if she was going to start being honest, there was much more she would have to tell him, and she just couldn't bring herself to tell him the truth.

"So, friend, do you have any advice?" Marcus persisted.

Unable to find the appropriate words, Paris remained silent.

"Paris, are you there?"

"Yes I'm here," she answered softly.

"Am I putting you on the spot?"

"Kind of," she admitted.

"I apologize. So what were you doing?"

"Nothing really," she said, "just watching TV."

Her thoughts raced to Cruz camping out on her sofa downstairs. *You can't even be honest with him about what you're doing at home. What would he think if he knew you had a bodyguard from a strip club downstairs on your couch right now?* Her internal thoughts mocked her.

"Have you eaten dinner?" he asked.

"No, I mean yes. Well, I mean I don't have much of an appetite," she stammered. Marcus was quiet. *He knows you don't want to see him you dummy*, a small voice inside her prompted. She wanted to relent, but she just couldn't let him see her vulnerability.

"Well, pretty lady, I think I am going to let you go, alright?"

"Okay," she agreed feebly.

"Paris?"

"Yes?"

"Whenever you're ready to talk, I'll be here. I just want you to know that."

Paris nodded. "I know."

"Goodnight, Paris."

She heard the receiver click in her ear before she was able to return his goodnight. She laid the receiver down next to her right thigh and stared at it. Her eyes began stinging and she shut them hard. *Get a grip,*

*Paris. You are really trippin', sitting up here crying over some guy you could never be with. You would have to tell him who you really are in order to be with him. If he knew you were a stripper, he'd be ashamed to be seen with you. Can you imagine how he'd feel if he knew he took a stripper to church with him?* Her conscious gave her a heart-wrenching dose of reality, far too bitter to swallow. She angrily swiped a runaway tear. *I should never have given him my new number. I'm just prolonging the inevitable,* she told herself sadly.

"No more phone calls. No more lunches, no dinners, none of that shit," she said to her reflection in her bedroom mirror.

Paris gave a superficial wave, complete with phony grin to her nosy neighbor Mrs. Hofer, then unlocked her door and disappeared inside her condo. Dropping her duffel bag and purse as soon as she stepped in the door, she locked all three locks and then peeked through her sheer curtains. She couldn't shake the feeling that someone was following her. It'd been three weeks since Cruz had left, and Kenton had told her that he was certain the psycho was long gone.

She got to the club ten minutes before she was due on center stage, but ten minutes was all she needed. Preparation was methodical, and she could do it in her sleep. Lots of mascara, dramatic eyeliner and there was no such thing as too much lipstick.

Onstage, Paris rolled her hips in a slow figure eight, licking her lips seductively.

"That's it baby girl," an old man in a red Kangol remarked snidely.

Paris let her eyes find the lights on the ceiling and continued dancing. She was trying her best to ignore the comments thrown at her, but her usual defenses had been shaken. Try as she might she couldn't gain her composure. She promised herself if she could just get through this evening, she would go visit Analise and do some serious soul searching. Battling her fear of the stalker, the guilt from hiding the truth from her mother and Marcus, the painful memories of her father's rejection, and the self-loathing that came along with her chosen profession wore heavily on Paris. Still staring into the lights, she longed for a better way, was afraid to pray for a better life. She knew the God her devout mother prayed to would never honor her prayers, not after all the things she'd done.

She decided not to take any offers for lap dances that evening. She couldn't look any of her customers in the eyes. If she did, she couldn't help wondering if this was the psycho that had turned her life upside down. The music changed to a slight upbeat track by Montell Jordan.

"Hey, Caramel, baby, you looking good tonight," a familiar voice leered.

She let her eyes roam "pervert row" until she placed the voice.

"Hey, Leroy." Relieved to hear a safe and familiar voice, Paris smiled. There was no way Leroy could be her stalker. He was sixty if he was a day.

"You know you lookin' too good in them pink panties, sweet thang," he said, licking his lips. "How 'bout a dance?"

"Not tonight, Leroy, I'm gonna chill tonight." She looked over the floor lights at him.

"Oh it's not for me. My great-nephew is in town with me for the night. I told him I had to introduce you to him. I told him you was the finest thing in here."

Paris smiled down at Leroy, but kept her eyes on all four corners of the club. "Yeah sure I'll meet him," Paris said, accepting the twenty-dollar bill Leroy was holding out to her.

She couldn't see the back of the club because of the red lights streaming down on the dance floor.

"Alright, fellas, get your seat and grab your dollas', cause it's that time again. It's the time we here at Under the Cherry Moon give all our faithful customers a little treat. That's right; it's time for the gentlemen's sundae. And you know we got your favorite flavas on the menu." The deejay's announcement served as the cue for Paris and Chocolate to begin their girl on girl number.

Raucous barks and chants erupted from the audience.

"You know who I'm talking about…Yeah baby, it's sexual chocolate and some of that smooth hot caramel. Aww yeah, it's on." The DJ's voice incited excitement over the booming bass line.

Paris looked over at Chocolate who was walking toward her with two bottles of whipped cream.

"Ooooh wee baby you got here just in time," Leroy said. "Caramel let me introduce you to my nephew real quick before you get bizzy. Come on boy, we just gonna get a quick look or so then be on our way. Uh huh look at that. I bet you never seen anything as fine as that in all your sheltered life." Leroy's voice was giddy with the excitement of watching his two favorite dancers perform every red-blooded man in America's fantasy.

"Unc, you'll never change. Now you know you're too old to be in here." Caramel felt her heart constrict when she heard the voice. She turned unbelievably toward Leroy.

"Caramel, I'd like you to meet my nephew, Marcus Rogers."

She felt sick, but she couldn't move. A fleeting image of shock then pain passed over Marcus's handsome features, then his eyes moved disdainfully from her teased hair to her exposed breasts and pink g-string.

"Ain't she the finest thing you ever seen?" Leroy nudged Marcus in his knit black polo.

"Naw, Unc, she's not my type," Marcus spat nastily.

Paris felt her knees weaken, then Chocolate was behind her tapping he shoulder.

"Come on girl, we got to get this show started. The sooner we start the sooner we'll be done," she whispered while caressing Paris's hair away from her face in an effort to stall.

"I can't do it," Paris rasped.

"What do you mean you can't do it? Girl, please don't have Kenton clown us in front of all these people."

She turned horror-stricken eyes on Chocolate but was unable to focus. "I can't," she whispered, her fingers gripping Chocolate's firm upper arms.

"Come on with the show!" an impatient customer bellowed.

"What the fuck is wrong with you? You turning pale," Chocolate asked hurriedly, letting her hands trail down to Paris's thigh.

Paris tried to tell her that the biggest lie she'd told in her entire life had just blown up in her face, but couldn't. She wanted to scream out in pain, but she couldn't. She wanted to run over to Marcus and erase this image of her out of his memory forever, but couldn't. All she could see was the raw disgust in Marcus eyes, and the pain felt like a hot knife slicing through her soul. She couldn't let him see her degrade herself anymore. Flashes of what she was preparing to do in the show panned before her eyes, and she felt the urge to throw up. There was no way she could do those things in front of Marcus.

There was no going back now. Marcus wouldn't even look at her. She had never felt so dirty in her life. She wondered how his refusal to look at her made her feel lower than the lewd comments men made to her while she gyrated over their laps over the past six years. Marcus was the first man to treat her with respect, and she was experiencing a new type of shame. One she didn't think she'd get over. She swallowed the sour bile that attempted to rise.

Chocolate grabbed her and shook her. "Snap out of it."

"I—I," she stammered.

"What happened to the music?" Chocolate asked, looking out to the deejays booth.

Chocolate and Paris had been oblivious to the murmuring getting louder and louder until the deejay completely shut off the music. All of a sudden, Paris was aware of the eerie silence captivating the club and her head whipped back toward the crowd.

"I'm gonna get that slut bitch!" an angry voice yelled.

"Paris, get down!" Chocolate screamed.

Paris felt Chocolate's body push her body to the ground. Then a jagged brick landed with a piercing thud next to Paris's leg. She screamed as Chocolate's tears began assaulting her neck, and they huddled together on the mirrored dance floor. Cruz's body blocked them from seeing the crowd, but she could hear Kenton yelling and another voice screaming her name and saying he was going to make her pay. Fear-stricken, concerned and angry male voices bounced loudly around her ears, causing her and Chocolate to clutch each other tighter. Her subconscious mocked her, making her think she heard Marcus call her name in a panic. She crammed her hands over her ears and shut her eyes. Within ten minutes, the entire club was empty and dark, mirroring her soul.

# *PART II*

Paris rushed out of the indigo-colored building. Eyes quickly adjusting to the dark of night, she checked her peripheral vision to ensure no one followed. Steps away from the deserted parking lot, she paused to squint up at the scripted sign. It blazed "Under the Cherry Moon" in red neon lights. She'd spent the last three years of her life here, but tonight had been her last shift. She fingered the cold metal in her soft leather purse then pushed teased hair out of her face. Tonight she would get answers to the haunting questions that plagued her all of her life.

Black t-strap heels three inches high made click-clack noises on the hard pavement as she made her way to her black Porsche Boxster with the vanity plate *CARAMEL*. She'd gotten the plate after her boss had taken one look at her and exclaimed, "Add butterscotch to chocolate and you get caramel." Paris smirked at the memory of his unexpected and unnecessary comment, then focused on more imminent matters.

Pressing the black button on her key ring, her Porsche bleeped, the headlights flashing in response. Paris input the personal code then paused as the door unlocked itself. She had a long drive ahead of her, so she hastily secured her safety belt and spared a quick glance to check the location of her mirrors. She'd stopped at the gas station earlier where she'd filled the tank, gotten a routine oil change, had the engine flushed and had her tires rotated. Pleased her car had received a clean bill of health; Paris knew there wouldn't be any interruptions in her journey. Paris slid the key in the ignition and smiled as the powerful engine trembled underneath her fingertips, resting on the steering wheel.

Every time Paris sat behind the wheel of this car, she appreciated it all over again. The power was intoxicating as it flowed from the engine. She felt empowered; driving at top speed always provided an immediate heady rush. Backing out of the parking lot, she checked her make-up in the rearview mirror, eased the car into the street then gunned the engine, taking off for the nearest exit. Paris was off to see her father.

# *CHAPTER TWENTY-TWO CONFRONTING THE PAST*

Paris's eyes shot incensed daggers at the overweight butterscotch colored man sitting in front of her. He looked pitiful, but offered no excuse. She had driven overnight, only stopping to fill her car twice. Once she reached Mississippi, it was as if she was reliving her visit there some thirteen years ago. She remembered every street corner and stop light as if it were yesterday as she drove to her father's house. Summers ago while visiting their grandmother, Paris, Ivan and Sharpe looked on with eager eyes as their grandmother pointed out the house where her father lived. The three children walked the twelve blocks several times over the course of their vacation, hoping to catch a glimpse of their father. Hoping to find something that would explain why he was too busy to spend any time with them.

He sat in a plain wooden chair pushed haphazardly against a matching table. Paris had taken him by surprise when she shoved her gun against his chest as soon as he opened the front door. She had instructed him to sit and not to move as she flicked on the light switch closest to the kitchen. The light flashed brightly before one of the bulbs shorted out and left father and daughter regarding each other for the first time in years through a dim yellow light.

"Everything started with you," Paris said softly. "Why I'm so fucked up. Why I can't be anything but tits and ass. Why I never fit in with everybody else," she finished, angrily wiping defiant tears.

Her mind flashed painful memories of a ten-year-old little girl being taunted by classmates because of her second hand clothes. A twelve-year-old sitting on a makeshift bed, clutching a tattered teddy bear, wondering what was so wrong with her that her father wouldn't want her. She blinked hard then aimed the pistol closer to his chest.

"I just couldn't figure out what was so wrong with me, Sharp and Ivan. It wasn't that you didn't want to marry Momma. Lot's of parents don't marry. Then they come around on their birthdays or on Christmas, or when they start feeling guilty," Paris rambled on, sniffling.

She pushed the gun at him again, angry that he wouldn't speak up. She wanted him to cry out for her to stop. She wanted him to tell her that she had it all wrong, that he'd loved her the entire time and had tried to be a part of her life. Even if she would've known he was lying, still she expected him to say something. What type of man just sat there, accepting that his daughter was threatening his life?

"I just can't understand how you have a child. Three, three children then just decide they don't exist anymore. Do you have any idea how we struggled?" she demanded, her voice cracking. Her eyes bounced wildly around the room then settled on her father's insolent face.

"No, there's no way you could know, because she moved us so far away from you. Well, I can tell you since you weren't there. I'll give you a recap. We went without food more times than I can remember. Without anything from you, Momma's checks weren't enough. Being hungry wasn't that bad for me. After a while I got used to it, but I had to explain to my brothers why we didn't have nothing," Paris's voice trembled as she remembered the burden she felt at being the eldest of three.

"How in the hell was I supposed to explain to them why you didn't want us? And I never even told them what Momma told me about the money you offered to get rid of me. I wonder how much your sons would have been worth. Cause it would've had to be more than just $1,000, cause a son is worth much more to a man right?"

Richard's silence was driving Paris insane. His face didn't betray any telltale signs of remorse or guilt. The lack of emotion reflected in his eyes mocked her as she recognized its familiarity, before pushing it out of her head.

Trying to gain focus of the pearl handled pistol held in her trembling ruby-tipped fingers, Paris's eyes stung with salty tears as she blinked rapidly. She cocked the gun, then turned her face, attempting yet again to make eye contact with her father.

"What was wrong with me?" she asked tearfully.

He raised sad, almond shaped eyes that mirrored her own, and she gulped harshly at the uncanny resemblance.

"What is wrong with me?" she repeated in a small voice.

He shook his head slowly. "There's nothing wrong with you, baby. It's me. It was always me," his melancholy voice lacked concern.

He seemed unmoved by her questions and her threats. Again, Paris closed her eyes against painful memories, this time they were of days as Caramel rather than an elementary aged Paris. How many men had shoved dollars down her panties to get her to perform for them, reinforcing her need for validation? Paris cocked her pistol nervously, rubbing the pearl handle. She wanted to kill him, kill the memories, which had to kill the pain.

"If there is something wrong with you there's something wrong with me," she stammered incoherently. "Whether you like it or not, I'm a part of you."

Paris narrowed her eyes at him. "You know, a thousand dollars is not a lot of money. But you know what? I make that in one night sometimes now, so I guess I proved you wrong."

Richard's non-expressive eyes didn't tell her if he remembered the deal he worked out to rid himself of his daughter or not. Not getting the response she wanted, Paris rambled on.

"I started out just trying to get someone who looked like you to say I was beautiful or I mattered. I thought if I found a customer that looked like you who liked me, it would mean maybe you would too if you saw what you left. I wanted to be a daughter you could be proud of, but soon they all looked like you. They all looked like you, and they were doing the same damn thing you did when you left Momma."

Richard leaned forward as if to decipher her mumbled rant, but quickly retreated when she pointed the gun at his head.

"I am proud of you, Paris. Deanne obviously did a much better job than I ever could have done."

"Shut up! Just shut up. I don't want to hear that. She couldn't have done a better job than she would have with a little help from you. Besides, how good of a job could she have possibly done? Did you hear what I said? I'm a fucking stripper. Every night I take off my clothes so some asshole can get his rocks off. Isn't that what all daddies want for their little girls?" she taunted bitterly

Paris repositioned the gun with one hand at her father to show him she meant what she said. The other hand she forced over her right ear to block out his pathetic voice.

"I hate what I am, a cheap-ass stripper. I can't even deal with a man on another level. Trust, you can forget that shit. It ain't happening. And it's all because of you."

Paris relived the moment Marcus's eyes met her. The guilt and shame she had for herself turned repeatedly in the pit of her stomach. She wanted the pain to stop, but screaming accusations at her father hadn't given her the relief she was seeking. She shook the gun at him again, causing him to shrink back against the chair. He was too much of a coward to even admit what he'd done and answer her questions. Paris ransacked her brain for plan B, but, again, she had forgotten to formulate a back-up plan. She'd come here for answers, and he couldn't or wouldn't give her anything. Should she kill him and go back home now? What was there to go back home to? She couldn't face going back to club. She was tired of being humiliated night after night. For some reason, after Marcus had seen her performing, she couldn't imagine herself dancing there again. In a burst of energy, she turned the gun and aimed it at her own temple. Richard lifted somber eyes to her.

"All I ever wanted was for you to love me. I wanted to be Daddy's little girl so bad. Do you know how many men I stripped for searching for your approval?" she asked in a small voice.

Richard reached out to her.

"Don't touch me!" she shrieked, pushing him back down against the wooden seat. "I wasn't worth your love then, and I'm not worth anyone else's love now. Not after all I've done."

Paris's eyes moved suspiciously over his features. She hadn't realized they were so much like her own. Everything began making sense. She knew what she had to do. She took one last look at her father and squeezed the trigger. She heard Richard scream, two ear-splitting pops, and then she was plunged into darkness.

Paris felt white lights surrounding her. The white heat radiated beneath her tightly shut eyelids. It felt as if her eyes were being pried open. She slowly opened one eye and saw Marcus's face above her.

"Marcus?" she asked faintly.

When she opened her jaws, a blinding pain shot through her head, causing her to gasp. She looked around and realized she was in a hectic hospital room that appeared to be spinning out of control. There were beeps, clicks, blaring lights and neon dashes everywhere. She gave up trying to make sense of her surroundings and focused on the face standing above her.

"Paris," he said softly, shaking his head, his brown eyes full of pity as he gazed down at her. "Calm down. It's okay. You're at the hospital."

"She's awake?" an anxious voice asked.

Marcus's eyes briefly left hers, and he quietly answered a pestering voice. She couldn't make out the question or the voice. Nor did she understand his hurried response.

"Marcus what happened?" she whispered.

Marcus shook his head sadly. "Damn, Paris," he said solemnly. Those were the last words she heard before darkness engulfed her again.

"She's not conscious, so I don't understand why you all are here."

"Mr. Rogers, I understand your concern for Ms. Jackson, but she is the only suspect in an attempted murder case and that is about as serious as it gets," a stern female voice explained.

"I understand that, Ms. Loren, but right now the doctors aren't certain that Miss Jackson will live another twenty-four hours, so your case is going to be put on hold. At least until we determine if she will live to explain what happened," Marcus retorted. A heavy door jerked opened and then closed with a soft thud.

"Mr. Rogers." Deanne's voice rushed into the room and surrounded Paris, reminding her of safer times.

"Please call me Marcus."

"How's my baby? Is she going to be okay? I heard there may be a bullet…" Deanne rushed on, oblivious to anyone around her.

"Ms. Jackson, Paris is stable for now. The bullet entered and exited at the very back of her head, so she doesn't need surgery. Right now, we're just waiting for her to wake up. There's a good chance Paris will be just fine." Marcus spoke in a calm voice, taking time to pause between the most important information to allow Deanne to ingest what he was saying.

Deanne's breathing was muffled with tears, but Marcus's briefing helped to settle her somewhat.

"Marcus, I can't thank you enough for being here. I am in total shock. I've heard so many things, horrible things about my Paris," Deanne's voice trailed off.

"Don't worry about that now. The important thing is, Paris is going to be fine. The doctors have been doing a good job. I've been checking in with them every thirty minutes or so, probably getting on their nerves," Marcus explained. "They're doing the best they can for your daughter."

"Do you know if she was really stripping? I mean Paris couldn't be dancing at some nightclub. I just can't believe my baby would do something like that. I talk to her at least two or three times a month," Deanne pressed on anxiously.

"Ms. Jackson, I just found that out myself a few nights ago. I don't know what to tell you about all of that. You'll have to wait and talk to Paris."

"I can't believe it. I don't think her brothers knew either. I just can't believe it. My baby, oh my baby Paris. I wonder if Richard knew. If that has something to do with why she was here, why she did this. I can't believe my baby tried to kill herself." Deanne's voice became increasingly frantic again.

"Herself and her father. I didn't even know she was in contact with him. Maybe he did something to her to make her come here and do this," Deanne rambled on, kneading her hands nervously in her lap.

Marcus's voice moved closer to Paris's bedside, and she knew he was attempting to comfort her mother.

"Ms. Jackson, please. Don't think about all of that right now. Right now we just need to make sure Paris is going to be all right. Once we know that she's safe, then she can answer your questions."

"Are you her boyfriend? I mean, how do you know Paris?"

"No, no I'm not her boyfriend. I thought...well, it doesn't matter what I thought. I'm her friend, Ms. Jackson. I'm Paris's friend. My number was the only one the hospital could find in Paris's belongings, so they called me."

"I can't thank you enough for coming as quickly as you did. Obviously you're a good friend, a very good friend," Deanne said solemnly.

Deanne's hands softly began caressing Paris's left hand, which was lying motionless on the bed.

"I just can't believe this. If only I'd known. I should've come to visit her regardless of the excuses she gave."

"Ms. Jackson, you can't blame yourself for this. Let's just wait until Paris wakes up before you start jumping to conclusions."

"She looks just like she did when she was a baby. She was such a beautiful little girl. When she was little I used to worry that she didn't have any idea how special she was, how beautiful she was," Deanne spoke softly, continuing to rub her daughter's hand.

"When she got older," Deanne paused. "It's funny, because when she got older I used to worry that she didn't know she was so much more than just beautiful."

Deanne began humming softly. The familiarity of her mother's humming quickly lulled Paris back into a deep unconscious sleep.

Paris's mouth felt dry and pasty as she pushed her tongue around inside her cheek. Snippets of conversations going on about her raced behind her tightly shut eyelids. The burden of opening her eyes was overbearing. There was something out there in the light. A sense of foreboding that sent chills down her spine. The incessant beep of the monitor and IV next to her hospital bed pulled her closer and closer toward consciousness. She fought until it was inevitable, and her eyelids fluttered then slowly opened. Her pupils struggled to focus on the figure sitting at the edge of her bed. Deanne's shoulders were slumped and her hair unusually unkempt, but Paris recognized her mother's forlorn shape. Deanne turned slowly and their eyes met.

"Oh my, Paris, my sweet baby girl," Deanne cried. She stood up and moved closer to sit near Paris on the bed. She caressed her face lovingly.

"You're awake. That means you're going to be okay," she smiled through her tears. Paris looked into her mother's face and felt tears teasing the corners of her eyes then slowly make their way down her cheek.

"Oh, baby, don't cry. Everything's okay, Paris." Deanne's voice cracked as she continued to caress Paris's face.

"Is Daddy?" Paris whispered hoarsely.

Deanne took her hand. "No, baby. Richard is fine. He's going home today in fact." She paused. "I can't believe I didn't know so much was going on with you. I should've known something was wrong; you were so secretive. You've been hurting for so long and we, I guess no one knew." Deanne's voice ended in a painful sob.

Paris weakly attempted to squeeze her mother's hand. "It' not your fault," she said, wincing.

"Oh baby, I'm sorry I shouldn't do this to you now. I can tell you're in a lot pain. You need your rest. Get some sleep, baby. I can't wait to tell your brothers you're awake. They went down to the…well, they went to take care of some business, but they'll be back. And your friend Marcus is here, too. He went with Sharp and Ivan."

"Marcus is still here?" Paris asked.

Deanne nodded happily. "He's been like a guardian angel. He's special, Paris. I just have a feeling about him."

Paris nodded limply then fell back into a dreamless sleep.

# CHAPTER TWENTY-THREE
# BACK TO THE BASICS

Two days later, Paris woke up to the doctor talking quietly to Deanne. When they noticed she was awake, they both turned their attention to her.

"You were very lucky, Ms. Jackson. The bullet you fired at your father struck him in the arm. He's fine except for a contact wound on his upper arm. When you aimed at yourself, the gun must've jerked and the bullet ended up going in the back of your head and exiting half an inch from your spinal column. You're lucky to be alive and even luckier not to be a paraplegic. Considering the circumstances, I think you're about the luckiest patient I've had."

"It has nothing to do with luck, doctor. As many nights as I've spent on my knees praying for my daughter, she has to have at least a dozen guardian angels," Deanne said, rubbing her daughter's hand. The doctor nodded nonchalantly and motioned for Paris to sit up.

"She needs to make sure to keep this wound clean and keep the rest of her hair off this area. As you can see, we had to shave a patch of her hair here about three inches wide and two inches high. When the wound heals, I'm sure her hair will cover it," the doctor addressed Deanne as if Paris were six instead of twenty-six.

"I'm giving you some fresh gauze and bandages. She needs to keep the wound wrapped for at least two weeks so it will heal properly. After that, you'll need to return after six months to make sure there is no long-term damage we can't foresee right now. The thing I'm most concerned about is the scar tissue putting pressure on the base of her brain and causing her to have migraines."

"Do you understand what he's saying Paris?" Deanne asked, rubbing Paris's hand calmly.

"Yeah Momma, I heard him," Paris answered.

The doctor's conversation with her mother floated around Paris like a pestering cloud. She knew she should feel grateful to be alive, but she didn't feel anything except a dull ache at the base of her head. The click from the hospital door being opened resounded loudly against Paris's temples. She smiled, in spite of her headache when she saw Ivan enter the room with a bottle of juice and a magazine.

"How do you feel now, sis?" Ivan asked.

"My head hurts," Paris mumbled.

The doctor stood up and closed the chart he'd been writing on. "You're nurse will be in shortly with your pain killers."

Paris watched him walk out of the room, then braced herself for more questions from her family. Sharp and Marcus took the doctor's exit as an invitation to enter the room. Deanne sat silently by the side of her bed.

"We need to figure out what we're going to do about the police. They want to talk to Paris, and I don't think that's a good idea right now," Sharp said sternly.

"Are they going to put me in jail?" Paris asked bluntly.

"They want to try your ass for attempted murder," Sharp snapped.

Paris glowered at him. She knew Sharp's sharp tongue was his only defense against the emotions going through him, but she didn't feel like hearing his sarcasm.

"They want to ask you some questions about what happened," Ivan, as usual, attempted to cover for Sharp's insensitivity.

"Do you all have a lawyer?" Marcus spoke up from a corner in the small room.

Sharp turned quickly on him. "Why would we have a lawyer? It's not like we had any idea our sister was going to be on trial for attempted murder. We didn't even know what happened. We get a call that our sister and our father are in the hospital in Mississippi, out of the blue. It wasn't until we got here that we realized what happened," Sharp snarled.

"She's not on trial for attempted murder. Right now she's not on trial at all," Ivan corrected.

"So I guess all the cops sniffing around here are just looking to get a statement and move on." Sharp laughed.

"Sharp will you stop?" Deanne pleaded. "Ivan's right. Paris is not on trial. Marcus you have the right idea. We should talk to a lawyer."

Paris listened without attempting to enter the conversation. She had never considered the possibility that she would go to prison. She'd left Louisiana in a daze. She didn't even really remember what had happened during the confrontation with her father. *Did I really want to kill my father? Did I really mean to kill myself? What is going on with me?* Desperately trying to summons a sense of composure, she closed her eyes, but nothing worked. The voices in her head clashed with those in the room. Her life had spun out of control, and there was nothing she could do about it.

"I know a lawyer that would give you all a consultation at no charge, just so we would know what we are up against. Maybe you all should talk to him before you let the police talk to Paris," Marcus offered.

"Who's the lawyer?" Sharp questioned.

"Paul is a family friend. If you'd like, you can come back to my hotel room and we can call him from there. I've got his number in my palm pilot back at the hotel."

Deanne moved from Paris's bedside and went over to stand directly in front of Marcus.

"That sounds like a wonderful idea. Marcus, I can't begin to thank you," she said, pulling him into her arms for a hug.

"It's okay, Ms. Jackson. I'm happy to help." He returned her embrace. "We can go now, if that's cool with you." Marcus motioned toward Sharp.

"I think I'll go with you, too," Ivan said. "Get some rest."

Paris smiled at Ivan as he bent down to kiss her on the cheek.

"Keep your ass in this bed and don't talk to anyone except Mom until we get back," Sharp demanded.

Paris rolled her eyes at him, but she wasn't fooled. She could read concern in his eyes as he tapped her lightly on the foot. Marcus, on the other hand, was a complete mystery. He didn't glance her way once while he spoke to her mother and brothers, and he left without so much as a backwards glance.

Marcus's family lawyer Mr. Paul Robinson agreed to take over as Paris's legal counsel and spoke with the police on her behalf. He suggested Paris begin seeing a psychiatrist in an effort to show she was making steps on her own toward becoming healthy and mentally stable. He told the family Paris should plead guilty to a lesser charge if he could get her probation as opposed to serving actual jail time. Mr. Robinson did advise the family that Richard could take Paris to civil court and probably win if he so desired. At Marcus and Deanne's insistence, Paris agreed to start therapy if it would help her case.

Paris asked that her family and Marcus be allowed to stay with her during her second session. While her first session had been very short and non-invasive, with most of the questions surrounding her health and the magnitude of what she'd done, she knew she would be asked some hard questions the second go round. She wanted to do something to alleviate the disappointment in her mother and brother's eyes. A small part of her acknowledged she wanted Marcus to understand also. The psychiatrist suggested Paris was reliving the rejection suffered from her father repeatedly every night as an exotic dancer. She explained that Paris projected her feelings of rejection by her father onto the men at the club.

"Why do you think you didn't reach out to your father before now?" the psychiatrist asked her pointedly.

Paris closed her eyes and tried to summon an answer from her soul, but failed. The last visual memory she had of her father was Richard driving off after dropping her Sharp and Ivan with their grandmother. After they'd returned home to Deanne and they learned of his girlfriend's impending pregnancy, Paris couldn't recall a single conscious thought of her father. She remembered brief mental comparisons of the money her father put up to relinquish his parental rights to her, but that was only while she was on the clock. She used that as a motivator. It kept her going in an environment where others used drugs and alcohol as their driving force—a place where she'd be surrounded with men that reminded her of the first man who put a dollar amount on her, her father.

"I never thought about my father. I'm not even sure why I thought to go after him that night. I can't even remember deciding to do that.

I don't even remember getting in my car to be honest," Paris answered honestly.

"You knew where to find him though. That's very odd, considering all the years that have passed since you saw him last," the psychiatrist pressed further.

"It was like my mind was following a map. I could see the route to his home like it was yesterday," Paris whispered.

"So what are you saying? Are you trying to say Paris had temporary insanity or something?" Marcus asked sarcastically.

"Not quite. It looks at if she had a breakdown. It will take further evaluation before I can make any conclusions," the psychiatrist replied patiently.

"I understand all that you're saying doctor, but... Well I guess to me this just doesn't make any sense." Marcus rubbed his hands over his curly black hair in frustration. Paris looked between him and the psychologist, then returned her gaze to Marcus.

"Well, Mr. Rogers, I understand this is an extreme situation, so perhaps we should move more slowly," Linda Clark said, standing up and patting Paris's hand. "I'll be back tomorrow, try to get some rest."

"Thank you," Paris said, attempting to smile at Linda before the door clicked behind her.

After the psychiatrist left, Paris's brothers convinced Deanne to go back to the hotel and rest. Ivan took Deanne to the hotel and said he was going to stick around for a while to make sure she rested. Sharp went to make some phone calls and get a break from the hospital. This was the first time Paris had been alone with Marcus since her first night in the hospital. She shifted uncomfortably in the bed and glanced cautiously over at him.

"Paris, don't even let that psychobabble get in your head. There's no excuse for what you did," he said firmly.

Paris's eyes traced the pattern on her white blanket solemnly. "You just don't understand," she interjected softly.

"Paris, do you know how many little girls grow up without their fathers? How many of them do you think go back to find their dad and try to kill them?"

"I didn't want to kill him," Paris muttered dismally.

"Paris, you shot your father. Stop making excuses. You keep making excuses for everything in your life. If you keep doing that, you are never going to get better."

Paris felt fat teardrops slide down her face onto her blue pajama top.

"Okay so your father messed up. Most people come from less than desirable backgrounds, but that doesn't make him responsible for you stripping for the last five years. And it doesn't excuse what you did. You almost killed him and yourself."

Paris's bottom lip trembled uncontrollably. Marcus looked at her, patted her on her head then picked up his jacket.

"How would you know, Marcus? You have no idea where I come from, or what my life was like before I met you. You couldn't possibly understand," Paris objected tearfully. "I mean, you have no idea what it feels like as a child to be rejected by a parent. I've heard you talk about your parents. Believe me, you couldn't possibly understand unless you've been there. I grew up knowing that my father didn't want me. I had to push it out of my mind in order to survive, and I did. Survive I mean," Paris finished, stuttering.

Marcus's eyes softened at her admission, and he patted her lightly.

"I guess I can't say I really understand, Paris. But you don't have to let that haunt you for the rest of your life. You shouldn't be talking about this now. Get some sleep," he said then turned to leave.

"Are you coming back?"

"I don't know. I didn't expect to be here this long. I'm sure you're going to be all right, so I guess I need to be looking at getting a flight back tomorrow or the next day. I'll call before I leave."

"Marcus I'm sorry about…"

He turned eyes on her that had lost their warmth, silencing her apology. "I should go," he said and quickly shut the door behind him.

The next morning, Paris was feeling more like herself. She gave a weak smile to the jolly nurse who entered her room to check on her, and was taken aback by the solemn expression on the woman's usual jovial face. "Your father would like to speak with you." The brown-skinned nurse held a beige phone receiver in front of Paris's face.

"We should give her some privacy," Ivan said, motioning for everyone to leave the room.

"Are you okay to talk to him?" Deanne asked, immediately becoming protective. Paris smiled and nodded at her mother. For as long as Paris could remember, Deanne had tried to act as a buffer, protecting her children from Richard's rejection. It hadn't worked then, and it sure wouldn't work now. This was something she had to own up to on her own.

"I'll be fine Momma," Paris assured her. She smiled at Ivan and Sharp, attempting to reassure them as well.

Her brothers left, then Deanne, the nurse, Mr. Robinson and finally the policewoman that had been working Paris's last nerve, followed.

Paris took a deep breath, then put the phone to her head, but quickly removed it before saying hello. She closed her eyes, gathered all her courage then placed the phone to her ear.

"Paris?" Richard asked hesitantly.

"Yes," Paris answered meekly.

"How are you doing?"

"I'm fine," she mumbled. She was still having a hard time admitting to herself that she had almost killed her father and herself. She was waiting for him to scream hate-filled curses at her. Her actions had surely justified his pre-conceived notion to disown her as his child.

"Paris, I don't know where to start. First, you need to know that I am not going to press charges against you, but the district attorney said something like he didn't need my permission. I don't know." He paused. "I guess after all you've been through, you needed someone to take everything out on. I guess I deserve it," he said slowly.

Paris gathered every bit of physical strength she had and sat up in the bed. She awkwardly held the phone to her ear. Regardless of everything that happened, a part of her couldn't help cherishing the fact that her father had actually called her. His voice was both strange and comforting at the same time to her ears.

"I talked to your doctor earlier this morning, and he told me you're going to be just fine."

"You're okay?" Paris asked in a small voice.

"I'm fine, Paris. I won't lie and say I wasn't damn relieved when I realized that bullet hadn't hit me anywhere but my arm," he joked. "For a minute I thought all the bad things I ever done had caught up to me, and I was about to be taken out of this world. By my own daughter no less."

Paris swallowed the lump in her throat but didn't respond to his comment.

"Now I want to say something to you, and then I'm never going to speak about what happened that night again. Paris, are you listening?"

"Yes, I'm here." She moved the phone even closer to her ear, clutching it until her knuckles were aching and nearly white.

"I am an old man, and I've done a lot of things in my past that I am not proud of. The main one being the way I treated my children. There's nothing I can do about that now. The three of you are grown, and the other child I had...well, her mother gave up and moved away years ago. I have no idea where they are. There are some wrongs you commit toward others that you can recover from, and some you can't. The wrongs I've done, I don't see a way to recover from, even if I had the strength to try. Now you on the other hand...Paris, you're not even thirty years old. You can take all the wrongs you've done because of growing up like you did and you can make all that right. Youth is one of the greatest gifts. The thing is if you don't take advantage of it, it'll be snatched away before you know it."

Hanging on to her father's every word, Paris didn't dare breathe too deeply. She realized her grip was so tight on the phone that her fingernails were cutting into her hand, but she didn't want to risk not hearing one word, so she remained frozen.

"You still there?" Richard asked.

"Yes, I'm here."

"I heard some of the things you've been doing, and there's no reason for you to be living like you are. Don't let an old fool like me ruin your chance at happiness. I'm not saying you shouldn't hate me or be angry with me, because you're right in the way you feel, but don't let those feelings claim your life and you end up being a disappointment to your mother like I was."

Silence crept onto the phone and captured the line for an awkward minute.

"Will I ever see you again?" Paris asked.

"I can't imagine why you'd want to. I wasn't good at being a father when you were born, and, honestly, I doubt I'd be much better now. I'm gonna leave that ball in your court. I've always thought I'd do you and your brothers more harm than good. But, Paris, you get your life straight and leave the past in the past. You don't have to relive it if you don't want to. Do you understand what I'm saying?"

"Yes," Paris repeated.

After asking brief formal questions about Sharp and Ivan, Richard wished his daughter a speedy recovery and excused himself from the conversation. Paris waited until she heard the busy signal and the request to hang up the line before she finally removed the receiver from her ear. Even after having the conversation she'd wanted to have for so long with her father, she still felt empty. It was the same emptiness she felt after counting the money she made from dancing after the performance was over. Part of her wished Richard would have apologized, then begged to be a part of her life. She'd desperately yearned for him to show an interest in taking up the mantle of fatherhood, even after all these years.

The actual turn of events was disappointing, but it felt right. Deep down she knew if he'd wanted to be a father, there had been almost twenty-seven years for him to change his mind and own up to the responsibility. Up until the past year, when things began to spin out of control, Paris would have accepted Richard's apology and gladly worked at building a father-daughter relationship. Now, she had to face the reality that it just wasn't meant to be. Richard hadn't given her a father figure, but he had given her some advice that in the end she knew would prove far more beneficial than him reentering her life.

# *CHAPTER TWENTY-FOUR CONSEQUENCES & REPERCUSSIONS*

"They arrested the guy who tried to attack you at the club," Marcus said slowly.

Paris winced, trying to find a comfortable position to hold the receiver away from her wound. "Oh my God, I forgot all about that. Did they say who he was?" She tried to sit up in the bed, but her head throbbed when she moved. She laid her head back on the pillow and closed her eyes.

"His name was Grey Luciano or something like that," he said.

Paris's eyes flew open, and she pushed herself upright despite the pain in her head. Her heart slammed into her chest suddenly.

"Lucette?" She clutched her sheet.

"That sounds right," Marcus said cautiously.

"Oh my God," Paris gasped.

She pulled the covers around herself self-consciously. *How could Grey have done all this to me?* Her mind flashed to the stunt he'd pulled in the Champagne room. She should have known he was capable of something, but she'd never given him enough credit. She remembered the incessant messages on her answering machine, the pleading in his voice that eventually morphed into hatred and mockery. Still, even with his neurotic messages and the stunt he'd pulled at the club, Paris never thought in her wildest dreams Grey would hurt her physically. Her head hurt as memories of her telling Grey tidbits about how the club was laid out backstage flooded her memories. At the time, she justified his questions by assuming he was trying to understand the layout of the club for a possible investment deal he was debating, but now she realized he'd been playing her for a fool the entire time. She'd never been in control of the relationship like she thought. Her memories flashed back to conversations she'd had with him about the stalker when things first began happening. He'd played her for a fool.

"I take it you know this person," Marcus spoke up, breaking the silence.

It suddenly occurred to her that Marcus was awaiting her reply. "Yes." She wished someone else could have told her the news, anyone but Marcus.

"Were you involved with this guy?"

Paris was at a loss. She desperately wanted to be honest with him, but she didn't know how to begin to tell him the truth. She willed herself to try to be honest with him, but he cut her off.

"Don't bother drumming up any more lies, Paris. It's obvious there was a reason this guy was coming after you like that." His voice seemed tired and irritable all over again.

"It's not like that. We were involved, but I called it off and he got angry and started coming to the club a lot. I should've known."

Marcus chuckled dryly. "Wow," he murmured under his breath.

Paris's heavy heartbeat resounded so loudly she was sure he could hear it over the phone line. She was sure she had stopped breathing all together, attempting to feel Marcus's reaction out.

"We weren't involved…" she began a feeble attempt to explain.

"The police picked him up, but he's out on bond. They said the owner of the club is pressing charges, so you don't have to worry about filing a report now. I understand he was the one that came in the club that night."

Marcus reference caused her heartbeat to speed up again. She didn't know what to say to him about that night. It seemed like eons ago. Besides being the night she ended up shooting her father, it was the night Marcus had learned the truth about her. She could feel the humiliation all over again and was thankful he was on the phone instead of sitting across from her, seeing the shame written across her face.

"Do you think he's going to try to come after you again?"

Paris squeezed her eyes against the pain and massaged her temples. "I don't know, Marcus. I wouldn't think so since he's been caught, but then I never thought he would go this far."

"So you two started out as boyfriend and girlfriend then he flipped out?"

"No it wasn't like we were boyfriend and girlfriend. I have never had a boyfriend, Marcus. Grey and I would hang out from time to time. He was okay at first."

"Let me guess, he would do things for you?"

"Yes," Paris admitted solemnly

"What type of things?"

"I don't know. He'd take me out and buy me things ever so often. He paid some of my bills from time to time. I never asked, he always offered," she added quickly.

Marcus didn't speak, and she was relieved that he seemed to be out of questions.

"Marcus I wasn't with him when you and I were—"

Marcus's voice abruptly cut her off. "I've got a lot to do right now. I just wanted to let you know what I heard."

"Thank you, Marcus. I just want you to understand that."

Again, Marcus cut her off before she could begin to explain. "Do you hear yourself?"

Although his tone was calm, Paris could detect anger in his voice.

"He flipped out? You pushed him to flip out. I bet you don't even see how you brought all this on yourself. Paris, I can't even begin to understand what is wrong with you. You're lucky he didn't kill you. You play with other people's feelings and that's a dangerous game. I just hope you learned from this."

Paris couldn't believe he was talking to her like this while she was laying in a hospital bed, recovering from fighting for her life. Maybe he didn't have any feelings for her. How could he say it was her fault that Grey had threatened to kill her?

"My flight leaves to go back to Louisiana in the morning. Tell your mother and brothers I said goodbye."

Paris started to thank him again, but he hung up before she could speak.

# *CHAPTER TWENTY-FIVE*
# *A PAINFUL TRANSITION*

Back in New Orleans, Paris was uncomfortable sitting in the lawyer's office. The walls were a dull shade of slate and everything from the official looking law journals and hard-backed textbooks was cold and uninviting.

Paris looked at the papers sitting before her, then slowly signed beside the spot marked with a red "x."

"Miss Jackson, I hope you understand that by signing this, you are agreeing to attend therapy sessions twice a week for a minimum of nine months, then your therapist will decide if the sessions should be reduced to one a week and for how long. You will also be on probation for three years. You will have a parole officer to check in with. If you leave the state you will need to notify your parole officer and your therapist," Mr. Robinson repeated.

Paris nodded glumly, then relaxed back against her chair.

"If you were to break this agreement, you will be remanded to prison for a period no shorter than five years in the great state of Mississippi. If that happens, you will not have the luxury of a plea bargain. This is a very serious contract." The lawyer looked steadily at Paris from beneath tiny bifocals, then pushed the papers across his desk to her.

"I understand." She nodded.

"Now some words off the record." He took off his glasses, folded them neatly in a case and clasped his hands together. "You have been given a chance to start over. You are very lucky not to be in jail or even dead for that matter. I don't know why you did what you did, and I don't think any of the people around here that care about you do either. The only person that knows that is you, and you're going to have to be the one to fix this thing. Whatever it is that made you drive down here and do what you did is serious, and you need to find its root. You're a beautiful, intelligent young woman. I suggest you start acting like one."

With that said, he picked up his glasses, put them back on and began shuffling through more paperwork. Paris's cheeks burned with shame at Mr. Robinson's blunt advice.

"So are we finished?" Paris asked.

"Yes, Miss Jackson we're finished. I'll ensure you have a copy of all of the paperwork and contact numbers."

Paris nodded and began gathering her coat and purse.

"Thank you, Mr. Robinson. I appreciate you doing this, especially on such short notice and all. I don't know what I would've done if you hadn't stepped in when you did," Paris said truthfully.

"Have a good day, Miss Jackson," he said without glancing in her direction.

Paris wished him the same, then turned to walk out of the office. There were questions she had for herself that she didn't have answers for. She'd never thought herself capable of shooting anyone, let alone her father. She was dreading the upcoming months of therapy, but she had no choice but to stick with it; jail was not an option.

Paris stretched her legs languidly, and glanced over at her mother.

"Sweetheart, you've got to straighten your life out, and you need to start doing it this minute. You can't go back to this lifestyle."

Deanne gestured at the extravagance of Paris's living room. "I just can't believe all this has been going on right under my nose. I would've never known if not for…" Deanne's voice faltered. "I've heard folks say you never really know what your children are capable of, and I finally understand what that means."

Paris winced at her mother's harsh words. "I'm sorry, Momma. I really am. I never wanted you to be hurt. I didn't want you to ever know about this."

Paris didn't bother to wipe the remorseful tear that left a trail down her left cheek. She had never wanted to expose Deanne, or the twins for that matter, to her life. Deanne moved from her seat across the room to sit next to her daughter.

"Paris, it's not so much that you're hurting me. I'm hurt because it tears a mother up to see her child like this." Deanne took a tissue out of her purse, then wiped the tear from Paris's cheek and lightly brushed her hair away from her hairline.

"Paris," she said softly, looking into her daughter's eyes. "You're better than this. I know you know that. You were always so strong as a little girl. I guess I should've been more attentive."

"No, Momma, it's not your fault. Don't blame yourself," Paris interjected quickly. "I've been an adult for a long time now. This was my decision."

Deanne shook her head but didn't release her hold on Paris's face. "You almost died. If you go back to this strip club or any other and keep this reckless behavior up, Paris, you will not make it. You have to know that. Beauty is not always a blessing. Men will use a beautiful woman up until there's nothing left, including her beauty."

"I never wanted to be the person I've become, Momma," Paris said quietly.

"Well you can change that, baby. It's never too late to change," Deanne said.

Paris realized that Marcus was right; much of the situation was her fault. She recalled several instances of Grey becoming more and more possessive with each gift or bill he paid. Now thinking clearly, she realized Grey had been far from weak. It would appear to anyone using their brain that he'd set her up. Paris remembered him asking her nonchalantly in the beginning if she would ever consider leaving the club behind if she met someone willing to take care of her. As they began spending more time together, Grey became insistent and demanding with her time and her future plans. She had never taken Grey's affections seriously. To her he'd been one of the many means to an end, which for her was a comfortable lifestyle. She had enjoyed his company, but she considered him entertainment.

Sex with Grey hadn't been very entertaining, but it had led to a fox fur jacket and after the first time, he'd paid her car note for the next three months straight. The few times thereafter resulted in expensive jewelry and cash gifts that helped supplement her income.

She thought about how angry Harley had been the last time they'd spoken. She remembered him saying pretty soon she would be too old to dance, and then she'd come looking for him. At the time she'd blown him off without a moments thought. Harley was entertainment for her just like Grey. Harley provided her with social status, and he loved buying her things that he could show her off in. She had enjoyed sex with him more than Grey, but she'd never even thought about him in relation to her future. He was a colorful toy that provided her with physical gratification and occasionally made her laugh. It never occurred to her that Harley or Grey may have been thinking they had a chance to win her heart. When they had begun talking about a future and pressuring her for more than a good time, she decided to throw them away, the same way she'd done many others.

*Is it any surprise that Grey objected to being tossed aside like a Christmas toy in February?* Her reflections took her to Dey and how he'd disappeared after finding the woman he wanted to marry. She'd been so caught up in her life, she refused to admit that her feelings were wounded that he'd never considered her more than a cheap arm piece. Guilt flooded through her as her memories went back even further. *Tariq.* Using him for everything he could give her, then moving on to his friend when she saw a better opportunity.

While she had never lied to Harley, Grey or any of the others about her future, she had encouraged them in some way or another to continue to pursue the relationship. Her goal had been to get as much money as she could from as many suitors as she could manage.

She decided she wouldn't press charges against Grey. She was certain Kenton would do everything in his power to get back at Grey for the damage done to the club and for the publicity he'd caused.

Paris hugged her mother as tightly as she could. They relaxed in each other's arms and let the tears that had been waiting since Richard Dennison abandoned his family flow between them.

# *CHAPTER TWENTY-SIX SKELETONS SOMETIMES ESCAPE THE CLOSET*

*Marcus was smiling down at her, and she could feel the heat on her cheeks as she struggled to return his smile. He leaned in to kiss her and she closed her eyes.* Paris woke up abruptly and sat up in bed. She'd been dreaming about Marcus for the third time this week. She pulled her legs up to her chin and closed her eyes. Maybe if she called him there would be a sense of closure, and she could put an end to this torment. Instinctively, she grabbed the phone from her nightstand and quickly dialed his number. By the time she heard the rings begin, the familiar lump of fear tightened in her throat. She moved closer to the night-stand to replace the receiver when he picked up.

"Hello?"

She opened her mouth to speak, but her voice caught in her throat.

"Hello?" Marcus repeated.

Paris bit her lip and inhaled sharply. *I should just hang up*, she thought angry at her weakness.

"Paris is that you?" Marcus asked. His voice betrayed his feelings, and Paris took strength from that to speak.

"Yes. I…ummm… I wanted to thank you for… for everything. I mean for being there and everything. My mom told me. I just wanted to say thank you," she stuttered.

"How are you doing?"

Paris sat up straight in bed and clutched the phone tighter. He'd ignored her gratitude, and she didn't know if that meant he was angry or just didn't care.

"Paris, are you alright? Are you in trouble?" Again, his concern was apparent and his voice rushed through the receiver and enveloped her.

"No, no I'm not in trouble. I'm fine. I mean I just wanted you to know."

"Is your mother still there?"

"No. She left yesterday. Marcus I'm sor—"

He grunted and stopped her in mid-sentence. "So you're staying by yourself, your brothers aren't there?"

"No, they're gone too, but I'm fine. This was probably a mistake. I did't mean to bother you. I only wanted to thank you." Her apology again went unaccepted. They both sat in silence, Paris could hear him breathing on the other end but didn't know how to excuse herself and get off the phone. It was obvious to her now that her first instinct had been right. There was no way Marcus would ever forgive her. At this point, it seemed he didn't even want an apology from her.

"I'd like to come and see you, just to make sure you're doing alright. That is, if you don't mind," he said seriously.

Paris was caught off guard. "You don't have to do that," she said quickly.

"I would like to check on you just to make myself feel better. If you don't want me to come, just say you don't."

"It's not that. I wasn't trying to hurt you." Tears burned at the corners of her eyes because of his blunt words.

"I'll call you tomorrow after I get off work. I can stop by on my way home."

"Okay." She could hear him breathing on the other end for a few seconds, then the line went dead. She sat listening to the dial tone, clutching her chest until the busy signal began blaring in her ear.

Paris sat staring at her reflection in the bottom of a coffee mug she'd left on the nightstand, as her heart painfully thumped in her chest. Again, Marcus hung up on her without saying goodbye. Paris observed her large brown eyes again. They looked so dark, unusually dark even considering everything, and somber. She pushed her hair out of her face, refastening the clip holding it off her neck, then changed her mind and took the clip out altogether. Maybe her unruly hair would take attention away from her eyes. Her fingers clasped the back of her neck and attempted to massage some of the tension that had been building since her first conversation with Marcus.

As usual, his actions befuddled her. On the phone, it was obvious he didn't want to hear her apologies, or her thanks for that matter. Yet, she could tell that he still cared. She could also hear pain in his voice. She hadn't understood why he'd volunteered to come over when it sounded like talking to her was torture. Furthermore, she wasn't sure if she wanted to face him in person. Although she'd seen him at the hospital, the most vivid recollection she had was of him seeing her for the first time at the club. Her eyes teared up again as she relived the humiliation she'd suffered that night.

Willing the tears to stop, she shook her head and pressed her fingers to her eyes, then took a deep cleansing breath.

She heard Marcus's footsteps well before he rang the doorbell. She froze for a second, then quickly got up to open the door. Her eyes went from his cream cable knit sweater to his chocolate cords and Italian loafers. Marcus was always like a breath of fresh air. Dressed to impress without being flashy, Marcus could have doubled for a *GQ* model on any given day. Paris greeted him, then watched as he walked past her.

"Are you feeling okay?" he asked.

She nodded.

"Let me look at your sore."

"I've been cleaning it with the pads I got. I think it's healing fine."

Paris obliged turning her back to him and lifting her hair off the back of her neck. Marcus was quiet as his fingers lifted the bandage then carefully replaced it.

"I will always have a scar to remind me that I once went crazy," she said, attempting to break the tension.

"Have you been sleeping?"

Paris looked curiously at him. "As much as I can. I have been having mild headaches at night, and it's hard to get in a sleeping position that won't put pressure on my head."

Marcus looked at his watch. "Have you taken anything today?"

Paris nodded. "I just took some pain pills about thirty minutes ago."

"Why don't you go lay down, I'll stay here for awhile," he said matter-of-factly.

"Marcus, I know you need to go to work. I'll be fine. I'll get some rest, but you go on."

"I can make phone calls from here, and I've got my laptop in the car. You go on upstairs and get some rest. I just want to make sure you're okay."

Paris attempted to protest again, but Marcus stopped her.

"Go on," he said nudging her toward the stairs. "If you need anything, just holler. I'll be right down here."

Paris lowered her head in defeat and headed up the stairs. She awoke later to voices coming from downstairs.

"Who the hell are you?" an angry voice demanded.

Paris couldn't hear Marcus's response, but the familiarity of the first voice pushed her out of bed and down the stairs in a panic.

"Ah, there she is." Kenton scoffed sarcastically up at her.

"Kenton, what the hell are you doing here?" she demanded, going over to stand in front of him.

"I thought you were supposed to be getting back at me. I know you're not trying to play me Paris."

"Nobody's trying to play you. I just haven't had a chance to get back with you since I've been back in town. I was going to call you today. How did you get in here anyway?" she questioned.

Kenton looked between Paris and Marcus. "I can see how busy you've been," he said sardonically. "Your girl Chocolate gave me the security code. She was sure you wouldn't mind," he taunted sarcastically.

"Paris, I'm going to let you handle your business." Marcus picked up his laptop and gathered a stack of papers together, preparing to leave.

"Marcus you don't have to go," Paris said, moving past Kenton to stand in front of Marcus.

"It's obvious you have some business you need to take care of, and I'm not trying to get in your way. I came over here to make sure you were doing okay. That's it. This is your business, and I don't want to be in it," Marcus said briskly.

"Marcus, please don't leave, not right now. This business is over." She turned to look toward Kenton, and her eyes narrowed furiously. *How dare you come into my condo like you own me!* She pushed her rage aside then returned her gaze to Marcus. "Please just let me clear this up. It'll only take a minute. I'd like to talk to you before you leave. Please."

Marcus's jaw softened, then he walked into the kitchen with his cappuccino. Paris took the opportunity to confront Kenton face to face.

"What the hell is wrong with you coming up in my house like this?" she demanded.

"So what, you got you a captain save-a-ho now and you tryin' to blow me off?" Kenton asked under his breath as he gestured toward Marcus.

"Fuck you, Kenton!" She immediately glanced over at Marcus to see if he'd heard her profanity. "I was going to call you and let you know that I won't be coming back, but since you're here, I will give you my resignation in person and you can get up out of my house."

A fleeting look of surprise passed across Kenton's face before his eyes blazed accusatory with fury. "I guess you're forgetting who saved your ass six years ago. I came over here to offer you a deal, but since you want to be stupid, I'm through with you. Trust me; you won't be shit in New Orleans without me."

"You do what you have to do, Kenton, but right now you need to get the hell out of my house," Paris spat angrily.

Kenton looked like he wanted to get physical with her but thought better of it. "It's probably for the best anyway. You ain't nothing but a high priced ho. I should've known you couldn't be a businesswoman. The only business you got is between your legs. Isn't that right, Caramel?" he laughed.

Paris's felt her face flush hot at his degrading words in Marcus's presence.

"You're lucky that crazy mutherfucka didn't kill your tramp ass. I was trying to protect you and your trick ass." He turned to leave. "You haven't heard the last of me, Paris. Just remember when the stuff hits the fan that you brought the shit on yourself." He laughed as he walked past Marcus. "I swear when niggas stop trying to turn ho's into house-wives, the world will be a better place. I'll see you soon, Paris."

He winked at Paris then slammed the door on his way out. Marcus walked back past her and began picking up his things. Paris went over to him and put a hand on his arm.

"Marcus, please just talk to me. I..."

He moved his arm away from her touch and turned stone cold eyes on her.

"What do you want to talk to me about?" he asked.

Paris was taken aback by his harsh tone. "It's not what it looked like. I mean, sounded like. Just let me explain," she asked.

"I don't want you to explain," he said simply. He gathered his items, turned his back to her and began heading toward the door.

"Marcus, why won't you at least let me apologize?" Paris voice was louder than she intended it to be.

Marcus whipped around on her. "Have I asked you for an apology?" he demanded.

Again, Paris felt heat flood her face and her stomach dropped. She shook her head no.

"Have I asked for an apology from you?" he repeated his question.

His lips turned up at the word you, and Paris was face to face with the look of disgust she'd ran from every time she closed her eyes.

"I'm out of here. I don't want to be here if your pimp comes back," Marcus said nastily.

"My pimp? Is that what you think? You think I'm a prostitute?" she asked unbelievably. "Marcus I told you I was a dancer," she faltered as his eyes shot daggers through her.

"And what makes you think I put stock in anything you say?" he asked mockingly.

Paris felt her stomach cramp up but refused to sit down. "I know that I wasn't honest with you. But I thought..." She stopped as he turned his back to her.

"You thought what?" he asked.

"Why are you here? Why are you checking up on me if you think I am a prostitute and don't want anything to do with me?"

Marcus shook his head. "Honestly, I don't know. I told your mother I would check on you," he answered truthfully.

Paris swallowed her tears. "I'm not your responsibility. You don't have to be here," she said, angrily pushing back tears.

She looked over at Marcus and could see his jaw muscles flexing.

He started to speak but just stood still.

"Paris, I am here because I was concerned about your physical health. That's it, nothing more, nothing less. I shouldn't have made the comment about your mother. I did tell her I would check on you from time to time, but I wouldn't have offered to do it if I didn't feel like I should."

Paris nodded.

Marcus rubbed his hands over his face and sighed. "It's time for me to leave. I need to be getting home."

Paris nodded. He turned his back to her and opened the door.

"Take care, Paris," he said over his shoulder. He pulled the door closed behind him quietly.

Paris sank down on the sofa next to the window and watched helplessly as he got in his Escalade, backed out of the parking space in front of her condo and drove away.

# CHAPTER TWENTY-SEVEN BETWEEN A ROCK AND A HARD PLACE

Paris slumped against the sofa and let her head drop onto her chest. It was inevitable that Marcus would walk out of her life. She had been living on borrowed time with him since he discovered the truth about her. Salty tears found their way to the corners of her eyes and made their way down her cheeks. The old Paris would've emerged from this second bout of rejection colder and angrier than ever, but she wouldn't allow herself to revert to her old ways. Her reaction to her father's rejection ended up causing her to self-destruct and had cost her what could have proven to be something more beautiful than she could've imagined. She wouldn't allow this rejection to have the same effect on her life. Instead of fighting the tears, for the first time she relented control and allowed them to flow freely.

Marcus's appearance at her door the following week was a welcomed distraction from the chaos running through her brain. After greeting her and asking about her head, it was apparent there was another reason he decided to drop by.

"I have to tell you something," Marcus said urgently.

Paris's heart dropped as she mentally ransacked their prior conversations. This was it; he was finally going to voice what she'd read in his eyes ever since the night he'd caught her performing at the club. He wasn't able to put her past behind him; her lies and her lifestyle were too much. She observed his nervous body language from under lowered lashes. He as awkward sitting next to her, his long brown legs bent uncomfortably between her sofa and coffee table.

"I received an offer a while ago from a firm in Michigan. They flew me out there twice and gave me ample time to consider their offer. I called them yesterday and told them I am accepting the position."

Paris instructed her lips to curve in a smile and her eyes to show encouragement. She would deal with her own disappointment later. Marcus deserved some happiness in his life. It was painfully obvious, and had been for some time, that she was unable to give him anything but heartache. She tried to focus on Marcus's hands instead of looking directly at him, watching his long slender fingers as they tapped on the edge of the table.

"Marcus, that's great." Willing her voice to sound cheerful, she smiled. "It sounds like you can really make a fresh start, I'm sure you'll really be able to shine up there."

Marcus was silent, his fingers tapping an uneven rhythm on the tabletop.

"I know that you would've done much better here if not for being so distracted with me for the last few months. I'm grateful that you're getting another chance. You're a very special person, Marcus. You've been such a good friend, much better than I deserved. I don't know what I would've done without you over the last few months," she finished truthfully.

She smiled at him again in an effort to convince him that she was being completely honest. Marcus nodded, his eyes glancing restlessly around the room.

"I leave next Friday," he said matter-of-factly.

"That soon?"

Suddenly she couldn't sit still any longer. She needed to move, put some distance between Marcus and herself before he was able to see through her flimsy exterior.

"I'll actually start two weeks from then, but I want to do some shopping around for a condo or maybe even a house. They're putting me up in a corporate apartment until I can find a permanent place to live."

"Wow," Paris breathed, "then I guess you're all set."

She walked over to her bay window and willed the tears threatening to betray her emotions not to spill over. She could hear Marcus pull himself up from sitting and follow her over to the foyer. She waited for him to speak, but he didn't. *You owe him this,* she reminded herself. She turned to face, but did not move.

"So did you want to get together before you leave? Maybe we could do something nice to celebrate your new job and all. I could fix you dinner or something if you don't want to go out, whatever you want," she offered nervously.

Marcus just nodded and moved closer to the door. Paris swallowed hard; the lump in her throat was growing by the minute. There was no way she was going to be able to hold the emotions swimming around in her stomach much longer. She quickly walked over to the door to open it for him.

"You must be in a hurry; I imagine you have a ton of things to do." She fumbled with the doorknob before finally getting it open. "Marcus I appreciate you coming by and telling me face-to-face," she said gravely. "I know you didn't have to do that."

He still did not speak. He just shifted the weight from foot to foot. His eyes betrayed the inner turmoil he was in. It was there, written all over his face from the first time she opened her eyes in the hospital. He cared but wanted desperately not to. She hoped after she was out of his life the light would return to his eyes and replace the ever-present torment in them now. *Yes, this move will be for best for you.* She would concentrate on being strong until he left and then she would pick up the pieces of her own life and start again.

"Just give me a call if you want that dinner or if there is anything I can do. And, Marcus, please don't feel obligated. If this is goodbye..."

She couldn't finish the sentence, but she was certain he understood what she meant. The open doorway created an awkward space between them, but he finally began to move forward. He reached for the opposite side of the doorknob to close it behind him.

*That's it Marcus please leave,* she urged silently. She didn't want him to see her cry. He suddenly stopped and awkwardly turned toward her.

"I was… I came over here because… I wanted to know if you

wanted... if you want to go with me," he stammered.

Paris's breath caught in her throat. "Do you want me to go with you, Marcus?" she asked, unable to believe her ears.

Marcus softly closed the door and walked back over to take a seat on the sofa.

"I've been thinking about this for a while because I wanted to make sure this is what I wanted before I asked you."

Paris took a seat directly across from him. Her heart was in her throat and she knew if she spoke a single word it would burst. Never in her dreams had she imagined Marcus would want her to be a part of his new life. His association with her had brought him nothing but deception and heartache. She had been convinced he wanted to remove her permanently from his life. Marcus's eyes mirrored hope and anguish as he twisted his hands in his lap then quietly spoke.

"I don't understand what we have or if we even have anything, considering everything," he began hesitantly.

Paris turned her face away from him. It hurt to watch him grapple with his feelings for her when it was obvious they brought him so much pain. Still, if there was a possibility he'd give her another chance, perhaps she could turn things around. *Is it possible?* She put the unvoiced question out of her mind and turned her attention back to Marcus.

"What I do know is the thought of leaving without trying to take you with me, isn't an option. It's not that I am promising the two of us will be together. In fact, I don't know if there is even a possibililty for us, but I know you could use a new start just like I could," he said, voice full of emotion.

Paris exhaled with breath that had been threatening to burst through her chest. "I don't know what to say, Marcus. I don't want to hurt you anymore. I never wanted that. If I could change—"

He held up a hand to stop her from finishing.

"Will you come?" he asked bluntly.

Paris nodded, but was afraid to smile.

# CHAPTER TWENTY-EIGHT ONE
# A NEW BEGINNING

Three weeks after she arrived in Michigan, Paris was second guessing her decision to move. She was proud of the progress she made in New Orleans. Turning down the job with Kenton was a major step for her, and she'd managed to complete the requirements necessary with her parole officer in order for her to leave the state. She had ninety days allotted with which to find a job, but she was optimistic about her new life in Michigan. The only situation not moving in her favor was her relationship with Marcus. He was doing everything in his power to avoid her. Even though he offered to help in anyway she needed, he was standoffish and still refused to listen to her apologies. He said she was welcome to stay with him as long as she needed, but everyday his demeanor toward her recanted that offer.

Paris made up her mind to confront the tension between the two of them once and for all. She had money in the bank and was perfectly capable of finding her own place. She decided to approach him as soon as he came in from work that evening. Lately, his habit was to come home late and head straight to his bedroom and shut the door. Paris sat on the sofa, determined to talk to him regardless of his mood.

At ten minutes until six, she heard Marcus's key turn in the lock. Surprised he was home so early, she swallowed her fear and prepared to attempt blocking him from heading to his room. She nervously smoothed her hair back as it had become wild and unruly while she napped, waiting for him on the sofa.

"I need you to let me apologize to you," she rushed nervously. "Marcus, there's no excuse for the way I hurt you. It wasn't because I didn't care. When we met, I didn't want to involve you in everything going on in my life, but then I started to care about you. I was afraid to be honest with you because I knew you would never be with someone like me. I never even thought I wanted to be in a relationship with anyone. I wanted to tell you the truth, and I was going to but then things started to get crazy, and there was so much going on."

Marcus held her gaze, his brown eyes softening as he took in her disheveled appearance and nervous behavior. Before Paris could assume he intended to hear her out, he broke the gaze looking off behind her.

She wanted to continue, but her feelings sounded lame now that she was hearing herself out loud. She started again but Marcus stopped her.

"I owe you an apology, too. I should never have asked you to come if I couldn't handle it. I also owe you an apology for not listening to you before now."

He reached down and picked up her hands. She knew he felt the electricity passing between them as their hands touched. All at once their heartfelt words, combined with physical contact, resurrected the intense attraction whenever they were alone.

"If I was being honest with myself, I would have to admit you did send me quite a few messages," he said. "I just didn't want to hear them at the time. I told you a long time ago that I would always be your friend, and I still mean that, Paris."

"Is that all you want to be, Marcus? My friend?"

His eyes held hers until she broke the gaze. She tried to catch her breath but was unable. It was as if she were suffocating in the sensually charged atmosphere they had created.

"What?" she asked, noting him staring intently at her body, clad in a silk pair of pale pink pajamas. Marcus's intoxicating cologne wrapped itself around Paris's senses and drew her into him. She was aware of the way his strong shoulders filled out his crisp white shirt. He'd loosened the first few buttons, and Paris had to force herself not to touch the almond skin peeking out.

She tilted her face up to look more closely at him. She found herself jolted by his lips suddenly capturing hers. His hands cupped her face, drawing her closer to him. Surprised by the onslaught of his passionate assault, Paris's body went limp against him. Her arms moved slowly and unsteadily until they were loosely clasped around his neck.

Trying to respond to the urgency of his kiss, she ended up sandwiched between him and the wall. His tongue pressed inside her mouth with an urgency that matched the frantic beating in her heart. She instinctively responded, hungrily tasting his mouth. Losing her senses amidst his hypnotic kisses, Paris felt heat flood her attention-starved body. His hands momentarily left her face to pull her waist harder against him, then down to her bottom, lifting her up and into him. Paris hands eagerly went to the buttons on Marcus's shirt, pushing it over his shoulders, hungry to see more of him. The sight of him in his undershirt motivated her to snatch the shirt up out of his slacks and over his head.

Feeding off her energy, Marcus moaned Paris's name and whispered suggestively in her ear, coaxing her legs to encircle his waist. He pressed her hard against the hallway wall until she could feel his heartbeat, and was sure he could in turn feel how tight her nipples had become at the feel of his chest pressed against them.

Emotions swirled around passion in Paris's stomach, making her dizzy and oblivious to everything but Marcus's mouth on hers. She fought to keep up with the intensity of his kiss, as his tongue tasted her mouth, then sucked gently on her bottom lip. She tightened her legs around his waist as he swooped her up and carried her to his room. Placing her gently on the bed, he removed his slacks and joined her, never breaking their kiss. It was as if his hands were everywhere, running through her hair, touching her breasts, cupping her bottom firmly against him. Like magnets without an option, they clung fiercely to each other, unable to distinguish where one body began and the other ended.

Paris's head was swimming; she couldn't believe this was actually happening. She had tried to keep herself from daydreaming about making love to Marcus, but idle thoughts had pushed their way through her resolve from time to time.

"Do you know how beautiful you are?" Marcus asked in a hoarse whisper, pulling away from her mouth to kiss her chin then her neck.

Paris tried to avoid making eye contact with him for fear he would come to his senses and stop completely. The thought of him stopping now was unthinkable. Her fearful thoughts were interrupted as Marcus pulled her face toward him and began kissing her thoroughly. His kisses, tender at first, quickly became more and more demanding. Her pushed her gently back on the bed and began unbuttoning her silk pajama top. Again, Paris tried to match the passion in his kiss but was unable.

There were so many emotions pushing up through her, wanting to be voiced, but she was afraid. She had never felt hands so strong, yet so gentle. Her body quivered uncontrollably as his hands pushed her top over her shoulders, then softly began kneading her back and shoulders. She attempted to say his name, but her voice sounded weak and foreign to her, so she concentrated on kissing him. She was oblivious to him removing the rest of her pajamas then bra and panties followed by his own boxer shorts.

Her eyes widened when she felt his skin against hers for the first time. No one had ever been this gentle or this loving with her before. She had always felt like the entertainment during intimacy, but Marcus kissed, held, and touched her as if she were the most precious thing in the world. His hands went firmly over her exposed breasts, pausing to caress her taut nipple. Each touch caused her to gasp sharply and seemed to excite him even more. She attempted to clear her head, trying to rationalize what was happening, but then he began suckling her nipples and she could do nothing but push her head farther back into her pillow, arching her back and pressing her chest towards his mouth and hands. His fingers moved lower then paused before slipping inside her. Paris opened her eyes and tried to focus but couldn't.

"Can I?" Marcus asked huskily.

She nodded eagerly and pushed her hips upward toward him. His fingers began stroking her so tenderly and sweetly she began to cry, the tears making slow trails down her face. She placed her palms on his shoulders and pulled him closer to her still. She wanted to feel him inside her so bad she was going crazy. A sweet agonizing ache that started in her lower stomach spread throughout her hips and inner thighs.

"Please Marcus," she whispered.

He pulled his mouth away from hers and tilted her head up with his free hand, forcing her to look at him.

"Paris," he said gently.

Paris heard him but could not answer. She couldn't open her eyes.

Her body was past yearning, and she just wanted him inside her.

"Paris, look at me," he repeated, again holding her head captive.

She lifted her eyelids slowly until their eyes met. It was hard to concentrate on keeping her eyes open with his fingers strumming her spot so sweetly. She shivered involuntarily, struggling to keep her eyes from shutting in sheer abandonment. His gaze was intense as he tenderly wiped a stray tear from her cheek.

"I have wanted to be with you since the moment I saw you," he professed hoarsely. She opened her mouth to speak, but then his fingers slid from inside her. Her body protested, and she needed to voice her objection but couldn't find the words. She was faintly aware of him reaching in his nightstand removing the foil silver packet that would protect them both. He then replaced his fingers by slowly guiding himself inside her.

On their journey to one, she moaned in ecstasy as her body became liquid silk and stretched to accommodate him. He groaned as he entered her, crushing her body against his.

"What are you doing to me?" he grunted, desperately trying to find a rhythm for their coupling. Pent-up frustration evident in their synergy, they pushed eagerly against each other, setting a frantically urgent pace.

"Slow down, Paris," Marcus rasped, attempting to refrain from meeting her bucking as she pushed wantonly toward him.

Her body was reacting on a purely exhilarating impulse, and for once, she abandoned the need for restraint or control. She gave in and followed Marcus's lead, allowing her body to relax and revel in unknown luxury of connecting with a man intimately. She couldn't get close enough to Marcus. She pulled him closer, her pelvis pressing upwards to take him deeper within her, to still the blissful torment building within. Paris felt waves building slowly, then more steadily until relief came in painfully sweet currents and enveloped them both.

Paris woke suddenly and turned over in bed. Yes she was in Marcus's bed, so she knew last night couldn't have been a dream, but the bed was empty. Not only was the bed empty, but she was wearing her lace black lace panties and the covers had been tucked around her exposed chest. She slowly put one foot on the floor and then the other and walked to Marcus's personal bathroom. Thinking she heard water, she pushed the door open, but the bathroom was empty. She looked around for something to cover herself with before going to look for Marcus.

She found a white button down work shirt of his and pulled it on. Something was wrong; she could feel it in the pit of her stomach. She walked through the hallway, slowly calling his name when she reached her room. Growing more worried with each step, she pulled his shirt closer about her and went into the living room, then into the kitchen. Her breath stopped in her chest when she saw him standing over the stove. Something was sizzling in the skillet on the top burner. It smelled like an omelet or scrambled eggs. He was standing motionless except for lightly turning his food with a spatula.

A frog formed in Paris's throat, and she couldn't find her voice. She grabbed a glass of water on the counter and took a sip. Her footsteps alerted him she was standing behind him, and he turned around. He slowly took in her appearance in his partially buttoned shirt then directed his attention back to the food.

"I got up to make breakfast. We need to talk," he said gruffly.

"Is something wrong?"

She placed one foot atop the other, forcing herself not to move away from the foreboding feeling enveloping the room.

"We have to find you an apartment," Marcus said.

Although his words were aimed at the stove, they boomeranged around to shoot daggers through her heart.

"Is it because of last night?" she asked softly.

He turned to face her. "I owe you yet another apology. Last night was my fault. I shouldn't have put either of us in this position."

"No, Marcus. It wasn't your fault," Paris said urgently.

She began walking toward him. When she reached him she could feel that he wasn't in the same place he'd been last night. There had been a world of change in a few short hours.

"I should have known better," he insisted coldly. "What we did last night wasn't supposed to happen. I thought I could handle you being here, but I can't. I still want to help you, but not like this. We have to find you a place to stay, or if you want to stay here, I'll find someplace else to stay until I find a house."

Paris inhaled too much disappointment too quickly, causing her to feel like she'd been kicked in the stomach. She turned her back for fear he'd see her true feelings. The pain she'd been running from her entire life had caught up to her. Now the pain was determined to reveal itself again and again. It seemed since her world collapsed at Under the Cherry Moon, she continued to experience rejection again and again.

"Today," he added, "we have to find it today."

Paris shoved the pain away and instead chose to embrace the more familiar anger she felt bubbling inside her.

"What just happened here, Marcus? I would expect this from anyone else, but not from you."

"What are you saying?" He placed both palms on the counter and gave her his full attention.

"I'm saying I hadn't pegged you for the type to hit it and trip out," she said bitterly. "You're damn good, because you had me totally fooled."

Paris narrowed her eyes at him angrily. *How could someone as naïve as Marcus have fooled me?*

"So you think this was my plan the whole time huh?" he asked.

Her eyes blazed through him, mirroring the rage evident in his own.

"If you really think that, Paris, then you are definitely more messed up than I gave you credit for. I guess you think I planned this whole situation out too, right? I must be damn good then. I guess I knew all along that you were a stripper, and I was just waiting until everyone else had you and the whole thing blew up. Then I decided to make myself look like a complete fool and ask you to move out-of-state with me. My master plan was to ask you to move all the way here just to make love to you before dumping you. Is that it, Paris?" His voice cracked during his tirade, and he picked the skillet up and slammed it on the stove angrily.

"Make love, is that what you call it when you get some, then throw the person out the next morning?" Paris asked snidely. "You know what? You are no different than any of the men I've ever met. You don't want me to be anything other than a piece of ass, isn't that right, Marcus? I was never good enough to be anything more to you. That's why you've got us living like this. I'm no fool, Marcus. I can see the signs. You barely come home, and when you do, you avoid me like the plague. Well now you got what you really wanted, so you can wash your hands of me totally now. I've never been one to stay where I'm not wanted."

Marcus moved around the countertop to stare her in the eye.

"You're wrong. I wanted you, Paris. I had no idea what you did. You know I didn't. You made sure of that, didn't you? What did you tell me you did? A choreographer wasn't it?"

Paris winced at his recollections but didn't respond.

"I would never have thought in a million years that you were the person you turned out to be. You are the one who doesn't want to be more than a piece of ass, Paris. I didn't put that label on you. You put it on yourself a long time ago. I just found out too late, and the joke was on me."

His words ripped fresh wounds through Paris's already aching heart. *How can he say such words to me after he'd been so gentle not five hours ago*. She turned away from him, but his arm reached out and grabbed her.

"No, you started this conversation, so you're going to listen. You seem to have forgotten what happened before I came to the club that night. I was the one pursuing you Paris. You didn't want to give me the time of day. I've asked myself repeatedly why I didn't just leave you alone when you asked. And the truth is, I couldn't. There was something about you that I thought I, or rather… I thought we connected. You must've thought I was a fool. Instead of just telling me I wasn't your type or you didn't want to be bothered with me, you strung me along, giving me just enough to stay involved but not enough to move forward."

Paris shut her eyes against the truth in Marcus's words. She hadn't allowed herself to calculate the club incident and the way she'd been dishonest with him into the equation this morning.

"Why are you realizing all of this now?" Paris bit back. "You've known I lied to you for months. But you wait until you've gotten me in bed to humiliate me. If you were so disgusted, you should've left me alone after you found out the truth," Paris challenged.

"Believe me, that was the plan. But there were some extenuating circumstances, if you remember," he replied honestly.

"You weren't obligated to come when the hospital called. They would've found my mother or one of my brothers eventually. I wasn't your responsibility. Or if you were just being the good Samaritan, you could've left when my family arrived. I've admitted I was wrong, Marcus, and I've tried to apologize to you, but you wouldn't let me. It's like you want to be the saint in all this and hang this shit over my head. I even tried to give you a way out. But you didn't want out. I tried to give you an out repeatedly, but you wouldn't take it. I guess it's more rewarding to hold the shit over my head."

Paris stopped when she noted the pained expression on his face. She had never let herself talk like this around him, and in a way, it was refreshing to let everything out. But that tiny, fleeting victory paled in comparison to the pain she knew she was inflicting on him that she wouldn't be able to take back. Still, she continued, unable to stop the pent-up flow of angry words tumbling from her mouth.

"If you want to punish me for what I did to you, I'm sure there were other ways, besides asking me to move up here with you. You should have gotten your revenge in New Orleans, moved here then made a fresh break. I'm sure you would've found a nice church girl by now to take to church with you and be that good little girlfriend slash fiancé slash wife you were looking for."

Marcus looked Paris defiantly in the eyes before shaking his head.

"You just don't get it do you? You're so wrapped up in your delusional world that you can't even function with a man if he's not stuffing money down your panties. You say you've been treated badly by all the men in your life. Well, look at where you choose to meet them. Look at what you did for a living. What about all the things you were doing to men, myself included? When are you going to see things the way they are, and realize you are not an innocent victim? Not by a long shot." He laughed bitterly.

Paris shook her head at him in an effect to block out his rationale that was resonating deep within her.

"I guess I'm the villain huh? Is that it, Marcus? I'm the one making the men at the club act the way they do." She snorted sarcastically. "Well if I'm such a villain, why were you with me, Marcus? What have you been doing all this time? Staying in the hospital, talking with the doctors? Asking me to move here? All this? If I'm so bad and all this is my own fault, why all the extra drama? I would've fucked you in New Orleans the first night you came over. Why'd you do all this?"

Marcus's eyes widened at her use of profanity, but he didn't back down. They stared boldly at each other until Marcus finally broke the silence.

"Because I had already fallen in love with you, Paris. I didn't want to fuck you that night. I wanted to get to know you. Considering the company you keep, I guess you can't comprehend that. You're used to getting paid to perform," he said sourly.

Paris inhaled sharply at his words, her breath catching in her lungs. His answer caused her to back down for the first time in her life. Defeated, she moved away from him and lowered her eyes.

"You've definitely showed me the truth in the statement sometimes love isn't enough," he admitted ruefully.

Paris nodded numbly, but without a verbal comeback, silently headed toward her bedroom.

# CHAPTER TWENTY-NINE
# CLOSING THE BOOK

Chocolate called Paris, and for the first time since she'd been in Michigan, Paris was happy to hear a familiar voice after almost two months. In the hospital, she'd had time to think about all the differences she had with Chocolate, and she decided her co-worker was doing the best she could with what she had. She couldn't fault Chocolate for falling prey to Kenton's charms. Deep down she knew Chocolate wasn't so much selling her out, as she was looking for validation in all the wrong places.

"How's it going up there? Are you all settled in now?" Chocolate ventured cautiously.

"Yeah I'm doing fine. Things are pretty cool here," Paris replied.

Chocolate started with small talk, bringing her up to speed on the other dancers. When she mentioned the sale of Paris's condo, a little red flag went up and Paris knew she'd been the topic of conversation at the club.

"I had no reason to keep the house. I don't plan on coming back to New Orleans any time soon," Paris answered Chocolate's unspoken question.

"You must be doing really well out there. Did you find another club or are you living with that guy you met?"

"Neither," Paris replied coldly.

She was offended that Chocolate automatically assumed that she was either stripping or living off the generosities of a man.

"I didn't mean it to sound like that," Chocolate apologized sullenly.

"No, it's cool. I actually got a job in a little boutique here, and I'm going to school in the evenings."

After the pause lasted longer than it should have, Paris thought the line had been disconnected.

"Chocolate, are you there?"

"Yeah, girl, I'm here. I'm just shocked I guess. So do you like your job? It must be paying well for you to be standing behind a counter."

Again, her comment pissed Paris off, but she struggled to keep her cool. "Actually, it doesn't pay that well at all. There weren't many jobs I could get without experience. I told you I was through with strip clubs, and I meant it. I needed to make some changes. Hell I was getting old anyway," Paris added in an attempt to keep the conversation light.

This time her comment seemed to rub Chocolate the wrong way.

"You're not old. I'm older than you anyway, so if you're too old to strip, that makes me past too old."

"It wasn't the years Chocolate. It just wasn't working for me anymore. You have to do what you got to do for yourself," Paris explained wearily.

"I hear you. Well, I was just giving you a call to see how things were going. I can't lie; I was hoping to hear you were coming back this way sometime soon. I guess Kenton was wrong this time."

Paris resisted the urge to tell Chocolate what she thought of her ex-employer. She knew the information would have fallen on deaf ears anyway. She had always been overly impressed with Kenton. Her esteem was dependent on the fact that he found her valuable.

"He was definitely wrong. So Kenton's the same old Kenton huh?"

"Naw, girl, he's been really sweet lately. We been chillin' a bit. I think he got fed up with Sundae. He's been doing a lot of nice stuff for the kids."

Paris bit her bottom lip in an effort to keep her cynical comments to herself. It was obvious with Paris out of the picture, Chocolate was his top moneymaker. It was just like him to be keeping a closer leash around his top earner.

"He's really not that bad, Paris. I wish you could've seen the side of him that I see."

Paris simply remained quiet, refusing to get into a discussion about Kenton.

"So are you still seeing that guy? What was his name, Marcus or something like that?"

"We aren't really seeing each other at the moment. I think everything that happened might have been a little too much for him."

"So have you met anyone down there yet? I know you got to be seeing somebody."

"Nope, I'm taking a break from all that right now. Between school and the job, I really don't have the time for all that right now. You know me, I don't meet that many people I vibe with anyway," Paris answered truthfully.

"If not for the sound of your voice, I wouldn't even believe I was talking with Paris Jackson right now. Damn, girl, you really have changed. I'm happy for you though. I mean if you're happy, that's all that matters."

Paris thanked her and told her to keep her chin up at the club. She did her best to smooth over the tension, but by the time they got off the phone, Paris knew they wouldn't be speaking again. Although Chocolate said she was sad Paris wouldn't be returning, Paris knew a part of Chocolate was relieved. With Paris gone, she was the center of attention with clients and more importantly, with Kenton. Chocolate had been the best friend she was capable of being, but they both knew she had struggled living in Paris's shadow. Paris truly hoped that the lifestyle wouldn't do the same thing to Chocolate that it'd done to her. She wished there were a way to reach out to Chocolate, but with her own life still being such a mess, she was in no position. That chapter to her life was over, and closure included letting go of all the players at Under the Cherry Moon.

# *CHAPTER THIRTY*
# *OVERJOYED*

Paris withdrew a couple hundred dollars from her savings account and treated herself to some pieces for her new home. Instead of the earthy tones her old home was decorated in, she opted for pastels this time. She purchased a beautiful Indian rug for her living room in a complimentary pale green. She accentuated that color with cream and silver pieces scattered throughout the sitting area. As Sunday was her only day off from both her fashion merchandising classes and the boutique, she reserved those afternoons for lounging around the house.

Today she'd worked from nine A.M. until around three P.M. She'd put a border up in her kitchen and polished her silver antiques for display. She sat Indian-style on the carpet, polishing a small silver butterfly she received as a present from Sharp on her last birthday. Only her family knew her birthday, so the only calls she received were from them. She'd never gotten the chance to share that piece of information with Marcus. She doubted he would have remembered after everything they'd been through anyway.

She's finished polishing the butterfly, then carefully set the tiny statue on its pedestal atop her coffee table. The sight of the intricately designed butterfly emerging from its cocoon and spreading its wings for the first time was a symbol of her new life. After removing it from the velvet box, she immediately got the message her brother was sending her. His card had read: *I'm proud of you, Happy Birthday, Sharp*. Ivan had sent her a bouquet of tulips and a card that read: *Sis, Never underestimate your inner beauty. It far outshines the outer.*

Beginning to tear up at the memory, Paris rubbed her eye and answered her ringing phone. She immediately sat up straight when she recognized the voice on the other end of the phone as Marcus's.

"Are you alright?" he asked. "You sound like you've been crying."

"Oh no, I was just thinking about something, and it had me tear up. I'm fine. How about you?"

Marcus ignored her question, choosing to probe deeper on her thoughts. "You were thinking about something that's bothering you?"

"No, Marcus. Actually, these are good tears. They come from happy thoughts. Honestly," she added for good measure.

"I'm glad. Paris, I said some things to you a while back that I will regret for the rest of my life. I hope you know that I never meant to hurt you. Honestly, when I said them I probably was trying to hurt you because I wanted you to feel what I was feeling. I know there's no excuse," Marcus continued awkwardly.

"Now I'm the one that doesn't want to hear your apology." She laughed, cutting him off. "Don't feel that way. You didn't say anything to me that wasn't true, or that wasn't deserved for that matter. And I hope one day you will know that I never set out to hurt you either. I have learned though that intentions really don't add up to much, so I just hope one day you will truly be able to forgive me."

"I hope it's okay that I called," Marcus said hesitantly.

"Of course, it's fine. I'm glad you did," Paris took a chance and said more than she usually would have allowed herself.

"Good. Well then I'm glad I did, too. I've been thinking about you a lot lately. Has your head been bothering you?"

"Not really. I'm doing well, Marcus. You shouldn't be worried."

Paris hesitated, afraid to share what she was thinking, but then decided to jump in and bare her soul. "I have missed talking to you."

"I've missed you, too," Marcus countered quickly.

Paris's face broke into a huge cheesy grin, which she was thankful Marcus was unable to see. He asked her about the boutique and she happily filled him in on the progress she was making learning the business. Her upcoming trip to market was a topic she couldn't talk enough about, and he seemed genuinely happy for her. His new job was proving to be a much better fit for him than the company in New Orleans. Paris gave a nervous laugh when he said that perhaps helping her had helped him find a better situation for himself. She was dying to ask him if he was dating anyone now, but she still felt uncomfortable being totally upfront with him. After they slept together, Marcus's attitude was strictly formal. He'd dumped cold water on any notion she had about the two of them getting to know each other on a more than friendship level.

"I called because I wanted to ask you a question," he finally admitted.

Paris got up and began busying herself with cleaning up her mess. Her heart was thumping heavily against her ribs, and she couldn't be still.

"I'd been visiting several churches, and I found one I liked a while back. Anyway, I joined two weeks ago, and they're having a celebratory dinner for all the new members." Marcus paused with his story, giving Paris time to connect the dots. Her lips were stretched so wide across her mouth she was sure she would have split them in two if she smiled any harder.

Marcus cleared his throat then jumped back into his story. "You know how church people are with signing folks up for the singles group and all, especially when you're new to the area. And well I don't particularly want to be fixed up with anybody in the choir or on the usher board."

Paris couldn't hold the laughter at the irony of the déjà vu. Marcus seemed motivated by her laughter and decided to reel the line in.

"I was wondering if you'd like to go with me to the dinner. It would keep the matchmakers disguised as deaconesses off me. I don't even know if you want to see me, but I'd really like to spend some time with you."

Paris found herself tearing up for the second time in less than an hour.

"I'd love to go with you."

The simple statement was a combination of all the warm uncontrollable feelings Marcus invoked within her. Marcus gave her the details of their date and told her he was looking forward to seeing her. Paris looked at the butterfly on the table again, found her reflection in it then watched as the joy bubbling over within her pushed itself up from her heart to her soul and finally broke through to her almond shaped eyes.

# *ABOUT THE AUTHOR*

**Christal Jordan-Mims** is a freelance writer and president of Enchanted PR, an entertainment PR firm in Atlanta, GA. Besides penning an advice column for a local magazine, she contributes to several Hip Hop/R&B magazines and is the originator of *Caramelized*, a T-shirt line celebrating a legacy of strength, beauty and grace in women of color. Her writing focuses on women's issues, specifically women of color.

Christal received her BA in Organizational Communication from the University of Oklahoma. She resides in Atlanta, GA with her husband and two children. She is currently working on her next novel.

You can learn more about Christal Jordan-Mims at www.getcaramelized.com.

*Excerpt from*

# *CAUGHT UP*

## *BY*

## *DEATRI KING-BEY*

**Release Date: February 2006**

# *CHAPTER ONE*

***Miami, June 15***

"This is not up for discussion, Rosa. You're not moving to Chicago." Ernesto stalked across her bedroom to the window. They'd moved to Miami when she was twelve to protect her from Harriet's drunken fits and distance himself from David.

"But, Daddy."

"The Senior Vice President of Marketing position was vacated a few months ago. I've held it for you to fill after your graduation." He checked his Rolex. "In two hours you graduate and take your rightful place as one of my Senior VPs. Someday Bolívar International will be yours."

Rosa twirled the tresses beside her ear between her fingers.

He crossed his arms over his chest. "Whatever you're calculating, forget it."

She released the hair. "Let's talk about this like the two rational adults we are." She motioned toward her beanbag chairs. "Please take a seat."

"I thought I told you to get rid of those things."

"That would be my fuzzy, pink dice chairs."

"This room is in need of serious redecorating," he grumbled as he situated his large frame onto the chair across from Rosa. "Order new furniture before you leave for Italy, so it will be here when you return."

"When I return, it will be to Chicago, not Miami," she stated calmly. "And thank you, but I won't be accepting the VP position at this time."

His expression matched hers, stoic. "Are you saying you need a longer vacation, maybe a year off? You've worked hard, you deserve it. I'll keep the temporary replacement until you're ready."

"No. I'm saying I'm moving to Chicago when I return from Italy and starting a computer networking firm with the hundred thousand dollar trust Mom gave me."

"I'll expand Bolívar International to include a computer networking unit. You'll be its VP."

"That won't work, Daddy. I'd still be working for you. Just as I have since I was nine. I want to be on my own. I want to build and run my own company. That's also why I'm not using the trust you've set up for me. I want to build my company from the ground up."

Ernesto had never been as proud of Rosa as he was at this moment. He could remember, many years ago, when he'd purchased the technology firm that grew into Bolívar International. At the time he'd wanted to be free of David to prove to himself that he could be a success on his own. "I admire that you wish to do this on your own, but run your company here. Not Chicago. You can't save Harriet." *Just as I can't save David.* He couldn't pinpoint the exact time it happened, but he no longer envied David's fire. He didn't want David's type of power—rooted in the fear of others. Ernesto craved the power rooted in respect: the respect he received for being an industry leader, the respect he received for improving the community, and most importantly, the respect he received from his daughter for being her hero.

Rosa looked away. He leaned forward and weaved his hands

through her long, bushy, black hair. "Your mother has to save herself."

She rested her caramel cheek on his shoulder. "I know I can't make her stop drinking. But I miss her. Maybe I can encourage her to seek help. I have to try. Please don't stop me."

Weighed down by family burdens, he knew he couldn't cut ties with David, just as Rosa couldn't cut ties with Harriet. "All right, I didn't get this far without knowing how to negotiate. You may go to Chicago and babysit your mother, but I expect you to stay up on Bolívar International business. And you will continue attending the strategy and status meetings. I want you ready when it's time for me to turn over the reins."

"Yes, sir." She backed away with a salute.

He chuckled with his own salute to her. "Go get ready for your graduation, soldier."

Later that night, David staggered across the hotel room, slurring, "I'm so proud of Rosa. *Mi* Rosa." He stumbled over nothing and fell onto the bed. "Damn, Ernesto, we did it. We're gonna pull this shit off."

Ernesto continued watching David from the chaise lounge in the corner. Though Rosa was going against his wishes, he was proud of her. "You need to sleep it off if you want to have a real discussion about Rosa, Paige and the DEA."

"My ass ain't drunk. What the hell's goin' on? You been actin' funny all night." He rolled onto his back. "Rosa's gonna be the head of the largest fuckin' drug syndicate ever! They won't know what hit 'em."

Ernesto hopped up from the chaise lounge. "What are you talking about? When did we ever agree to something like that?"

"What the fuck?" David stood with his arms out to his sides. "So you sayin' you don't remember the original deal?" Accent thickening, he harrumphed. "And I'm the one who's drunk. Don't let your white ass get this shit twisted, amigo. Not now. Not after we've come this far. Now when does Rosa return?"

Ernesto reined in his anger. Rosa was his to protect, and he had no intention of relinquishing control. "Four, maybe five months."

"Shit! My girl will finally be at her rightful place, by my side. You hear me, Ernesto? Rosa is my baby! When she returns, she'll be all mine!"

"She's mine!" Ernesto glared down on David. "No blurring of power! I decide what we do with Rosa!"

The two stood toe-to-toe staring at each other. Ernesto had never noticed just how short David really was. Ernesto was as tall for a man as David was short. Looking back, Ernesto realized David's presence had made him seem bigger than life. Ernesto internally chuckled at himself for all of the years he'd chosen to stand in this little man's shadow.

David drew in several deep breaths, calming himself. In Spanish, he said, "This is a time to celebrate our daughter. We have time to discuss Rosa's future when she returns from Europe. Grab a seat." He motioned to the chaise lounge, then sat on the bed.

Guard at an all-time high, Ernesto took his seat. This was one fight David wouldn't win. He'd protect Rosa at all cost.

"We need to talk about the DEA," David continued in Spanish. "I've made sure those bastards won't bother you again. I know you want out, but I need you're ass to continue laundering for me. I don't trust anyone else with my money. And that fucking Barry Paige." David nodded his head "I'm thinking about having his ass whacked."

Unsure how to handle this new change-of-subject tactic of David's, Ernesto half-listened while figuring out what to do to protect Rosa.

"Damn, damn, damn!" Ernesto stormed into his study with Harriet close behind. He regretted allowing her to stay with them for the few days she'd be in Miami for Rosa's graduation. He wouldn't have agreed, but having Harriet close meant so much to Rosa.

"You're just angry because Rosa's decided to move to Chicago to be with me," Harriet taunted. "I told you, you couldn't keep her away from me. You're losing control over her, and you can't stand it."

"I never kept Rosa from you. Your drinking did. Now leave me alone so I can think."

She pursed her lips. "I saw David at the graduation ceremony. He's getting closer and closer to telling Rosa the truth every day. Wait until she finds out her precious daddy is nothing but a lackey for a drug dealer."

"Shut the hell up! David isn't telling Rosa shit." He thumped his chest. "I'm her father, that's the only truth she'll ever know."

Harriet's drunken laugh filled the room. "Not if David has anything to say about it, lackey."

**2006 Publication Schedule**

**January**

A Lover's Legacy
Veronica Parker
1-58571-167-5
$9.95

Love Lasts Forever
Dominiqua Douglas
1-58571-187-X
$9.95

Under The Cherry Moon
Christal Jordan-Mims
1-58571-169-1
$12.95

**February**

Second Chances at Love
Cheris Hodges
1-58571-188-8
$9.95

Enchanted Desire
Wanda Thomas
1-58571-176-4
$9.95

Caught Up
Deatri King Bey
1-58571-178-0
$12.95

**March**

I'm Gonna Make You Love Me
Gwyneth Bolton
1-58571-181-0
$9.95

Through The Fire
Seressia Glass
1-58571-173-X
$9.95

Notes When Summer Ends
Beverly Lauderdale
1-58571-180-2
$12.95

**April**

Sin and Surrender
J.M. Jeffries
1-58571-189-6
$9.95

Unearthing Passions
Elaine Sims
1-58571-184-5
$9.95

Between Tears
Pamela Ridley
1-58571-179-0
$12.95

**May**

Misty Blue
Dyanne Davis
1-58571-186-1
$9.95

Ironic
Pamela Leigh Starr
1-58571-168-3
$9.95

Cricket's Serenade
Carolita Blythe
1-58571-183-7
$12.95

**June**

Cupid
Barbara Keaton
1-58571-174-8
$9.95

Havana Sunrise
Kymberly Hunt
1-58571-182-9
$9.95

Bound For Mt. Zion
Chris Parker
1-58571-191-8
$12.95

**2006 Publication Schedule (continued)**

**July**

Love Me Carefully
A.C. Arthur
1-58571-177-2
$9.95

No Ordinary Love
Angela Weaver
1-58571-198-5
$9.95

Rehoboth Road
Anita Ballard-Jones
1-58571-196-9
$12.95

**August**

Scent of Rain
Annetta P. Lee
158571-199-3
$9.95

Love in High Gear
Charlotte Roy
158571-185-3
$9.95

Rise of the Phoenix
Kenneth Whetstone
1-58571-197-7
$12.95

**September**

The Business of Love
Cheris Hodges
1-58571-193-4
$9.95

Rock Star
Rosyln Hardy Holcomb
1-58571-200-0
$9.95

A Dead Man Speaks
Lisa Jones Johnson
1-58571-203-5
$12.95

**October**

Who's That Lady
Andrea Jackson
1-58571-190-X
$9.95

A Dangerous Woman
J.M. Jeffries
1-58571-195-0
$9.95

Sinful Intentions
Crystal Rhodes
1-58571-201-9
$12.95

**November**

Only You
Crystal Hubbard
1-58571-208-6
$9.95

Ebony Eyes
Kei Swanson
1-58571-194-2
$9.95

By and By
Collette Haywood
1-58571-209-4
$12.95

**December**

Let's Get It On
Dyanne Davis
1-58571-210-8
$9.95

Nights Over Egypt
Barbara Keaton
1-58571-192-6
$9.95

A Pefect Place to Pray
Ikesha Goodwin
1-58571-202-7
$12.95

**Other Genesis Press, Inc. Titles**

| | | |
|---|---|---|
| A Dangerous Deception | J.M. Jeffries | $8.95 |
| A Dangerous Love | J.M. Jeffries | $8.95 |
| A Dangerous Obsession | J.M. Jeffries | $8.95 |
| A Drummer's Beat to Mend | Kei Swanson | $9.95 |
| A Happy Life | Charlotte Harris | $9.95 |
| A Heart's Awakening | Veronica Parker | $9.95 |
| A Lark on the Wing | Phyliss Hamilton | $9.95 |
| A Love of Her Own | Cheris F. Hodges | $9.95 |
| A Love to Cherish | Beverly Clark | $8.95 |
| A Risk of Rain | Dar Tomlinson | $8.95 |
| A Twist of Fate | Beverly Clark | $8.95 |
| A Will to Love | Angie Daniels | $9.95 |
| Acquisitions | Kimberley White | $8.95 |
| Across | Carol Payne | $12.95 |
| After the Vows | Leslie Esdaile | $10.95 |
| (Summer Anthology) | T.T. Henderson | |
| | Jacqueline Thomas | |
| Again My Love | Kayla Perrin | $10.95 |
| Against the Wind | Gwynne Forster | $8.95 |
| All I Ask | Barbara Keaton | $8.95 |
| Ambrosia | T.T. Henderson | $8.95 |
| An Unfinished Love Affair | Barbara Keaton | $8.95 |
| And Then Came You | Dorothy Elizabeth Love | $8.95 |
| Angel's Paradise | Janice Angelique | $9.95 |
| At Last | Lisa G. Riley | $8.95 |
| Best of Friends | Natalie Dunbar | $8.95 |
| Beyond the Rapture | Beverly Clark | $9.95 |
| Blaze | Barbara Keaton | $9.95 |
| Blood Lust | J. M. Jeffries | $9.95 |
| Bodyguard | Andrea Jackson | $9.95 |
| Boss of Me | Diana Nyad | $8.95 |
| Bound by Love | Beverly Clark | $8.95 |
| Breeze | Robin Hampton Allen | $10.95 |

**Other Genesis Press, Inc. Titles (continued)**

| | | |
|---|---|---|
| Broken | Dar Tomlinson | $24.95 |
| By Design | Barbara Keaton | $8.95 |
| Cajun Heat | Charlene Berry | $8.95 |
| Careless Whispers | Rochelle Alers | $8.95 |
| Cats & Other Tales | Marilyn Wagner | $8.95 |
| Caught in a Trap | Andre Michelle | $8.95 |
| Caught Up In the Rapture | Lisa G. Riley | $9.95 |
| Cautious Heart | Cheris F Hodges | $8.95 |
| Chances | Pamela Leigh Starr | $8.95 |
| Cherish the Flame | Beverly Clark | $8.95 |
| Class Reunion | Irma Jenkins/John Brown | $12.95 |
| Code Name: Diva | J.M. Jeffries | $9.95 |
| Conquering Dr. Wexler's Heart | Kimberley White | $9.95 |
| Crossing Paths, Tempting Memories | Dorothy Elizabeth Love | $9.95 |
| Cypress Whisperings | Phyllis Hamilton | $8.95 |
| Dark Embrace | Crystal Wilson Harris | $8.95 |
| Dark Storm Rising | Chinelu Moore | $10.95 |
| Daughter of the Wind | Joan Xian | $8.95 |
| Deadly Sacrifice | Jack Kean | $22.95 |
| Designer Passion | Dar Tomlinson | $8.95 |
| Dreamtective | Liz Swados | $5.95 |
| Ebony Butterfly II | Delilah Dawson | $14.95 |
| Echoes of Yesterday | Beverly Clark | $9.95 |
| Eden's Garden | Elizabeth Rose | $8.95 |
| Everlastin' Love | Gay G. Gunn | $8.95 |
| Everlasting Moments | Dorothy Elizabeth Love | $8.95 |
| Everything and More | Sinclair Lebeau | $8.95 |
| Everything but Love | Natalie Dunbar | $8.95 |
| Eve's Prescription | Edwina Martin Arnold | $8.95 |
| Falling | Natalie Dunbar | $9.95 |
| Fate | Pamela Leigh Starr | $8.95 |
| Finding Isabella | A.J. Garrotto | $8.95 |

**Other Genesis Press, Inc. Titles (continued)**

| | | |
|---|---|---|
| Forbidden Quest | Dar Tomlinson | $10.95 |
| Forever Love | Wanda Thomas | $8.95 |
| From the Ashes | Kathleen Suzanne<br>Jeanne Sumerix | $8.95 |
| Gentle Yearning | Rochelle Alers | $10.95 |
| Glory of Love | Sinclair LeBeau | $10.95 |
| Go Gentle into that Good Night | Malcom Boyd | $12.95 |
| Goldengroove | Mary Beth Craft | $16.95 |
| Groove, Bang, and Jive | Steve Cannon | $8.99 |
| Hand in Glove | Andrea Jackson | $9.95 |
| Hard to Love | Kimberley White | $9.95 |
| Hart & Soul | Angie Daniels | $8.95 |
| Heartbeat | Stephanie Bedwell-Grime | $8.95 |
| Hearts Remember | M. Loui Quezada | $8.95 |
| Hidden Memories | Robin Allen | $10.95 |
| Higher Ground | Leah Latimer | $19.95 |
| Hitler, the War, and the Pope | Ronald Rychiak | $26.95 |
| How to Write a Romance | Kathryn Falk | $18.95 |
| I Married a Reclining Chair | Lisa M. Fuhs | $8.95 |
| Indigo After Dark Vol. I | Nia Dixon/Angelique | $10.95 |
| Indigo After Dark Vol. II | Dolores Bundy/Cole Riley | $10.95 |
| Indigo After Dark Vol. III | Montana Blue/Coco Morena | $10.95 |
| Indigo After Dark Vol. IV | Cassandra Colt/<br>Diana Richeaux | $14.95 |
| Indigo After Dark Vol. V | Delilah Dawson | $14.95 |
| Icie | Pamela Leigh Starr | $8.95 |
| I'll Be Your Shelter | Giselle Carmichael | $8.95 |
| I'll Paint a Sun | A.J. Garrotto | $9.95 |
| Illusions | Pamela Leigh Starr | $8.95 |
| Indiscretions | Donna Hill | $8.95 |
| Intentional Mistakes | Michele Sudler | $9.95 |
| Interlude | Donna Hill | $8.95 |
| Intimate Intentions | Angie Daniels | $8.95 |

**Other Genesis Press, Inc. Titles (continued)**

| | | |
|---|---|---|
| Jolie's Surrender | Edwina Martin-Arnold | $8.95 |
| Kiss or Keep | Debra Phillips | $8.95 |
| Lace | Giselle Carmichael | $9.95 |
| Last Train to Memphis | Elsa Cook | $12.95 |
| Lasting Valor | Ken Olsen | $24.95 |
| Let Us Prey | Hunter Lundy | $25.95 |
| Life Is Never As It Seems | J.J. Michael | $12.95 |
| Lighter Shade of Brown | Vicki Andrews | $8.95 |
| Love Always | Mildred E. Riley | $10.95 |
| Love Doesn't Come Easy | Charlyne Dickerson | $8.95 |
| Love Unveiled | Gloria Greene | $10.95 |
| Love's Deception | Charlene Berry | $10.95 |
| Love's Destiny | M. Loui Quezada | $8.95 |
| Mae's Promise | Melody Walcott | $8.95 |
| Magnolia Sunset | Giselle Carmichael | $8.95 |
| Matters of Life and Death | Lesego Malepe, Ph.D. | $15.95 |
| Meant to Be | Jeanne Sumerix | $8.95 |
| Midnight Clear (Anthology) | Leslie Esdaile<br>Gwynne Forster<br>Carmen Green<br>Monica Jackson | $10.95 |
| Midnight Magic | Gwynne Forster | $8.95 |
| Midnight Peril | Vicki Andrews | $10.95 |
| Misconceptions | Pamela Leigh Starr | $9.95 |
| Montgomery's Children | Richard Perry | $14.95 |
| My Buffalo Soldier | Barbara B. K. Reeves | $8.95 |
| Naked Soul | Gwynne Forster | $8.95 |
| Next to Last Chance | Louisa Dixon | $24.95 |
| No Apologies | Seressia Glass | $8.95 |
| No Commitment Required | Seressia Glass | $8.95 |
| No Regrets | Mildred E. Riley | $8.95 |
| Nowhere to Run | Gay G. Gunn | $10.95 |
| O Bed! O Breakfast! | Rob Kuehnle | $14.95 |

**Other Genesis Press, Inc. Titles (continued)**

| | | |
|---|---|---|
| Object of His Desire | A. C. Arthur | $8.95 |
| Office Policy | A. C. Arthur | $9.95 |
| Once in a Blue Moon | Dorianne Cole | $9.95 |
| One Day at a Time | Bella McFarland | $8.95 |
| Outside Chance | Louisa Dixon | $24.95 |
| Passion | T.T. Henderson | $10.95 |
| Passion's Blood | Cherif Fortin | $22.95 |
| Passion's Journey | Wanda Thomas | $8.95 |
| Past Promises | Jahmel West | $8.95 |
| Path of Fire | T.T. Henderson | $8.95 |
| Path of Thorns | Annetta P. Lee | $9.95 |
| Peace Be Still | Colette Haywood | $12.95 |
| Picture Perfect | Reon Carter | $8.95 |
| Playing for Keeps | Stephanie Salinas | $8.95 |
| Pride & Joi | Gay G. Gunn | $15.95 |
| Pride & Joi | Gay G. Gunn | $8.95 |
| Promises to Keep | Alicia Wiggins | $8.95 |
| Quiet Storm | Donna Hill | $10.95 |
| Reckless Surrender | Rochelle Alers | $6.95 |
| Red Polka Dot in a World of Plaid | Varian Johnson | $12.95 |
| Reluctant Captive | Joyce Jackson | $8.95 |
| Rendezvous with Fate | Jeanne Sumerix | $8.95 |
| Revelations | Cheris F. Hodges | $8.95 |
| Rivers of the Soul | Leslie Esdaile | $8.95 |
| Rocky Mountain Romance | Kathleen Suzanne | $8.95 |
| Rooms of the Heart | Donna Hill | $8.95 |
| Rough on Rats and Tough on Cats | Chris Parker | $12.95 |
| Secret Library Vol. 1 | Nina Sheridan | $18.95 |
| Secret Library Vol. 2 | Cassandra Colt | $8.95 |
| Shades of Brown | Denise Becker | $8.95 |
| Shades of Desire | Monica White | $8.95 |

**Other Genesis Press, Inc. Titles (continued)**

| | | |
|---|---|---|
| Shadows in the Moonlight | Jeanne Sumerix | $8.95 |
| Sin | Crystal Rhodes | $8.95 |
| So Amazing | Sinclair LeBeau | $8.95 |
| Somebody's Someone | Sinclair LeBeau | $8.95 |
| Someone to Love | Alicia Wiggins | $8.95 |
| Song in the Park | Martin Brant | $15.95 |
| Soul Eyes | Wayne L. Wilson | $12.95 |
| Soul to Soul | Donna Hill | $8.95 |
| Southern Comfort | J.M. Jeffries | $8.95 |
| Still the Storm | Sharon Robinson | $8.95 |
| Still Waters Run Deep | Leslie Esdaile | $8.95 |
| Stories to Excite You | Anna Forrest/Divine | $14.95 |
| Subtle Secrets | Wanda Y. Thomas | $8.95 |
| Suddenly You | Crystal Hubbard | $9.95 |
| Sweet Repercussions | Kimberley White | $9.95 |
| Sweet Tomorrows | Kimberly White | $8.95 |
| Taken by You | Dorothy Elizabeth Love | $9.95 |
| Tattooed Tears | T. T. Henderson | $8.95 |
| The Color Line | Lizzette Grayson Carter | $9.95 |
| The Color of Trouble | Dyanne Davis | $8.95 |
| The Disappearance of Allison Jones | Kayla Perrin | $5.95 |
| The Honey Dipper's Legacy | Pannell-Allen | $14.95 |
| The Joker's Love Tune | Sidney Rickman | $15.95 |
| The Little Pretender | Barbara Cartland | $10.95 |
| The Love We Had | Natalie Dunbar | $8.95 |
| The Man Who Could Fly | Bob & Milana Beamon | $18.95 |
| The Missing Link | Charlyne Dickerson | $8.95 |
| The Price of Love | Sinclair LeBeau | $8.95 |
| The Smoking Life | Ilene Barth | $29.95 |
| The Words of the Pitcher | Kei Swanson | $8.95 |
| Three Wishes | Seressia Glass | $8.95 |
| Ties That Bind | Kathleen Suzanne | $8.95 |
| Tiger Woods | Libby Hughes | $5.95 |

**Other Genesis Press, Inc. Titles (continued)**

| | | |
|---|---|---|
| Time is of the Essence | Angie Daniels | $9.95 |
| Timeless Devotion | Bella McFarland | $9.95 |
| Tomorrow's Promise | Leslie Esdaile | $8.95 |
| Truly Inseparable | Wanda Y. Thomas | $8.95 |
| Unbreak My Heart | Dar Tomlinson | $8.95 |
| Uncommon Prayer | Kenneth Swanson | $9.95 |
| Unconditional | A.C. Arthur | $9.95 |
| Unconditional Love | Alicia Wiggins | $8.95 |
| Until Death Do Us Part | Susan Paul | $8.95 |
| Vows of Passion | Bella McFarland | $9.95 |
| Wedding Gown | Dyanne Davis | $8.95 |
| What's Under Benjamin's Bed | Sandra Schaffer | $8.95 |
| When Dreams Float | Dorothy Elizabeth Love | $8.95 |
| Whispers in the Night | Dorothy Elizabeth Love | $8.95 |
| Whispers in the Sand | LaFlorya Gauthier | $10.95 |
| Wild Ravens | Altonya Washington | $9.95 |
| Yesterday Is Gone | Beverly Clark | $10.95 |
| Yesterday's Dreams, Tomorrow's Promises | Reon Laudat | $8.95 |
| Your Precious Love | Sinclair LeBeau | $8.95 |

# Order Form

**Mail to: Genesis Press, Inc.**
**P.O. Box 101**
**Columbus, MS 39703**

Name ______________________________
Address ______________________________
City/State ____________________ Zip ____________
Telephone ____________________

*Ship to (if different from above)*
Name ______________________________
Address ______________________________
City/State ____________________ Zip ____________
Telephone ____________________

*Credit Card Information*
Credit Card # ____________________ ☐Visa ☐Mastercard
Expiration Date (mm/yy) ____________ ☐AmEx ☐Discover

| Qty. | Author | Title | Price | Total |
|---|---|---|---|---|
| | | | | |
| | | | | |
| | | | | |
| | | | | |
| | | | | |
| | | | | |
| | | | | |
| | | | | |
| | | | | |
| | | | | |
| | | | | |
| | | | | |



Use this order form, or call 1-888-INDIGO-1

**Total for books** ____________
**Shipping and handling:**
**$5 first two books,**
**$1 each additional book** ____________
**Total S & H** ____________
**Total amount enclosed** ____________

*Mississippi residents add 7% sales tax*